BAACP

the
Promise

**Also available from
Patricia Davids
and HQN**

The Amish of Cedar Grove

The Wish
The Hope
The Promise

PATRICIA DAVIDS

the Promise

HQN

If you purchased this book without a cover you should be aware that this book is stolen property. It was reported as "unsold and destroyed" to the publisher, and neither the author nor the publisher has received any payment for this "stripped book."

ISBN-13: 978-1-335-13694-7

The Promise

Copyright © 2020 by Patricia MacDonald

Recycling programs for this product may not exist in your area.

All rights reserved. No part of this book may be used or reproduced in any manner whatsoever without written permission except in the case of brief quotations embodied in critical articles and reviews.

This is a work of fiction. Names, characters, places and incidents are either the product of the author's imagination or are used fictitiously. Any resemblance to actual persons, living or dead, businesses, companies, events or locales is entirely coincidental.

This edition published by arrangement with Harlequin Books S.A.

For questions and comments about the quality of this book, please contact us at CustomerService@Harlequin.com.

HQN
22 Adelaide St. West, 40th Floor
Toronto, Ontario M5H 4E3, Canada
www.Harlequin.com

Printed in U.S.A.

This book is dedicated to my charming sister-in-law
Theresa Stroda. We need another girls' day out.
I'm game if you are. Let's go explore
a new Kansas Amish community.

CHAPTER ONE

"I KNOW YOU don't want to hear this, but I'm going to say it anyway. I'm tired of waiting for the two of you to settle down. I want grandbabies."

Levi Raber choked on a sip of his strong black coffee and set his mug down hard enough to splash hot liquid on his fingers. He shook his hand as his gaze flashed to his mother's face.

Henrietta Raber's eyes were narrowed with determination, her lips set in a tight line. She might look like a meek Amish woman with her white *kapp* pinned to her brown-and-silver–streaked hair, but when Henrietta took the bit between her teeth there was no stopping her.

"Grandbabies require a mother, and that means a wife for one of us," his brother, Isaac, quipped, wagging his eyebrows at Levi. "I'm not baptized, so it looks like it will be you, *brudder.* That's one game I'd be happy to let you win."

Levi gave him a sour glance. "I don't know why you feel the need to top me at everything except how much work I put into the stables."

"That's because I don't care for horses. I'd rather drive a car."

Their mother glared at Isaac. "Your *rumspringa* has

gone on long enough. You are twenty-two. You will make up your mind to join the faithful this summer, or you will move out of my home."

"You don't mean that," Isaac sputtered.

"She means it." Levi leaned back in his chair. "What is this all about, *Mamm*?"

"Exactly what I said. I want you to find wives. Isaac goes from girl to girl like a hummingbird from feeder to feeder and wastes his time with those rowdy *Englisch* friends. You only pay attention to those ridiculous horses."

Since he was running the family's broodmare farm almost single-handedly, Levi wasn't sure how he was supposed to ignore the animals that were their livelihood.

She sniffled and closed her eyes. "I expected to have the company of your father long into our old age, but *Gott* had other plans for my Walter. He's been gone a year next month." Her voice trailed away as her lower lip quivered.

She glanced between her sons and settled her gaze on Levi. "Now I look to you to provide me with grandchildren to care for me in my declining years."

Fifty-two didn't qualify as declining years to Levi, but it was evident that his father's death had taken a toll on his mother's health and certainly her happiness. She had lost weight and rarely left the house anymore. It was exactly what his father had feared would happen.

The memory of his last moments with his father flashed into Levi's mind. The young horse limping away from the shattered remains of the practice cart that Levi had to toss aside to reach his father. His *daed*'s pale face

twisted with pain, his eyes wide as he tried to breathe
through the blood frothing at his lips.

*"Look after...your brother...and your mother. She'll
fall apart...without me. Keep the...farm going,"* he managed to say in a ragged whisper.

"You don't need to ask, Daed. *I will. I promise."*

"Wing's gonna...be...our...champ..."

Levi stared into his coffee cup. He had asked his father to exercise the skittish new gelding while he finished
cooling down Wing and a Prayer. He'd seen the new
horse panic, watched in horror as the racing cart flipped,
throwing his father into the railing. He had rushed to his
father's side shouting for help, but it came too late. All
he had been able to do was hold his father's hand and
promise to care for the people and the things he loved.

Levi pushed the sad memory aside. It had been God's
will. If he told himself that often enough he might someday believe it. "I don't have time to look for a wife. I
have a stable to run."

Wife hunting wasn't on the list of things he needed
to make Raber Stables profitable again. His father had
poured his blood, sweat and heart into the place. Levi
owed it to his father to continue his legacy.

"You'll never find time as long as you pay more attention to those dangerous animals than you do people."

She wiped her eyes. "That is going to change. I have
sold this farm. We're moving to Cedar Grove, Kansas,
to my childhood home. My parents left the property to
me years ago. I wanted us to move there, but your father would never consider leaving this place. He tried
to get me to sell my farm so he could buy more of those

worthless horses, but I knew to keep it. I rented the farm to a fellow, but now he is ready to retire."

Levi couldn't believe what he was hearing. When had she done this? How could she sell what his father had spent a lifetime building?

She nodded to him. "You and Isaac will farm it together. I intend to deed it outright to the one who marries first."

Isaac's mouth dropped open. "We can't leave Lancaster. What about our friends?"

"The moving van will be here the day after tomorrow. You'll have time to say goodbye to your *Englisch* so-called friends. You'll be well rid of them. Besides, you made friends in Kansas the summer you stayed with my folks. That girl Sarah still writes to you."

"She's just a kid, but that's not the point. I don't want to leave."

"You've failed to keep a steady job. You have no means of support. You will come with me and that is the end of it."

Isaac's brows drew together in a frown. "We'll see about that!" He pushed away from the table and stormed out.

Levi gaped at his mother. "Our family has raised standardbred horses on these eighty acres for a hundred years. *Daed* loved this place. How could you sell it?"

"He loved it, and it killed him."

"It was an accident, *Mamm*," he muttered, swallowing his guilt.

"It was a crazed racehorse. I lost my husband, but

I won't lose my sons to this business. I have sold the mares along with the property."

Levi's breath caught in his throat. The mares and their foals were the foundation of the farm's future. Without them it was little more than eighty acres of grass with a barn and a practice track. He leaned forward. "What about Wing and a Prayer? You can't have sold her. She's mine."

The horse had been a gift from his father. Their Amish church district was one of the few in Lancaster that allowed members to own and breed racehorses. Raising and training trotters and pacers along with keeping the winnings a good horse earned was acceptable, but no gambling was permitted. A man could quickly find himself shunned for placing wagers.

Levi had high hopes for Wing and a Prayer. She was a promising filly. It had been more than ten years since Raber Stables had produced a major money winner, but Levi believed that Wing would be the next one.

His mother leaned back in her chair and folded her hands in her lap. "We will need a buggy horse in Kansas. You can bring her along."

"She's a racehorse, not a buggy horse. Who bought the place?"

"Arnold Diehl. He will take good care of it."

Arnold was an *Englisch* neighbor with his own stables. Levi had trained several of his horses who went on to win big at major racetracks. He couldn't believe the man had purchased the place without talking to him first. He got up from the table. "I must speak to Arnold."

"It won't change anything," she said behind him as he walked out the door.

Once he was outside, the sick feeling growing in his stomach made him brace his hands on his knees and take slow, deep breaths. How could she do this? From the time he was old enough to walk, Levi had loved everything about raising and training standardbreds with his father. The excitement of each birth, of wondering if the new foal might be that one in a thousand with the speed and endurance needed to become a champion, was only eclipsed by the thrill of flying along behind a great horse.

He would never love anything as much as he loved this farm.

He stood up straight. His mother was going to be bitterly disappointed if she thought plowing a Kansas wheat field would be a satisfying life for him. He would find a way to get back what she had sold.

As he neared the stable, he was surprised to see Arnold's pickup parked beside it. Arnold appeared in the open doorway. He was a big man with silver-white hair under his red ball cap. "I see she told you."

Levi walked over to lean against the white board fence. "She told me. Why didn't you?"

Arnold came to stand beside him. "I promised Henrietta I'd let her break the news. I know it's tough, but you've been hanging on to this place by a thread for the past three years. Your pa made some bad business decisions."

"I could have turned it around. In another three months Wing and a Prayer will be ready to compete."

Arnold clapped a hand on Levi's shoulder. "She's a beautiful filly, but we both know there's a big difference between owning a promising two-year-old and a winning one."

"She's a champion. *Daed* said she was the horse he'd waited a lifetime to see born here."

Several of the mares with foals at their sides walked up to greet Levi. He rubbed the face of each one in turn. He couldn't imagine his life without these magnificent animals.

Arnold stroked the nose of a curious foal. "Your dad knew horses, but he wasn't so good at business. He put too much heart into his decisions instead of using his brain. If you want to stay on, I'll give you a job right now. You're one of the best trainers I know."

Levi lifted his straw hat and raked his fingers through his dark curls as he realized he had no choice but to turn down Arnold's offer. "I appreciate that, but I promised *Daed* I'd look after *Mamm*. She's set on moving to Kansas. I can't let her and Isaac go by themselves."

"Maybe once Henrietta is settled, she won't object to you coming back."

Levi rolled his eyes. "She wants to see Isaac and me saddled with wives."

Arnold laughed. "My mother was that same way, but once my kid brother got hitched, she stopped nagging me. Which was a good thing. A wife that doesn't understand and love racing the way you and I do can put a damper on a man's career and his business decisions. Your father was a prime example. Before he married he was as good a trainer as you are. Afterward, he gave it up because your mother hated the risks that came with the job."

"He told me." It was the main reason Levi had avoided serious relationships.

"Take my advice. Find a nice gal for Isaac, and then you can make your escape."

Levi rubbed a hand down the silky neck of the nearest mare. Arnold might be on to something. Maybe one wedding would satisfy his mother.

Isaac was always sure he was in love with each new girlfriend who came along. Until he met the next one. He did his best to entice any woman who gave Levi a second look to go out with him instead. They usually did. Isaac's blond good looks paired with his smooth-talking ways had captured the hearts of many young women, whereas Levi's stoic personality kept them at bay. It was amazing Isaac wasn't married already.

Maybe he simply needed a push in that direction from his big brother. Would the prospect of owning his own farm be enough to convince Isaac to settle down? Was that their mother's reason for saying she'd give the land to the first one who married?

Levi turned to Arnold. "If Wing and a Prayer is as good as I believe she is, will you sell this place back to me?"

Arnold met Levi's gaze without flinching. "Talk to me after her first race."

Levi looked out over the green pasture dotted with mares and foals. *I'll get it back,* Daed. *I promise.*

SARAH YODER STOPPED hoeing at the persistent weeds in the vegetable garden and straightened to stretch her back. The spring sunshine was warm on her shoulders.

The moist soil under her bare feet was cool and soft. A few puffy clouds drifted across a bright blue Kansas sky. The brisk breeze that cooled her cheeks and fluttered the ribbons of her Amish *kapp* against her neck carried the sweet scent of the lavender fields to her. Summer would be here soon with hot days and sticky nights, but for now she would enjoy every nice day that early May had to offer.

Her brother-in-law, Joshua, and her sister, Laura Beth, were each working their way down adjoining rows. They stopped, too. Joshua leaned over and gave Laura Beth a quick kiss. It was easy to see they were in love.

Both had been married before and lost their spouses. Sarah wondered if that was why they seemed to treasure every moment together. Stolen kisses throughout the day were the norm for those two on the farm. So were lingering glances and holding hands. They had been married for two years, but their romance showed no sign of fading.

Sarah wanted a love like that.

She closed her eyes. To have a husband who loved her and to raise a family of her own in Cedar Grove, Kansas, was all she wanted out of life. A simple, plain life among the people she knew and cared about. It wasn't too much to ask, was it?

Sarah sighed. The shortage of marriageable men in her Amish community was the real problem. Unless the Lord did something about that, she might remain a spinster.

Two and a half years ago Laura Beth had made plans for the sisters to move to Ohio for that very reason. Sarah had resisted the notion with tooth and nail. She hadn't been ready to settle down. At nineteen she couldn't imagine moving away from her dear friends. Sarah, Angela, Ella and Melody had often been referred to as the Four Peas. As alike as peas in a pod, their teacher used to say. The girls had done everything together through elementary school and beyond. But two years ago things started to change.

Joshua arrived in Cedar Grove with his infant son, Caleb, and Laura Beth fell in love with them both. Melody met an Amish boy from Haven, Kansas, and married him. She was expecting her first baby soon. Ella had gone to visit her grandparents in Missouri, where she met Zack Hostetler. The two had been married last year and returned to Jamesport, Missouri, to live with Zack's family. Angela and Sarah were the only two peas left, and Angela was walking out with Bishop Weaver's grandson Thaddeus. They were quietly planning a fall wedding. Unless the Lord had a surprise up His sleeve, Sarah would soon be the last lone pea in the pod.

Maybe she should have taken Isaac Raber up on his offer to marry her. The thought made her smile.

Handsome Isaac, the young man from Pennsylvania who had stolen her heart the summer she turned sixteen. Isaac had spent a few brief months in Cedar Grove working on his grandfather's farm, but he'd spent every free minute courting Sarah. She had some wonderful memories of their time together. On his last day she had gone with him to the bus station where he proposed to her. She had laughingly refused him because she knew he wasn't serious. Isaac had seldom been serious. Their summer romance ended once he returned to his family's home in Lancaster, Pennsylvania. They had both been too young and immature to make a long-distance courtship work, but they had remained friends, occasionally exchanging letters.

"Is something wrong, Sarah?" her sister asked.

Sarah opened her eyes to see Laura Beth staring at her. She smiled. "*Nee.* I was just thinking about a friend I haven't heard from lately."

"Who would that be?"

"Isaac."

Laura Beth looked puzzled. "Do I know him?"

"He's the boy from Pennsylvania that I had such a wild crush on a few years ago."

Laura Beth smiled. "Now I remember. You still write to each other?"

Sarah nodded and resumed hoeing around the young beet plants. Isaac hadn't answered her last letter yet. He was such a poor correspondent. Often she mailed him four or five letters before he got around to writing back. His missives were short and all about his life in Pennsylvania, his annoying older brother or the fun he and his friends were having during their *rumspringa.* He never wrote about settling down.

Sarah had enjoyed her *rumspringa,* too. The "running around" years when Amish teenagers weren't required to live by the church's rules. It was their time to experience the world before they took their vows to remain separate from it. She'd had some fun times with her friends, but she was ready to settle down and start a family if that was what God had planned for her. She was ready to put her childish ways aside.

At the next church gathering she would start her baptismal classes with the church elders. The first of nine over a period of eighteen weeks. Following the classes, the baptized members of the community would vote whether or not to accept her into the church. If they were all in agreement, she would be baptized into the Amish faith in the fall.

"Have you heard from Ella?" Laura Beth asked. "Her mother thought she would enjoy having you visit her in Missouri. We can spare you from the farm if you want to go."

Sarah shook her head. "Ella only wants to introduce me to some of Zack's cousins."

"Would that be a bad thing?" Joshua asked.

"Not if I didn't mind living hundreds of miles away from you, Laura Beth, Caleb and everyone I know."

Laura Beth sighed in exasperation. "Ella would be close. Anyway, no one said you have to marry one of them."

Sarah forced herself to smile. "Don't fret about me. I'm a sensible woman. I'm content to wait until the Lord sends the right fellow to me." If there was such a man.

Joshua moved to stand beside his wife. "*Sensible* isn't a word I would use to describe you. *Loving*, *loyal* and *brave*, *ja*. *Sensible?* Not so much. It wouldn't hurt to keep an open mind and consider going out with fellas from other Amish districts."

Sarah knew he was right, but the thought of marrying someone who didn't want to live in Cedar Grove was a frightening prospect. Laura Beth was her only family. Their parents and grandparents were gone. How could she get along without her sister now that her friends were scattering? It didn't bear thinking about.

The sound of a horse and buggy coming up the lane made them all look toward the road. Sarah's friend Angela Beachy waved as she drew her black mare to a stop beside the garden gate. Her eyes were wide with excitement as she hopped out of her buggy and rushed to grab Sarah by the hand. "Guess who has moved to Cedar Grove. Go ahead—guess. You won't get it right in a hundred years."

"Don't leave us in suspense that long," Joshua drawled, leaning on the handle of his hoe.

"Mother's cousin Henrietta Raber and her sons from Lancaster, Pennsylvania. They're moving into the old Helmuth place. I'm on my way to welcome them. Sarah, I knew you'd want to come along."

Sarah gave a shriek of delight and squeezed her friend's hand. "Isaac is back? We were just talking about him. Oh, Angela, of course I'll come with you, but I have to change my dress first. I won't be a minute." Sarah bolted up the porch steps of the old farmhouse, her bare feet hardly touching the wooden treads.

She washed her hands and face, put on a clean *kapp* and her best Sunday dress after kicking her grimy work dress and apron into the corner.

Laura Beth came into the room carrying her stepson, Caleb, on her hip. At two years of age, Caleb was a chubby armload of sleepy sweetness, having just gotten up from his nap. "You seem very excited," Laura Beth said in amusement.

Sarah closed her eyes and pressed her hands against her chest. "You heard Angela. His family has moved here. This is wonderful news. *Gott* is truly amazing. Here I have been worrying that I won't find a husband who wants to live in Cedar Grove, and He delivers one."

Laura Beth's brows snapped into a frown. "That's putting your cart before the horse, Sarah. For all you know, Isaac may already have a wife."

"He would have told me if that were the case." Sarah struggled to calm her racing heart and reassure her sister. "I'm excited and happy to see Isaac again. I'm not expecting him to propose the minute he sees me, but we once had strong feelings for each other. It's possible those feelings still exist and can grow into something serious."

"It's possible," Laura said slowly. "Only don't start planning the wedding until after you two have spent plenty of time together. You may find you've grown apart and have nothing in common."

Sarah rolled her eyes. "Don't worry. I'll be sensible."

Isaac was back and she couldn't wait to see him again. "I've got to go. Angela is waiting. I'll be back before supper." She smiled at her sister and kissed Caleb's white-blond curls. "Bye, pretty boy."

He pulled his fingers out of his mouth, opened and closed them. "Bye-bye."

She chuckled as she hurried out the door. Someday in the future, God willing, she would have a beautiful baby of her own.

Outside, Sarah climbed in the buggy with Angela. "Why didn't you warn me that Isaac was moving here?"

"We didn't know about Cousin Henrietta's plans until yesterday. For some reason her letter was delayed."

"Are they really settling here or are they just visiting?" Sarah held her breath.

"According to Henrietta's letter, her sons are going to take up farming. That certainly sounds like they're staying. She told *Mamm* she has been longing to return since before her husband passed away."

"Isaac doesn't have a wife, does he?" Sarah asked, trying not to sound too interested.

The sidelong glance Angela cast her way proved she wasn't fooled. "Neither of Henrietta's sons are wed."

Sarah breathed a sigh of relief. He wasn't married, and he would be living just five miles from her. She fell silent for the remainder of the trip. On one hand, she wanted Angela to hurry, but on the other hand, she was afraid she wouldn't know what to say when she was face-to-face with him. Or his mother, for that matter.

She needed to present herself as a modest and mature Amish woman. It was important to make a good first impression on his family and to show Isaac that she wasn't a giddy girl any longer. She sat up straighter and patted a few stray hairs into place as their destination came into view at last.

Sarah was familiar with the Helmuth farm. It had become something of an eyesore in the community over the last few years. Jake Helmuth had rented it from the Raber family, but he had never put much energy into keeping up the property. The barn wasn't in great shape,

but it was better than the house, which badly needed
a coat of paint.

A large moving van and a pickup pulling a horse
trailer sat in front of the house. Several men were closing up the van. The horse trailer stood empty. A beautiful black horse with a white patch on her forehead
was prancing around a small corral beside the barn
with a second brown gelding pacing close beside her.
She whinnied when she caught sight of Angela's horse,
who promptly whinnied back. Sarah scanned the yard
eagerly but didn't see Isaac.

A small woman in Amish clothing came out of the
house. Angela jumped down from the buggy and went
to embrace her. "Cousin Henrietta, it is so nice to see
you again. Welcome. My mother wanted me to tell you
that she is bringing over supper for you and your boys
tonight so you don't have to worry about cooking after
your long trip."

"Bless you and your mother, Angela dear. I have to
admit that I'm exhausted. I don't enjoy traveling the
way I once did. Who do you have with you?"

Sarah walked up to stand beside Angela. "Hello,
Mrs. Raber. I'm Sarah Yoder. Your son Isaac and I became friends when he spent the summer here with your
parents."

"You are the one who writes to him. I know he enjoys your letters." Henrietta swayed a little.

Alarmed, Sarah took her arm. "Are you ill?"

"*Nee*, I'm merely tired. It was a long trip."

"Don't let us keep you standing here. I'm sure you'll
be more comfortable inside," Angela said.

"I'm afraid the place isn't fit for company, but I believe I will go in and lie down. Isaac is in the barn. Sarah, you should go say hello."

Angela tipped her head in that direction. "Go on. I'll take care of Cousin Henrietta."

"Are you sure?" Sarah bit her lower lip. Angela nodded and helped the older woman inside.

Sarah began walking toward the barn. Her pulse raced as butterflies filled her stomach. What would Isaac think of her? Would he be happy to see her again? What should she say? She stepped through the open doorway and paused to let her eyes adjust to the darkness. She spotted him a few feet away. He was on one knee tightening a screw in a stall door. His hat was pushed back on his head. She couldn't see his face. He hadn't heard her come in.

Suddenly she was a giddy sixteen-year-old again about to burst out laughing for the sheer joy of it. She quietly tiptoed up behind him and cupped her hands over his eyes. "Guess who," she whispered in his ear.

"I have no idea."

The voice wasn't right. Strong hands gripped her wrists and pulled her hands away. His hat fell off as he turned his head to stare up at her. She saw a riot of dark brown curls, not straw-blond hair. She didn't know this man.

A scowl drew his brows together. "I still don't know who you are."

She pulled her hands free and stumbled backward as embarrassment robbed her of speech. The man retrieved his hat and rose to his feet. "I assume you were expecting someone else?"

"I'm sorry," she managed to squeak.

The man in front of her settled his hat on his head. He wasn't as tall as Isaac, but he was a head taller than Sarah. He had rugged good looks, dark eyes and a full mouth that was turned up at one corner as if a grin was about to break free. "I take it you know my brother, Isaac."

He was laughing at her.

The dark-haired stranger folded his arms over his chest. "I'm Levi Raber."

Of course he would be the annoying older brother. So much for making a good first impression on Isaac's family. She wasn't sure she could feel more embarrassed if she tried.

Isaac walked past her with a load of harnesses in his arms. He nodded toward her. "Hey, Sarah. Nice to see you again." He continued into the depths of the barn.

She stood openmouthed in shock. That was it? After all this time the only thing Isaac had to say to her was "Nice to see you again"?

This was not the reunion she had hoped for.

CHAPTER TWO

LEVI WATCHED THE young woman's expressive features shift from embarrassed to confused to annoyed. Crossing her arms, she stared toward the back of the barn, waiting for his brother to reappear.

She was slender with blond hair neatly parted in the center beneath a white *kapp* the way all Amish women wore their hair. A sprinkling of freckles dusted her nose and tan cheeks. Her dress was a dark blue that matched the color of her eyes. The white apron tied over it accentuated her small waist. She was barefoot. And very attractive. He rarely gave a second glance to most young women. Why was she different?

Several silent moments slipped past. Levi gestured toward the open barn door. "Should I leave? I have the feeling that you'd like to speak to my brother alone."

Her frown deepened. "He doesn't appear eager to speak to me."

Levi wasn't sure why he felt the need to tease a smile from her. "He got the answer right," he drawled. "You should give him credit for that."

She switched her intense gaze to him. "What answer?"

"Guess who. He got the name right if you are Sarah."

She managed a tentative smile. "I am Sarah, Sarah

Yoder. I'm sorry about that childish stunt. I thought you were Isaac." She grew flustered and dropped her gaze.

The feeling of her small, warm hands lingered on Levi's cheeks as her husky whisper echoed in his ears. "So I assumed. I think you're the first person to mix us up. We don't look much alike."

"I couldn't see your face or your hair until your hat fell off, and then it was too late. You're his older brother, aren't you? He has mentioned you in his letters."

"Nothing flattering, I imagine."

She didn't answer but a faint flush brought heightened color to her cheeks as she stared at the ground, so he knew he was right. "You must have known each other pretty well if you thought he'd remember your voice."

"We became *goot* friends the summer he visited here. Please forgive my foolish behavior."

"There's nothing to forgive."

"Tell Isaac I'll wait for him on the porch." She turned on her heels, left the barn and crossed the farmyard. Levi couldn't help but notice the sway of her hips as she walked away. Sarah Yoder was attractive from every angle.

His brother came back from the tack room minus the harnesses a few moments later. He looked around. "Where did Sarah go?"

"She said she'd wait for you on the porch. I take it she is someone special?"

"Not really. She's one of the local kids I was friends with when I spent the summer here with *Daadi* and *Mammi*."

Sarah Yoder with the dainty hands and husky voice

had an interesting way of greeting old friends, but she was no kid. His brother needed glasses if he hadn't noticed that. "She has fond memories of you."

"What makes you say that?"

"Just a hunch." Levi picked up the screwdriver he had dropped when Sarah surprised him. He finished tightening the bottom hinge on the stall door. "She said the two of you were *goot* friends. She's been writing to you, hasn't she? What did you tell her about me?"

And why was that important? He didn't normally care about the opinions of others.

Isaac laughed. "I told her you are a pain in the neck. You're always after me to do more work around the place even though you know I'm not fond of horses the way you and *Daed* were."

Levi arched one eyebrow. "More work or *any* work?"

Isaac's expression soured. "See what I mean? No matter what I do, you aren't satisfied with it, so why should I put out the effort?"

"I don't know. Maybe to impress me?"

"Like that will ever happen."

"You should go speak to Sarah. She's more than happy to see you again."

"I know. I hope she doesn't make it awkward."

"Why would it be?"

"Because we thought we were in love back then."

"Is that so?"

"You know how it is. She was the prettiest girl in the neighborhood—I was a long way from home. She was…likable, but we were just teenagers. I got over her. I hope she got over me."

The reluctant affection in Isaac's voice caught Levi's attention. Arnold's words came back to him. *Find a nice gal for Isaac, and then you can make your escape.*

Was he being handed a potential spouse for Isaac on their first day in Kansas? That was almost too good to be true. Who was he to doubt the wisdom of the Lord? His chances of returning home suddenly seemed brighter. His mood lightened. "She's still likable, and she's not a kid. You shouldn't keep her waiting."

"Okay. The only things left in the trailer are the boxes of horseshoes you brought along. Those lightweight aluminum racing shoes aren't practical for a buggy horse."

"Wing and a Prayer is not going to be the family buggy horse. Jasper will keep that position. Wing is used to wearing those shoes, and I don't want to put anything heavier on her."

"Look around, big brother. There isn't a racetrack in sight for two hundred miles."

"That doesn't mean I'm going to stop training her."

Isaac shook his head and left the barn.

It might be foolish, but Levi couldn't give up the belief that he would watch Wing break the one-mile speed record someday. She was born to race, an athlete that God had given the heart of a champion. She was also the key to getting his father's farm and stables back. He couldn't trust her training to anyone else.

When the time to race her drew close, he would need to hire a driver. He knew several men and one woman who drove well enough and could handle her. Wing and her *Englisch* driver could enter the winner's circle and pose for photos and interviews. His church didn't allow members to seek fame or notoriety. That wasn't his goal anyway. He was happiest working in the background. He enjoyed bringing out the best God-given talent in every horse he trained.

Levi carried the screwdriver to the worn workbench beside the front door and returned it to the row of his tools he had set out earlier. He moved to the doorway to watch his brother walk toward the house, where Sarah sat on the porch steps.

Pretty little Sarah just might be the answer to his prayers. If Isaac showed an interest in her, Levi would do everything in his power to see that the two of them spent plenty of time together.

SARAH SAT WITH her hands clasped tightly together in her lap. She was afraid to look up as Isaac approached. Her butterflies had returned. So far their reunion wasn't going as she had imagined. She thought of all the things she wanted to say to him but didn't know where to start.

To her relief, he sat down beside her. "How have you been?" he asked.

"Fine. And you?" She kept her gaze modestly lowered.

"I could be better."

She glanced up, surprised at the bitterness in his tone. "I'm sorry. Is there anything I can do?"

He looked at her then. "Good old Sarah. Always eager to lend a helping hand."

Not exactly a flattering comment, the way he made it sound. "Is there anything wrong with that?"

"*Nee*, I reckon not."

"I'm really happy you have come back, Isaac."

"That makes one of us."

She grew a little impatient with his sour mood. "Then why are you here?"

"Because I didn't have a choice."

This didn't bode well for renewing their relationship. She folded her arms tightly across her chest and forced herself to be cheerful. "I've never forgotten the good times we had when you were here last. We went to all the singings and picnics. We hung out together a lot."

He gave a little nod and smiled at her. "That was a fun summer. I was so excited when my grandfather let me drive his truck and run his combine during the wheat harvest. I wish our church district in Pennsylvania let us own tractors and farm equipment the way your church does. I'd much rather drive a tractor than a team of horses."

"Now that you're here, you can farm with tractors, too."

"Are you trying to get me to look on the bright side?"

"Maybe." She wanted to nudge the conversation toward the happy times they had once shared. "We used to have such fun together. I've missed you," she added softly.

"I'm sorry I was so bad about writing."

"It doesn't matter. You're here now. We can say things face-to-face. I'm going to be baptized next month." She hoped he understood the broad hint that she was ready to settle down.

"That's nice."

"What about you?"

"No plans for that yet. I'm not sure I want to stay Amish."

She sucked in a quick breath and pressed a hand to her chest. Unless he joined the church, he couldn't marry a baptized member of the Amish faith. "This is the first time you've mentioned that to me."

He didn't seem to notice her shock. "I thought I had my mind made up, but things have changed."

"I'm sure the Lord will lead you to the right decision if you pray about it."

He rolled his eyes. "Now you sound like my mother."

A buzzing sound came from his boot. He quickly pulled a cell phone from inside his sock. "We can talk later, Sarah. I have to take this call." He stood up and walked away with the phone pressed to his ear. She was surprised by his abrupt departure, but she wasn't shocked to see him use a cell phone.

Many Amish youth carried such phones. Sarah's Amish community had phone booths located throughout the area where several families could share them. The church didn't allow members to have phones in their homes. Once a youth was baptized, the use of cell phones wouldn't be permitted. Sarah had only recently given hers up.

She stared after Isaac's retreating figure. She couldn't tell if he wanted to renew their relationship or not. His brother seemed more interested in her feelings than Isaac did. At least Levi had laughed off her bumbling attempt to surprise Isaac and tried to put her at ease.

Angela came out of the house. "Are you ready to go?"

Did she stay and wait for Isaac to come back? No, she had made the first overture. It would be up to him to make the second if he wanted to see her again. She didn't want to give the impression that she was desperately chasing after him.

The two women headed toward Angela's buggy. Levi walked out of the barn and came up to stand by the passenger-side door, but he didn't open it. He nodded to his cousin. "It's good to see you again, Cousin Angela. I wanted to tell you that my mother and I appreciated you and your *mamm* coming all the way to Pennsylvania for *Daed*'s funeral. Are you gals leaving so soon?"

Angela nodded. "Your mother isn't feeling well. I helped her lie down. Has she been ill?"

"She took *Daed*'s passing really hard. Do you think it's more than that?" A worried frown creased his forehead.

"I can't say. *Mamm* will be over later with supper for all of you. Perhaps your *mamm* will be feeling better by then."

"Your kindness is deeply appreciated." He shifted his gaze to Sarah. "Were you able to renew your acquaintance with my *brudder*?"

"Not as much as I would've liked. He had to take a phone call."

"That's too bad, but I'm sure there will be plenty of time for you to catch up now that he has moved to Cedar Grove for good."

Angela tilted her head slightly. "Aren't you staying here, too?"

"I'm hoping to return to Pennsylvania, but I'll be here for as long as my mother needs me."

The black horse trotted to the fence and whinnied from the corral. Sarah couldn't help but admire the beautiful animal with her shiny coat gleaming in the sunlight. She walked toward the fence. "Is she one of your racehorses your brother wrote about?"

Levi followed and stopped beside Sarah. Angela stood on the other side of him. The horse stretched her neck over the fence and allowed Levi to rub her face. "This is Wing and a Prayer. She's the best horse to come out of Raber Stables in many years."

It was easy to see the pride in Levi's eyes and to hear it in his voice. Isaac hadn't written much about the horses they raised, only that his brother was more interested in them than he was. "She has an unusual name."

Levi smiled. It brightened his face and crinkled the crow's-feet at the corners of his eyes. "*Daed* named her. Do you see the white mark on her forehead? It's shaped like a bird's wing. He said he knew the minute she was born that she was the answer to his prayers. Hence a Wing and a Prayer."

The horse pressed her face against Levi's chest. He rubbed the filly's cheek as Sarah gazed at him. She sensed the bond between the pair went deep. "You're very fond of her, aren't you?"

He grinned at Sarah. "I guess it shows. *Daed* and I cared about all the horses we raised, but Wing is something special. She'll be in the winner's circle one day."

Sarah studied him as he lavished affection on the pretty filly. The conviction in his voice when he spoke about her future touched a chord in Sarah. He believed in his horse wholeheartedly. His faith in her ability was absolute and appealing.

Sarah wanted someone to care about her in that same way. With unmistakable certainty, without hesitation or reservations, she wanted to know that she was his one and only love.

Levi glanced at her again, still grinning, and Sarah looked away. Levi was an attractive man in his own right, but he wasn't the one she wanted smiling at her. She looked around for Isaac, but he was nowhere in sight.

LEVI WASN'T USED to sharing his feelings so openly, but talking to Sarah was easy. Isaac could do a lot worse. As he was musing about the interesting young woman, the *putt-putting* of a tractor on the road caught his attention. Instead of passing by, the driver turned into the farmyard, pulling a trailer loaded with hay bales behind him. Wing wheeled away from the fence and galloped to the far side of the corral.

An older Amish fellow got down from an antique model John Deere. He wore dark blue pants with black suspenders crisscrossed over a light blue shirt. He had on a slightly battered straw hat, but he was beardless. It was odd for an Amish fellow his age not to be married.

Hitched behind the tractor was a trailer loaded with fresh-looking prairie hay and dark green bales of alfalfa. The fellow smiled and waved to the group standing by the fence. "I saw this hay just sitting in the field across the way and thought maybe you could use some. If not,

I'll put it back and the owner will never know it went for a ride."

Levi chuckled. "I've heard of kidnapping but never hay napping."

"You never napped in the hay? What kind of country boy are you?" He laughed heartily at his own joke. "I'm Ernest Mast. I know Angela and Sarah. Hello, girls."

Levi held out his hand. "Levi Raber."

A soft expression came into Ernest's eyes as he took Levi's hand. "You have the look of your father, that's for sure and certain, but I see your mother in you, too."

"You knew my *daed*?"

"Best friend I ever had."

The name clicked and Levi's grin widened. "Ah, you would be 'That Clown Ernie.' I've heard so many stories about you."

"None of them are true unless they involved fishing."

Levi chuckled. "I think they all involved fishing. Ice fishing with you was the story *Daed* told most often."

Ernest held up one finger. "It wasn't my fault that he fell through the ice. I told him not to walk there."

"Gigging frogs was another story he liked to tell about you."

Ernest rolled his eyes. "In my defense, your *daed*'s big foot looked just like a frog when it was covered in moss. I only grazed him with my spear once. It did not go clean through his toe."

Levi grinned and shook his head. "He did have big feet."

Ernest laid a hand on Levi's shoulder the way his father used to. "I think I'm gonna like you. Only one way to tell for sure. Do you fish?"

"Do ducks quack?"

A grin spread across the older man's face. "I'll show you where I catch the big ones. Bring that little brother of yours along. Seems I remember he liked to go fishing, too."

"I'll do that. Come inside and say hello to *Mamm*."

Angela laid a hand on Levi's arm. "She's sleeping now. Best to let her rest."

The smile left Ernest's face and disappointment filled his eyes. "Another time, then. Tell her I came by."

"I will," Levi assured him.

Ernest gestured toward the hay. "I'll unhitch the trailer and leave it so you can unload it when you have time. I'll pick it up later this week." He tipped his head toward the horses gazing at them over the fence. "That's a real fancy filly you have there. Trotter or pacer?"

"Trotter," Levi said, always happy to talk about Wing.

"Is she fast?"

Levi rocked back on his heels. "As lightning. She hasn't been in an official race yet, but when she is, she'll leave everyone in her dust."

Ernest's eyebrows shot up. "In a race? I knew your *daed* raised standardbreds, but does your Amish church let you own racing horses?"

"They allow members to breed, raise and train them, but once the horses are ready for the track, we have to hire someone from outside of our faith to race them. As the owner, *Daed* got to keep a percentage of the winnings. Sometimes those winnings covered the bills, sometimes they didn't. Wing is going to do more than pay the bills. She's going to be a champion."

Ernest cackled. "Now you sound like your *daed*. I don't know what our bishop will say about owning a racehorse. It's never come up before."

"I'll face that hurdle when I reach it."

"A wise plan. Sarah, what are you doing here?"

SARAH SMILED AT Ernest and prayed Levi wouldn't share the story of their first meeting with him. It was embarrassing enough without the community hearing an embellished version from everyone's favorite *onkel*. "I came with Angela to welcome her cousins to Cedar Grove."

"That was kind of you. I thought they could use some hay. I cut it off their meadow last week. It seemed only natural to offer to let them use it."

Levi laughed. It was a deep, hearty sound that made her want to smile. He shook his head. "You kidnapped my hay and now you're offering to let me have some of it. No wonder *Daed* liked you."

Ernest hooked his thumbs under his suspenders. "He was a fine judge of character. I knew it the first time we met. I'll tell you the story one day. It's a funny tale."

"Speaking of funny meetings." Levi glanced at Sarah.

She could feel the heat rising in her cheeks. She sent him a pleading look.

Please don't say anything about our first meeting. He'll tell everyone I made a fool of myself.

Levi grinned and turned to Ernest. "I once mistook

the mayor of Lancaster for a stable hand at the racetrack. I handed him a rake and a shovel and told him to clean stalls four and five. I couldn't figure out why everyone was taking his picture. The headline in the paper the next day said Mayor Keeps Campaign Promise to Clean Up Horse Racing. His photo was underneath."

Ernest cackled. "That's a *goot* one. I hope you don't mind me repeating it."

Angela tugged on Sarah's arm, forcing her to look away. "Here comes Isaac."

He strolled around the corner of the barn with an unhurried stride. "Hey, Ernest. It's been a long time. You haven't changed a bit. Angela, nice of you to come visit."

Ernest grinned at him. "I was about to invite your brother to go fishing the day after tomorrow. Will you join us?"

"Sounds great. I love fishing."

"Goot." Ernest rubbed his hands together.

"Mamm sent over some of her special poppy seed kolaches. They're in a basket on the table," Angela said cheerfully.

"Danki. I am kinda hungry. Levi?" Isaac nodded toward the house.

Levi shook his head. "Later."

Isaac shrugged. "Suit yourself."

Levi cast Isaac a speaking glance as he nodded toward Sarah. "Did you and Sarah have a chance to get reacquainted?"

"Sure." Isaac nodded to her. "We've already done our

catching up. I hear those kolaches calling my name. See you later, Sarah."

She frowned as he walked away. What was she supposed to make of that? Was he telling her that he would be coming around to visit her when they could be alone? Or was he uninterested in seeing her again?

Ernest clapped Levi on the shoulder. "I imagine you have plenty of settling in to do. Don't forget we have a fishing date for the day after tomorrow. Early."

Levi nodded. "Sounds good."

Ernest pulled the pin from the wagon tongue, climbed up on his tractor and drove off.

Angela started toward her buggy. "We had better get going, Sarah."

Levi followed them and opened the door for Sarah. He took her hand to help her up. The brief contact brought the heat of a flush to her cheeks. Something about him unnerved her. "Thanks for not telling Ernest I mistook you for Isaac," she said softly.

"It never crossed my mind." He stepped away from the buggy and touched the brim of his hat. Sarah glanced back as they drove away and noticed he was still watching them.

Angela had driven less than a quarter of a mile when she turned to Sarah. "Okay, how did it go? What did Isaac say?"

Sarah rolled her eyes. "Ugh. I don't want to talk about it."

"It can't be that bad."

"It was. I made a total fool of myself. I mistook Levi for Isaac. I practically had my arms around him before

I realized my mistake. Then Isaac acted like it was no big deal to see me again. He showed more interest in your mother's kolaches. I feel like an idiot rushing over to greet him."

Angela slipped her arm around Sarah and gave her a hug. "I'm sorry. I was really hoping the two of you might get back together."

Why would God bring Isaac back to Cedar Grove at this time of her life if not for them to be together? Maybe her sister was right and she was putting her cart before the horse. "It's like he doesn't remember what we meant to each other."

Angela withdrew her arm. "Sarah Yoder, I have never heard you sound so discouraged in my life. You are always upbeat and ready to take on any challenge. I can't believe you're giving up on Isaac after one brief visit."

"What do you think I should do?"

"If he doesn't remember what you meant to each other, then you need to remind him."

"You really think so?"

"I do. True love is worth any effort. You don't think it was easy to get Thaddeus to ask me out, do you? I had to corner him after the singing at the bishop's place last winter and tell him he needed to take me home. Then I had to ask him to kiss me at the spring picnic before he finally got up the courage to ask me out again. Don't give up on Isaac so easily."

"You're right." She needed some way to be alone with him.

Angela chuckled. "That Ernest is sure a funny fellow." She glanced at Sarah. "Thaddeus has a fine sense of humor, too. I think it's as important to be able to laugh together as it is to pray together."

Sarah couldn't recall what Isaac sounded like when he laughed. They must have laughed a lot when they were together. Why couldn't she remember the sound of it?

His brother, Levi, had a nice laugh. She liked the way his humor lit up his dark eyes and she liked the way he gave his full attention to the person he was talking to. Almost like he was trying to read what that person was thinking. She couldn't shake off the image of him joking with Ernest.

Sarah sat up straight. That was it. "Ernest said he is taking them fishing the day after tomorrow."

"Did he? I can't stand fishing. All that waiting for a catfish to find your worm in the murky water. Half the time they get away. If you do haul one in, you've got to clean it. I don't mind cooking fish, but I hate cleaning them."

"You don't understand. Isaac used to take me canoeing on the lake."

"Now, that sounds like fun."

"It was. We had a glorious time together."

Sarah chewed on her bottom lip as she began to formulate a plan. It was simple, really. All she had to do was borrow a canoe, have someone help her put it in the lake near where Ernest liked to fish, and then she would simply paddle into Isaac's view. He was bound to remember what fun they'd had together. She would invite him to come along and share a picnic lunch on that secluded beach near the dam.

It would be like it had been before. She had captured his attention once. There was no reason she couldn't do it again.

A canoe ride on a lovely spring morning. What could be better than that?

CHAPTER THREE

ON THE MORNING of the planned fishing trip, Levi fixed a breakfast of scrambled eggs and toast for himself and Isaac. The day was cool, almost chilly. His mother wasn't up yet, and he wasn't about to wake her. He was growing concerned about her.

After his father's death she had lost interest in many of the things she once enjoyed. Quilting, reading, sewing, visiting with friends. He hoped she would pick up those activities again as time healed her grief, but her determination to come to Kansas troubled him. What was here that she needed? For the past two days she wandered around the house as if seeking something that was no longer there.

Why had she given up her home in Pennsylvania to come here? She could have rented this farmland to another local family without leaving Lancaster. There were plenty of single women in their church district back home, if she truly wanted to see her sons married. Maybe it was to force him to give up raising racehorses. Maybe, but he suspected she had another reason. He wanted to know what that was.

His mother came in the room as he was transferring half the eggs to Isaac's plate. He scooped the rest onto another dish. She looked pale in her somber gray dress with a black apron and a black *kapp*. They were her work clothes. He hoped that meant she was feeling better.

She stared at the skillet he held. "What a poor *mudder* I am to make my *kinder* cook for themselves."

He slid the plate of eggs toward her, hoping she wouldn't notice that all he had was toast and coffee in front of him. "I thought a *goot mudder* taught her children how to take care of themselves."

"I reckon you are right. *Danki*." She sat down with a sigh, bowed her head to say a silent grace and then took a forkful of eggs. "These are *goot*. I may let you cook all the time."

"Scrambled eggs are the only meal I can turn out." He buttered his toast and took a sip of coffee.

"What do you boys have planned today?"

"We are going fishing with Ernest Mast this morning," Isaac said between mouthfuls.

She looked up from her plate with panic in her eyes. "Ernest? Is he here?"

Levi tipped his head slightly. "Not yet, but he should be here soon."

She pushed the eggs around with her fork but soon put the utensil down. "I reckon I'll have to face him sometime."

"Face him? Is there something we should know about?" Isaac asked.

She shook her head quickly, making the ribbons of her *kapp* tremble. "Ernest is a fine man. He reminds me of your father, that's all. They were friends."

Isaac looked satisfied. Levi wasn't. "Is something troubling you, *Mamm*?"

She glanced at him and looked down. "Troubling me? *Nee.*" She pushed her eggs around again. She could be tight-lipped when she wanted to be.

He folded his arms on the table and leaned toward her. "I think there is. I wish you would tell me what really prompted this move."

"I wanted to come home. How is that a bad thing?" She didn't look at him.

Because neither of your sons wanted to leave Pennsylvania and you sold my business out from under me.

He could have said as much, but he didn't. He had forgiven her, but that didn't mean he was ready to stay in Kansas. He couldn't shake the feeling that she was hiding something. "You know we will help however we can," he said gently.

"I have a lot of unpacking to do." She pushed back from the table, leaving her eggs on her plate, and left the room.

Levi looked at Isaac. "I think it would be best if I stayed here with *Mamm* this morning. You and Ernest go without me."

"I can hear you," she called from the other room. "I don't need a *kinder heeda*, Levi."

"I wasn't offering to babysit, only to help with unpacking," he called back.

"The boxes can stay packed until tomorrow if I don't get things put away today. Go fishing."

The *putt-putt* sound of Ernest's tractor approaching came through the open kitchen windows. Levi's mother walked back into the kitchen. She wore a thick gray cape over her thin shoulders. It was trimmed with two-inch-long black fringe. Levi was sure he'd never seen it before. Their previous church district would have considered it too fancy and insisted she remove the decorative fringe. Maybe this church had more lenient rules.

"That's a pretty cape. Is it new?"

She drew the ends together across her chest. "It's one I've had for many years. I couldn't wear it in Lancaster, but I couldn't bear to part with it. It was a wedding gift from a friend."

She walked outside with her head up. Levi followed. Ernest was coming up the walk. He froze at the sight of her. She nodded to him. "*Guter mariye*, Ernest."

He snatched off his straw hat. "*Goot* morning to you, too, Henrietta. You are a sight for these old eyes. As pretty as ever."

"Flattery is not our way," she said sharply, but Levi could tell she was pleased. "I hear you are taking my boys fishing."

"That's right. Grab a pole and come with us."

"My time is too valuable to spend it sitting on a creek bank."

"Ah, that's where you're wrong. We're headed to the lake. You know the spot I mean. You can't have forgotten it."

Her brows drew together in a fierce frown. "Creek or lake, it's still a waste of time in my eyes, but I know I can't talk you out of it. You always go your own way. It would be best if you didn't visit us again."

Puzzled at her abrupt tone, Levi stared at her as she

turned on her heels and went back in the house. Five minutes ago she had said Ernest was a fine man who reminded her of her husband. Now she was telling him to stay away. What was going on?

Ernest settled his hat on his head. "At least she spoke to me. That's more than I expected. Come along, boys. The fish are up and wanting their breakfast."

Levi wasn't willing to ignore what had just happened. "Why wouldn't my mother speak to you?"

"Because she doesn't like me much. Or at all."

"I'm sure there's a story that goes with that remark." Levi waited. Was Ernest somehow behind his mother's insistence on moving back to Kansas?

Ernest let out a long sigh. "There is a story right enough, but that's between your mother and me. We'll work it out. Are we going fishing or not?"

Isaac walked past the two men with his pole in his hand. "I'm going."

Levi put his curiosity aside for the moment, but he intended to find out what was behind Ernest's cryptic remarks and his mother's sudden animosity.

He and Isaac settled themselves in a small trailer equipped with folding chairs behind the tractor. Twenty minutes later they reached the turnoff to the lake. Ernest took a winding road back into the woods and stopped in a small clearing. "Hop out. This is the best fishing spot in the state. It's only about five feet deep here, but the south wind brings lots of food into this cove and the big catfish and bass sit down there waiting for the buffet to open."

Levi had to admit it was a pretty place. Trees lined the shore and leaned out over the water on either side. Off to his left a tall honey locust was in full bloom. The strongly scented cream-colored flowers hung in clusters and dropped petals onto the lake's surface each time the breeze stirred them. A finger of grassy land jutted about ten feet out into the water. It was just wide enough to line up their chairs. They settled themselves and had their poles in the water for about fifteen minutes when a canoe came around the point hugging the shoreline. Levi recognized Sarah as the only occupant. He glanced at his brother, who was busy baiting his hook. He hadn't seen her.

"Hello," she called out.

Isaac looked up and scowled. "What is Sarah doing here?"

"My guess would be canoeing," Levi said, holding back a laugh. Sarah wasn't being very subtle in her attempt to capture his brother's attention.

She raised her paddle to wave at them and hit a branch of a willow leaning out over the water. Something dropped into the canoe. Sarah screamed and shot to her feet. The canoe wobbled a second then flipped over. Sarah disappeared under the water. A snake slithered away from the canoe toward shore.

Sarah came up flailing wildly. Isaac and Ernest burst out laughing. Levi ran down the shore and dived into the water without a second thought. He was a lousy swimmer, but she was in trouble.

SARAH STRUGGLED TO keep her head above water. She couldn't swim. She tried to shout for help, but water rushed into her mouth, making her choke. Her head slipped under. Was this how she was going to die?

A strong arm circled her waist and lifted her. She gasped when she came up. The water burned her eyes. She couldn't see anything. She wrapped her arms around her rescuer and raised herself farther out of the water. "I knew you would save me, Isaac."

"Put your feet down."

The voice wasn't quite right. Again.

She squinted at the man who held her. It was Levi, not Isaac. She thought about letting go and sinking under the water but decided facing the embarrassment was better than drowning. The sound of raucous laughter made her glance toward the shore. Isaac and Ernest were slapping their thighs and laughing like a pair of fools.

"Put your feet down," Levi said again. "It isn't that deep."

"I can't. My shoes keep floating up. I think it's because the soles are thick rubber."

"Kick them off."

"*Nee!* They are brand-new. I'm not gonna leave them in this lake." She was still clinging to his neck. She remembered the snake that had fallen into the canoe with her and clutched Levi in a tighter grip as she looked all around. "Where's the snake?"

"Long gone. And you're choking me."

"Sorry." She relaxed her grip.

He began trudging toward the shore. Isaac and Ernest had recovered enough from their laughing fit to help Levi out of the water. He set her feet on dry ground. She couldn't make her arms release him. Tremors shook her, making it hard to talk. The water was miserably cold, but the breeze blowing over her wet skin was making her colder.

"I know it's childish to be frightened…of a snake that's probably harmless. I'm not usually so—"

"Childish," Levi finished for her.

She nodded and realized her hair had come undone. It hung in long, wet dirty-blond strands down her chest and back. Bits of moss, twigs and creamy flower petals decorated it. Isaac came over and held out a stick with her wet *kapp* dangling on the end. She managed a slight smile. *"Danki."*

"He gets thanks for fetching your prayer covering and I don't get anything for saving your life?" Levi still had his arm around her as she clung to his shoulders.

"I'm more grateful than words can express. I thought I was going to die." She laid her forehead against his chest and drew comfort from his solid presence.

He patted her back and scowled at the other two. "Glad I could help while these two were laughing their heads off."

"You have to admit it was funny," Isaac said, still grinning. "Don't get me wrong. I'm glad you're okay, Sarah, but the timing of it all was so perfect. Paddle up, snake down, Sarah up, Sarah down. Snake scoots away, Levi dives in."

"It landed in my lap. You would have jumped, too." Her scolding tone was undone by her chattering teeth.

"It was only a green snake. They don't bite," Ernest said. "Levi, I don't believe I'll be able to top your fishing story. As soon as you toss out your bait, you pull in a pretty gal. Who will believe it?"

Sarah was fed up with all of them. "Can you please take me home?"

Ernest gestured to a footpath leading into the dense woods. "Harold and Susan Miller live a few hundred yards that way. I'm sure they'll get you some dry clothes. It will be much quicker and more comfortable than a trip home in those wet things. You and Levi go ahead and get dried off. I can't get a tractor through those woods. I'll have to go around on the roads, but I'll take you home when I get there. No point in fishing here now. I'm sure they've all been scared off. Isaac, gather the poles and chairs."

"Thanks a lot, Sarah," Isaac called as he began to reel in his line. He wasn't happy.

She had managed to ruin his outing and make a fool of herself. How was she going to fix this? She was still shaking as she walked beside Levi.

"Hey, I've got one," Isaac shouted behind them. "Ernest, bring the net."

She and Levi turned to look. Isaac's pole was bent almost double. Ernest was hurrying toward him with the dip net.

Levi shook his head. "I don't believe it."

Sarah wrapped her arms around herself. "I'm so cold."

He gently brushed strands of wet hair away from her face. "What you need is a warm bath."

"I'm not sure I'll get in water deeper than my big toe for as long as I live." She glanced over her shoulder, wishing Isaac was the one walking beside her, but he was still trying to land his fish.

Levi smiled at her. "My suggestion is to stay away from boats. I reckon you know Isaac likes to go canoeing."

She remained silent.

"You were going to invite him to go with you. Am I right? Is there a picnic lunch at the bottom of the lake?"

What was the point of denying any of it? "Please don't tell him. I look foolish enough."

"Don't worry. Your secret is safe with me."

Sarah gazed at his face, wondering if she could trust him. "*Danki.* I appreciate that."

They began walking again. "I hope my brother's behavior just now hasn't given you a disgust of him."

Sarah shook her head. "Of course not. I'm sure it did look funny from where he was sitting. I don't mind being laughed at. He would have come to my rescue as soon as he realized I was in trouble."

She looked over her shoulder again. "I know he would have."

This woman liked his brother a whole lot if she could defend his lack of action. Levi took her elbow and guided her along the path through the trees. "Don't test your theory anytime soon."

The walk to the Miller place didn't take long. The elderly couple were out in their garden and spotted them right away. They called out greetings, but their welcoming expressions changed to concern as they took in Levi and Sarah's bedraggled condition.

Mrs. Miller held open the gate for them to come into the garden. "My goodness, Sarah, what happened to you?"

"I went for a swim in the lake. I don't recommend it. Susan, this is Levi Raber. He and his brother were fishing with Ernest near where my canoe tipped over. Levi pulled me out. Levi, this is Susan Miller and her husband, Harold."

"You poor children. Wait here." Susan went into the house and came out moments later with a pile of towels in her arms. She handed half of them to Levi, then wrapped one around Sarah's head and one around her shoulders before leading her into the house.

Levi waited on the front porch until Harold Miller brought out some fresh clothes. "The pants and shirt will be big, but they're dry." The older man tried not to smile. "The suspenders will keep the pants up despite the loose waist. Why don't you step into the garden shed and change? I'll hang your wet things on the line if you'll hand them out."

Levi stepped inside the shed lined with gardening supplies and tools. He quickly toweled off and got into the dry clothing. The pants and shirt were too big, but he wasn't going to complain. He opted to go barefoot instead of putting his wet boots back on. Harold knocked on the door frame. "Can you hand out the wet stuff?"

Levi opened the door and walked out. "I'll just throw them over the fence. Ernest should be here soon."

Harold chuckled. "I can't wait to hear the tale Ernest spins out of this adventure."

"He seems like a pretty funny fellow. Have you known him long?" Levi followed Harold back to the front porch and into the kitchen. Susan was setting out mugs and a coffeepot.

"We've known Ernest our whole lives, haven't we?" Harold took over the job of spooning the coffee grounds into the basket and adding water. Levi noticed that Susan's hands were crippled with arthritis.

She grinned and sat down at the table, letting her husband finish putting the coffeepot on the stove. "I've known Ernest almost since the day he was born. He was an ornery one in school. I can't tell you all the tricks he got up to."

Levi sat across the table from her. "Then you must know my mother, too."

"Henrietta? Of course I know her. How is she? We were sure surprised to hear she was moving back to Cedar Grove."

"She's not feeling the best."

"I'll have to get over to visit. I haven't seen her in ages."

"I got the feeling this morning that she and Ernest don't get along. Do you know why?" He was hoping the Millers could shed some light on his mother's behavior.

Susan shared a speaking glance with her husband. He gave an almost imperceptible nod of his head. Susan stood and went to the refrigerator. "Everyone thought Henrietta and Ernest would marry. They were almost inseparable growing up. It came as quite a shock when Walter's name was announced at the reading of the banns. No one knows what happened between them. That is something you'll have to ask your mother about," she said without looking at him. "Do you take cream in your coffee? I know Sarah does."

"Just black." He wasn't any closer to finding answers, but he wasn't going to give up. "I understand my *daed* and Ernest were friends, but *Daed* wasn't from around here."

Harold leaned back against the counter as he waited

for the coffee to perk. "There was a big tornado outbreak in southern Illinois when we were teenagers. Ernest and I traveled there with a group of a dozen Amish fellows to help with the cleanup. That's where we met your *daed*. Ernest and Walter hit it off the first day. Over the next several years Ernest would go to Lancaster for a few months a year and stay with Walter's family, and then your *daed* would come stay with Ernest's family during the summer harvest."

"That explains how he met my *mamm*."

Sarah entered the kitchen. Her dry clothes fit her trim figure perfectly, as she and Mrs. Miller were about the same size, but it was her hair that caught and held Levi's attention. She wore a white kerchief on her head tied at the nape of her neck instead of a *kapp*, but her blond hair was unbound and hung loose in wet tendrils that reached to the backs of her knees. She must have washed it because there wasn't a trace of moss or a single petal to be seen.

She noticed him staring. Her cheeks grew rosy red. "I need to get my hair dry. Susan, I'll be out in the flower garden letting the sun and wind do the work."

"All right, dear. Do you need help getting the tangles out?"

Sarah held up a wide-toothed comb. "I can manage. I would like some of that coffee when it's done."

"I will bring you some. How is my grandbaby?"

Sarah rolled her eyes as a smile brightened her face. "Getting big. You won't believe how much Caleb can eat. It seems that every month we have to sew new clothes for him. I think he's going to be as big as Joshua, maybe even as big as your husband."

Susan laughed. "I won't be able to pick him up much longer. They grow up much too fast."

"I know. Since he has learned to walk, there's no stopping him. He took a tumble down the stairs last week. Wound up with a goose egg on his forehead. He cried for a few minutes and then he was off again."

Sarah turned to Levi. "Their grandson, Caleb, is my nephew. I guess he is actually my stepnephew. Joshua, my brother-in-law, was married to Susan and Harold's daughter before he married my sister."

Susan's eyes grew sad. "God called our Amy home before us, but He gave us a beautiful grandbaby to ease our pain."

Sarah laid a hand on the older woman's shoulder. "My sister loves him like her own."

Susan patted Sarah's hand. "I know. Is Laura Beth expecting yet? One grandson is fine, but I'm looking forward to making clothes for a little girl."

Sarah pressed one hand to her lips. "If she were, it might explain a lot. Laura Beth and Joshua have been holding hands, sneaking kisses when they think I'm not looking. They both seem so happy lately. That would be an amazing blessing. Laura Beth feared she would never have children of her own."

"She is a *goot* stepmother to our grandson."

Harold tipped his head to the side. "Sarah, did you say you were out canoeing alone? I've never known you to go paddling around the lake by yourself."

Sarah glanced at Levi and smoothed the front of her skirt. "I was going to meet a friend. Now I need to let the Novak brothers know their canoe got away from me. I hope they won't be angry."

Mrs. Miller dismissed Sarah's worry with a wave of her hand. "Harold can slip over and tell them this afternoon. They'll be able to pick it up easily enough with those Jet Skis. Zoom, zoom, zoom, every weekend on that lake. It makes me wish the *Englisch* could create a quiet engine. Go out and start drying your hair."

At the door Sarah cast Levi an imploring glance. He nodded slightly and she smiled in relief. He figured she didn't want the Millers to know she had been angling for his brother's company. Levi was happy to keep her secret and earn her gratitude. From the way things were going, he might need to offer his assistance in her future efforts to gain his brother's attention, and Levi wanted her trust.

OUTSIDE IN THE garden Sarah sat on a small bench and waited for Ernest and Isaac to arrive. She absentmindedly pulled the comb through her wet hair as the sun warmed her. The more she thought about it, the more it troubled her that Levi was the one who came to her rescue and not Isaac. She had to believe Isaac would have saved her if Levi hadn't acted first. Had Isaac been the one with his arms around her, she wouldn't have felt the cold of the water.

She had to laugh at her own assumption. The lake water was too cold even for true love to warm it. She had made such a fool of herself.

She heard the screen door bang shut and looked over her shoulder. Levi was coming toward her with a mug of coffee in each hand. She quickly began to braid her hair. It wasn't proper for Levi or anyone outside of her family to see her with her hair loose.

He took a seat beside her on the bench and held out a cup of coffee. "They should have been here by now. Maybe the fish kept biting after all."

She took the mug he handed her. "You would think a basket of fried chicken, potato salad and apple pie would have tempted any fish away from Ernest's worms."

"Was that the lunch my brother missed out on? No wonder the snake jumped in the boat with you. He must have been hungry."

She shivered and stared at the coffee in her mug. "Don't remind me."

"Sorry."

He bent to look at her face. "Have you considered that Isaac might be too old to enjoy the antics of a love-sick *maedel*?"

Sarah gripped her mug as heat bloomed in her cheeks. Levi had been front and center at both her humiliating episodes. She was seriously starting to dislike him. "I don't appreciate you laughing at me."

"Take a *goot* look at my face. I'm not laughing."

She brought her chin up. "I'm not a lovesick girl."

"Then I'm going to offer some free advice. Stop acting like one."

She put her mug down and folded her arms over her chest. "If you have something to say to me, Levi Raber, just say it."

CHAPTER FOUR

SARAH BRACED HERSELF to hear Levi's opinion of her.

"My brother isn't a teenager anymore. It could be that he's looking for a more mature woman."

"What makes you think I'm not a mature woman?" she snapped. "Anyone can make a mistake. Even you."

"I apologize if I have offended you. I know you like my brother, and he used to like you."

She raised one eyebrow. "Did you know that Isaac proposed to me when I was sixteen years old?"

"I did not. I assume you refused him?"

"I knew he wasn't serious, but I was willing to wait for him. Are you aware he intended to return to Cedar Grove and farm with your grandparents the following summer?"

"He talked a lot about returning to Kansas for a year or so. His interests changed after our grandparents passed away."

"Circumstances kept us apart, but we cared deeply for each other in those days. I still care for Isaac and I believe we are meant to be together."

"I'm not sure Isaac sees it that way, but I believe you. In fact, I hope you are right."

"Danki." She relaxed a little. "He is considering leaving the Amish. Has he told you that?"

Levi frowned. "Do you think he's serious?"

"He may be."

Levi was silent for a long moment. "It would break *Mamm*'s heart."

"And mine," Sarah added softly.

"Our mother is eager to see Isaac wed. I want to see him settle down, too. Maybe I can help the two of you."

"How?"

"He was very angry with *Mamm* for springing this move on us. To tell the truth, so was I. Let me speak to Isaac about you. It could be he isn't ready to give up his *rumspringa* and he resents our mother's attempt to force him into a decision. Sometimes he can dig in his heels and refuse to budge out of pure stubbornness."

"So maybe I have a chance with him?" she asked hopefully.

"Give me a couple of days. I'll be your go-between."

Among the Amish, a go-between was usually a male relative of the woman a young man wanted to court. The go-between would find out if she was open to the idea and report back.

"Why would you want to help me? I haven't made a good impression on you so far."

"It could be because I'm a nice guy. I did pull you out of the lake."

"Or?" She waited to hear his real reason.

"Okay. I intend to return to Lancaster and buy back my father's broodmare farm. I can't do that until I'm sure Isaac is settled with a wife who can help him care for our mother when she gets older. I promised my father I would look after her and that's the best way I can see to do it. I'm not about to stay here for the rest of my life, and I don't plan to marry until I have restored my family's business."

"I reckon that's a pretty honest answer." She resumed braiding her hair. "I should be flattered that you think I'm the right person to help care for your *mamm*."

Sarah heard a tractor approaching. "Sounds like our ride is coming."

Levi rose to his feet. "Finish your coffee before it gets cold." Then he walked back into the house.

When Isaac and Ernest pulled into the farmyard, Sarah saw that Isaac was driving the tractor. She remained seated on the bench. She wasn't about to throw herself at Isaac again today. To her delight, he came into the garden and dropped down onto the bench beside her. He was grinning from ear to ear. When he smiled he looked like the boy she used to know.

"Did you see that Ernest let me drive?"

"I did." She finished the rest of her coffee.

"He said this church district not only lets members drive tractors and farm vehicles, but a fellow can get a driver's license. Not just before he joins the church, but even after he is baptized if he has a job where he needs to drive for his work. I don't remember my *daadi* telling me that."

"Perhaps because you were too young to get a license then, so it didn't matter."

"I reckon. Are you sure you're okay?"

He did care about her. She smiled. "I'm much better now that I'm warm." She put her empty mug down and continued to crisscross the sections of hair without looking at him.

"I knew it would take more than a little dunking to rattle Sarah Yoder."

"It was more than a little dunking," Levi said, coming up behind them. As grateful as she was to Levi, Sarah wished he would go away. She was finally having a conversation with Isaac and she didn't want his interference.

She handed him her empty coffee mug and rolled her eyes toward the house. "Would you take this back to Susan with my thanks and make sure Ernest has a chance to enjoy some coffee, too?"

She saw comprehension dawn on him. He nodded, took the mug and walked away. She wished Isaac was that attuned to her wants.

Sarah glanced at Isaac's face. She saw embarrassment and what she hoped was concern for her. He cleared his throat. "I didn't mean to make light of your ordeal. I'm glad you're okay. I should have jumped in to help you, but Levi thought of it first. The next time you need rescuing, I'll be there for you."

She kept her gaze down, but inside her worries were fading. They would grow close again. All they needed was more time together. "I'm sorry I spoiled your fishing."

"Oh, I landed a big one after you left. Ernest said he would take me again one of these days. He also mentioned your brother-in-law has an engine repair business."

"Joshua King is my brother-in-law. He and our neighbor Thomas Troyer have a business together, but Joshua also farms. We grow corn and hay for our livestock, but our cash crops are lavender and pumpkins."

"I don't care much for flowers and pumpkins, but I would like to see Joshua's workshop. I enjoy tinkering with engines."

"Joshua would be delighted to show you around. Most of the work is done at the Troyer place in Thomas's big shed. Our worship service is going to be held at the Troyer farm next week. You'll have a chance to see the place then."

He leaned closer. "Do I really have to wait more than a week?" His cajoling tone sent ripples of happiness along her nerve endings.

"Of course not. You can visit anytime. I will show you around if Joshua and Thomas are busy."

He chuckled and leaned back. "What does a woman know about repairing gasoline engines?"

"More than you might think. I know the difference between a diesel and a gas engine. I have even set the timing on the spark plugs for a gas pickup."

"Is that so?" He looked impressed.

Joshua had shown her how to do it once. She wasn't certain she could do it again, but she wanted to impress Isaac and let him know she could be interested in the things he liked.

"I'm happy we are getting a chance to catch up," she said, casting a sidelong glance at him. She needed to change the subject before he could quiz her on exactly how much she knew about engines. "Your brother told me that the move came as a surprise to the both of you. He said you were upset about it."

"Did he? I'm surprised he even noticed. *Mamm* sold the farm without any discussion and she sold all the horses Levi cares so much about. I didn't mind that, but I left behind some close friends."

The sadness in his voice stirred pity in Sarah's heart. "I'm sorry. That must've been hard for you." She laid her hand on top of his.

His lips curved in a half smile. "You're the first person who acts like they care about what I'm going through."

"I do care, Isaac. You and I used to be close friends. I missed you when you left, so I understand a little of what you're going through."

He gazed into her eyes. "That means a lot, Sarah."

Her heart soared. "Why don't you tell me about your friends. You mentioned a few of them in your letters, but I'd like to learn more about them and about you. I used to know you quite well, but a lot of time has passed for us, hasn't it?"

He stuck his legs out and crossed one boot over the other as he leaned back. "There really isn't much to tell."

"Most of the people you wrote about were *Englisch*, right? Have you spoken to them on your phone?"

"A couple of them have called me." His expression grew guarded.

"Just because you've moved away doesn't mean those friendships will fade. Our friendship has survived being apart." She tried to sound encouraging and cheerful.

He stood up abruptly. "I'd rather not talk about the

friends I left behind. We should get you home. Ernest is going to look at our tractor and see if he can get it going. It wouldn't start for me yesterday."

Sarah finished the end of her braid quickly and wished she had a piece of string to tie around it. She flipped the heavy, wet hair over her shoulder, knowing it would come undone, but hopefully not before she reached home.

Levi, Harold and Ernest came out of the house followed by Susan. She handed over Sarah's wet things in a pillowcase. "I pray you don't suffer any ill effects from your dunking. A nice bowl of chicken soup will ward off any ill effects. Make sure you get your hair dry. My *mudder* always said if you go to bed with a wet head, you'll wake with a cold."

Isaac grabbed the end of Sarah's braid. "It must take forever to get this much hair dry. *Englisch* women have it so much easier. I think it's too bad Amish women can't cut their hair." He seemed unaware of the shocking statement he had just uttered as he walked toward the tractor.

Sarah felt a headache coming on.

LEVI COULDN'T BELIEVE Isaac had spoken against one of the most sacred edicts of the Amish church. An Amish woman never cut her hair. It was her glory to be viewed only by her husband and by God. It was clear Sarah was already uncomfortable having hers on display. Isaac drawing attention to it didn't help.

Levi turned to Harold and Susan. "I apologize. My brother has not been baptized and sometimes speaks foolishly."

"He lacks an understanding of our ways," Harold said dryly.

"It's nothing that time can't fix," Ernest said. "We were all young and impulsive once."

Levi was grateful for Ernest's understanding, but he knew Isaac's comment would be repeated to the elders in the church.

Levi helped Sarah into the small trailer. Isaac settled himself in the driver's seat on the tractor. Ernest climbed up and sat on the fender beside him. He looked back and winked at Sarah. "I'll see that he doesn't put us all in the ditch."

Mrs. Miller stepped up to the trailer. "Unbraid your hair, Sarah, and let the wind blow it dry on the way home."

"I don't want to appear vain." Sarah bit the corner of her lower lip.

Mrs. Miller waved away her concern. "No one who sees you with wet hair will think such a thing. We may be plain folks, but we are practical, too."

Sarah nodded. "You're right."

"Isaac, why don't you leave the driving to Ernest and entertain Sarah," Levi suggested.

"I need to learn how to run a tractor if I'm going to run the farm. You can entertain her." Isaac turned the key and the engine roared to life.

Levi gave up trying to talk to Isaac and climbed in the trailer with Sarah. The trailer jerked forward as Isaac let out the clutch, sending Levi stumbling backward until he landed in Sarah's lap. He struggled to his feet. Embarrassment made him scowl at Isaac, but Sarah giggled, drawing Levi's attention to her. She was loosening her hair. "He's right. He needs some practice."

Levi sat down as the tractor and trailer lurched again. "Apparently a lot of practice," he said, a little grin creeping out as he met her smile. "Remind me not to ride with him again anytime soon."

Isaac brought the tractor to a stop at the end of the Millers' lane. When he took off again, he nearly unseated Ernest. Sarah grabbed hold of the side of the trailer. "I agree completely. None of us are safe."

She continued undoing her braid and soon had her hair fanned out behind her. He tried not to notice how beautiful it was. Being wet made it look darker, but the drying ends were a bright golden color, like wheat straw. It was impossible to ignore it, especially when the wind flipped some of it against his face.

He had seen his mother's hair down any number of times, and even some of the women in his church district, if he happened by their homes early in the morning or late in the evening. He shouldn't find Sarah's hair so attractive, but he did. He was tempted to reach out and draw his fingers through it the way she was doing as she spread it to dry.

He swallowed hard and looked the other way. "This region is different from our Amish country."

"How so?"

"Amish farms back east normally have large white barns and white houses with multiple smaller houses cobbled together. Here in Kansas the Amish houses don't look different than any other farmstead."

"I imagine a casual observer might miss the fact that

electric lines strung along the roads bypass one house but lead to another. A tractor in the front yard doesn't tell you it's an Amish farm unless you notice the trailer behind it is a refurbished pickup bed. Most of our buggies are stored in sheds until we take them out to go to church every other Sunday morning."

They passed a field where a man on a tractor was plowing. Levi knew he was Amish by his dress and his beard. "I miss seeing the draft horse teams. It is strange to know an Amish fellow is using a massive piece of farm equipment that is gas or diesel operated and not pulled by horses."

Sarah nodded in understanding. "A combine harvester or even a large grain truck traveling down the road might be driven by an Amish farmer or by an *Englisch* one. The only way to tell the difference is if you get a glimpse of a ball cap or a straw hat."

It was a different lifestyle. It would take a lot of getting used to. Except he didn't want to become accustomed to Kansas farm life.

A green pasture dotted with sheep drew his attention. A little girl holding a large white puppy in her arms waved and called out to them as she ran to the fence. Ernest tapped Isaac on the shoulder, and he pulled the tractor over to the side of the road. The little girl came running up to them. "Hello, Onkel Ernest. Hello, Sarah. Did you lose your *kapp*?"

Sarah leaned her arms on the side of the trailer. "Hello, Grace. My *kapp* came off when I fell in the lake. Now I'm trying to get my hair dry."

The child's eyes grew wide. "*Mamm* can lend you one. Shall I go ask her?"

"*Nee*, I have it here. My friend Isaac fished it out of the water for me. Isaac is driving the tractor, and this is his brother, Levi. They have just moved into our church district along with their mother."

Levi smiled at the child. "That's a mighty fine dog you have."

The little girl lifted the big puppy higher. "This is Muffin. When she grows up she's going to help Meeka guard our sheep, isn't she, Onkel Ernest?"

"I hope so. But what did I tell you about making her a pet?" Ernest asked.

Grace gave him a sheepish look and put the puppy on the ground. "She has to live with the lambs, so she knows they are her family. But I'm her family, too. She likes me a lot." The puppy danced around her feet, begging for attention.

A Great Pyrenees came loping across the pasture to check out the activity. Ernest gestured toward the big white dog. "Meeka has to teach Muffin her job. She can't do that if you are always taking Muffin away from her."

Grace's contrite expression made Levi grin. She gave Sarah an imploring look. "Can you come visit us?"

Sarah nodded. "We will one day soon."

Grace brightened. "And Caleb, too. Don't forget to bring him."

Sarah laughed. "I'm certain Laura Beth and Joshua will remember to bring the baby."

"Okay, g*oot*. Bye." She waved and began running

toward a farmhouse in the distance. The puppy and several of the lambs raced beside her.

"She's a cute kid," Isaac said.

Ernest grew uncharacteristically somber. "She is my great-niece and we are blessed to have her. If it weren't for Sarah, Grace might not be here at all."

Levi glanced at Sarah. "How so?"

She shrugged. "*Gott* put me in the right place at the right time, that's all."

"You are being modest, as you should be," Ernest said. "I will tell the story. A year ago last winter, Grace was found on my porch by my nephew Owen during a blizzard. No one knew who she was. Owen took her to our neighbor Ruth while we tried to find out where Grace belonged. Several weeks later her mother was found dead. She had been shot. The man who did it was Grace's father, a criminal who wanted to take Grace away. Owen, Ruth, Sarah and Grace were trapped by him in their barn. He threatened to shoot them if they didn't give him Grace. Owen and Ruth hid Grace and tried to stall the man while Sarah climbed through a skylight in the roof and went to call for help. The sheriff arrived in time to save them."

"What happened to the criminal?" Isaac asked eagerly.

"He was killed in a shoot-out with the sheriff," Sarah said quietly.

Levi could see she was distressed at having the story repeated. He read the sadness in her eyes. The loss of any human life by violence was tragic. It seemed there was more to Sarah Yoder than the silly girl trying to gain his brother's attention that he had seen so far. "That was very brave of you."

She shook her head. "Not really. I just happened to be small enough to fit through the skylight."

"You've got to tell us all about it," Isaac said, clearly wanting more details.

"Maybe another time," Levi said. "I think we should get Sarah home. She has had a trying day."

She sent him a look of gratitude. *"Danki."*

"Okay, sure." Isaac gazed at Sarah for a long moment. Then he started the tractor again.

Levi hoped his little brother was seeing Sarah in a new light, too.

SARAH HAD A full-blown headache by the time the tractor chugged and jerked up the final hill to her home. Laura Beth and Joshua came out of the house to meet them as Isaac came to a stop. The scent of the lavender fields in the sun lifted her spirits, as did the sight of their dainty blooms nodding in the wind. The look of surprise on her sister's face told her she had a lot of explaining to do once their company departed.

Joshua looked up at Ernest. "Your old tractor is running a little rough. Do you want me to take a look at it?"

"Would you mind?" Ernest got down to stand beside Joshua and Isaac as they gathered beside the front of the machine.

Levi got out and helped Sarah down from the trailer.

"What happened to you?" Laura Beth asked, eyeing Sarah's loose hair and borrowed clothing. "That isn't the dress you left the house in this morning."

"It belongs to Susan Miller. I fell in the lake and she gave me some dry clothes to wear."

"It's a mighty fine story," Ernest said from his spot beside the tractor. "Young Levi here dived in to save her after her canoe tipped over. Fortunately, the snake got safely away."

Sarah scowled at him. "And you would still be laughing as I went to a watery grave. At least Levi was brave enough to save me."

Ernest looked taken aback. It wasn't like her to be snappish, but she was tired, her head hurt, she wanted to lie down and for some reason she felt like crying.

Laura Beth slipped an arm over her shoulder. "Come on in the house, dear. I'll make you a cup of hot tea."

Tears sprang to Sarah's eyes. "*Danki.* I would like that."

She allowed her sister to lead her inside and she promptly burst into tears. Laura Beth gathered her into her arms and held her close as she patted her back. "There, there. Everything is okay now."

"I don't know what's wrong with me," Sarah wailed.

"It's obvious you have had a stressful ordeal. Come into the kitchen and tell me about it. Start at the beginning. What happened after you left home this morning?"

Sarah wiped her eyes and followed her sister into the kitchen. She sat down at the table and used a paper towel to dab her eyes and blow her nose. "I walked over to the Novak place. I borrowed their canoe."

"What on earth for?" Laura Beth filled the kettle at the sink.

"You're going to think I don't have the sense *Gott* gave a goose. I know I used to say that about you, but in this case I'm the guilty one."

Laura Beth laughed. "It wouldn't be the first time."

Sarah managed a tiny smile. "True. I thought Isaac would be as happy to see me as I was to see him. We've been apart for so long."

Laura Beth carried the kettle to the stove and turned on the burner. "Are you saying he wasn't?"

"He almost ignored me. It's like he has forgotten how close we were. We were more than friends."

"I'm sorry."

"I know. I was just so certain of his feelings."

"Not to make light of your disappointment, but what does that have to do with a canoe?"

"On our way home the other day I told Angela that Isaac didn't seem to remember how close we used to be. She said that I needed to remind him. That true love is something worth fighting for. I had overheard Ernest offer to take Isaac and Levi fishing. I knew the spot where he liked to go. I packed a picnic lunch, borrowed the Novak brothers' canoe and paddled over to where I thought they would be. Isaac and I went canoeing at least a dozen times the summer he was here. I thought seeing me in the canoe might prompt him to want to join me and we could go enjoy a nice picnic lunch together."

"Things didn't go as planned?"

"A snake fell from a tree into the canoe with me. I jumped up and tipped over."

"How awful."

"The awful part was hearing Isaac and Ernest laughing their heads off. Fortunately, Levi didn't see the humor in it and came to my rescue."

"Thank *Gott* for his presence and quick thinking." Laura Beth left the room and came back with a brush in her hand. "Let me get those tangles out."

Sarah untied the kerchief on her head and leaned back as her sister began brushing her hair. "Levi guessed what I was trying to do. He wants his brother to settle down. He thinks he might be able to help rekindle the romance between myself and Isaac."

Laura Beth stopped brushing. "What is he suggesting?"

"He has offered to be a go-between for us. He's going to find out exactly what Isaac's feelings are for me."

"That certainly seems sensible."

"I thought so, too, but…"

"But what?"

Sarah turned her head to look at her sister. "I'm afraid to hear what Isaac tells him."

Laura Beth smiled at her. "That's understandable. You hope that his feelings haven't changed but it appears they may have. My question is, have your feelings changed now that you have spent some time together?"

"We haven't really spent more than a few minutes together. I'm so confused by his behavior that I don't know what to think."

She rubbed her throbbing temples. "When Angela told me Isaac had moved here with his mother, I was sure it was part of *Gott*'s plan for me. I thought we would take up where we left off. We would court and eventually marry and be neighbors with you and Joshua."

Laura Beth stopped brushing Sarah's hair. "We can't know *Gott*'s plan for us until it unfolds. Joshua and I are the perfect example of that."

Sarah looked up at her sister. "I know you both suffered before you found each other. It is a joy to see the two of you so happy together. Oh, Susan Miller wants to know if you're expecting. Are you?"

Laura Beth leaned down. "I am," she whispered, "but it's too soon to share the news. If all goes well, I'll let Susan know in a few weeks."

"She's praying for a little girl."

"I'm praying for a healthy baby." Laura Beth laid her hand on Sarah's shoulder.

Sarah reached up and squeezed her sister's fingers. "That's what I pray for, too."

Laura Beth and her first husband, Micah, had been childless through the ten years of their marriage. Sarah knew the anguish her sister had endured during the months when her husband was ill and eventually died. Laura Beth deserved every happiness the Lord could shower upon her.

"My problems are small in comparison to the ones you have faced. I will stop feeling sorry for myself and do what I can to regain Isaac's affections."

"If you don't mind some advice from your sister, the most enduring marriages begin with friendship. Be a friend to Isaac. And please avoid any more brazen behavior like today."

"I had to leave my hair down to dry."

"I'm not talking about your hair. I'm talking about chasing after Isaac in a canoe."

Chastised by her sister's words, Sarah nodded, but she knew her future happiness depended on what Levi learned from Isaac. How soon would he speak to Isaac and how soon could she see Levi again to hear what Isaac had to say about her?

CHAPTER FIVE

THEIR MOTHER WAS standing by the kitchen sink rubbing her temples when Levi and Isaac entered the house after their fishing trip. She straightened and raised her chin. "Well? What did that man have to say about me?"

"What man?" Isaac asked, hanging up his hat.

"I think she means Ernest," Levi said.

Her lips thinned. "Of course I do. What did he say? Tell me now."

Levi shrugged. "Nothing."

Mamm didn't look like she believed him. "Nothing? He didn't say anything about me? He didn't talk about your father?"

"What did you expect him to say about you? Are you okay? Do you have another headache?" Her brow was creased with pain.

"I think Ernest said, 'At least she spoke to me,' or something like that." Isaac sniffed the air. "Smells *goot*. What's for lunch?"

She gestured to the stove. "There is a meat loaf and vegetables in the oven. I have already eaten." She turned and left the room without answering Levi's question. She had been suffering from headaches a lot lately.

He took off his straw hat and hung it on one of the

pegs by the kitchen door. "I would like to know the story between our mother and Ernest."

Isaac lowered the oven door, picked up a pair of hot pads and brought out a foil-covered pan. "You won't learn it from *Mamm* until she is ready to share."

"I'm afraid you are right about that." Levi found a pitcher of lemonade in the refrigerator and filled two glasses at the table.

Isaac dished up a plate for himself and one for Levi. The two men ate in silence. When they were finished, Levi carried the plates to the sink and washed them. He returned to the table and sat across from his brother. "Would you care to explain your relationship with Sarah to me?"

Isaac donned a wide-eyed puzzled expression. "What do you mean?"

Levi wasn't fooled. "Sarah says you asked her to marry you before you left Cedar Grove. Is that true?"

"I was joking. Did she think I was serious?"

Levi folded his arms on the tabletop and leaned toward his brother. "Why don't you tell me your side of the story? I have already heard from her."

Isaac stirred a spoonful of sugar into his drink. "It was such a long time ago. I don't really remember what went on."

"Did you propose to her?" Levi kept his gaze fastened to Isaac's face. He could usually tell when his brother was being less than truthful.

"I was seventeen. I might've said something that she took for a proposal. I'm not sure."

Levi leaned back in his chair. "'Will you marry me, Sarah?' Is that what you said?"

Isaac stirred his lemonade a little faster. "I know I never used those words."

He stopped stirring and laid down his spoon, but he didn't look at Levi. "I might've said something like I could see myself spending the rest of my life with her. Now, that isn't a real proposal."

Levi blew out an exasperated breath. "Isaac, that's pretty close. A sixteen-year-old girl who fancies herself in love with you could easily see that as a will-you-marry-me moment."

Isaac finally met Levi's gaze. "I have never thought of us as anything other than long-distance friends. We exchanged letters but they weren't love letters."

Levi sat back. "She's kind of cute and funny in an odd way. Would you consider going out with her?"

"Nee."

So much for fostering a romance between the two of them quickly. Levi moved to his backup plan. "Okay, that's *goot*."

Isaac shot him a puzzled look. "It is?"

"Mamm intends to deed this land to the first son that marries."

"Oh, so you're interested in going out with Sarah to get this farm. Why? To spite me because you know I'd love to own my own land? You don't want to be a farmer. You want to raise horses."

"I do want to raise and train horses. This is valuable land, and the owner can sell it. Like I said, Sarah's cute.

Right now she has her eye on you, but I can change that." Levi hoped his words were enough of a challenge.

"You're giving yourself too much credit, *brudder*. Face it—the girls have always liked me better than you."

That was exactly what Levi wanted to hear. "She also mentioned that you are thinking about not joining the faith. Is that true?"

"If you must know... I'm in love with someone back in Pennsylvania. She isn't Amish. Her name is Brittany."

Levi drank the last of his lemonade as he processed this new information. "How serious are you about this *Englisch* woman?"

"Plenty serious."

If that was the case, why hadn't he stayed in Pennsylvania? He could have gone to work for any stable. Arnold Diehl would have hired him out of respect for their father. Something didn't add up. "How serious is she about you?"

"Her folks don't approve of me. I'm not educated enough. She's attending college, but I'm not giving up on her."

This was an unexpected complication, but Isaac had been in and out of love a half-dozen times in the past. What he needed was someone to take his mind off the girl he'd left behind. A nice Amish girl who was eager to go out with him. Levi sighed heavily. "You're going to break Mother's heart if you don't join the church."

Isaac looked pained for a moment but shook his head. "It can't be helped."

Levi didn't want his brother on the defensive. "I understand."

Isaac's eyes narrowed. "You do?"

"The mind can't tell the heart what to do. Take Sarah. She's still into you after all these years. You must be flattered by that."

Isaac moved his head from side to side. "Maybe a little."

"I like Sarah. I'd ask her out, but feeling the way she does about you, she'd turn me down flat. Why don't you take her out on a date or two so she can see that you don't click anymore now that you're both older. That way you can let her down easy. What do you think? As a favor to me."

Shaking his head, Isaac looked unconvinced.

Their mother walked into the room with unsteady steps. She leaned heavily on the back of a kitchen chair. "What are you both still doing in here?"

"We were talking about Sarah Yoder," Levi said quickly. "She has a crush on Isaac."

Henrietta's eyes brightened as she turned to Isaac. "Does she? I think that's wonderful. She seems like a nice girl. She's been writing to you for years. As I recall, you were very taken with her the summer you stayed with my folks. Are you planning to walk out with her?"

He held up one hand. "I'm not interested in going out with Sarah. We're barely friends."

She frowned at Isaac. "I think you should ask her out. What have you got to lose? You may find you like her as more than a friend. You owe her that much consideration for keeping in touch after all this time."

Isaac rose and picked up his hat. "We need to get the hay off the trailer and into the barn. The forecast is for rain tomorrow and we have already wasted the entire morning."

Henrietta glared at them both. "If there is so much work to be done, why are you still sitting at the table?"

"I was just on my way out." Levi rose and snatched his hat from the peg. "I want to repair the roof on the porch, too. I see where it has been leaking."

"And Ernest says we need to get the corn cultivated this week," Isaac added.

"I don't care to hear any opinion voiced by that man." She turned around and left the room.

The two brothers stepped out onto the porch and Levi closed the kitchen door behind him. Isaac settled his hat on his head. "I wish you hadn't said anything about Sarah. I was afraid *Mamm* was going to insist I marry the girl. I can see her trying to force my hand."

Getting his mother to help put pressure on Isaac was exactly why Levi had mentioned Sarah. "She knows we Amish are free to choose our spouses, but she can make your life miserable by nagging you about it. Which would be worse? Going out with Sarah a few times or listening to *Mamm* harp on the subject day in and day out?"

Isaac turned to face Levi. "Did you notice how pale she was and how unsteady she was on her feet?"

"I did. Do you really want to upset her more?"

Levi saw Isaac struggle with his decision before he shook his head in resignation. He tapped one finger against Levi's chest. "I'll go out with Sarah twice. Then I'm done."

Levi grinned. "That's reasonable, and it should satisfy *Mamm*."

"I don't know what you're smiling about. She's still going to like me more than you." Isaac's phone buzzed. He pulled it from his sock and walked away to answer it.

Levi's grin widened. "I'm smiling because I'm not the one that's getting married, little brother. You are. The sooner the better, if I have anything to say about it."

As long as Sarah did her part. Which shouldn't be hard. She was already half in love with Isaac, although Levi couldn't see why.

SARAH WAITED A full day and a half without hearing a single word from Levi, and she grew increasingly impatient. That afternoon she kept staring out the kitchen window willing him to show up while she helped her sister trim and tie lavender into bundles. What was keeping him? Was he afraid to bring her bad news?

"Why are you putting two ties around those?" Laura Beth asked.

Sarah looked down at her work. A half-dozen bundles had two rubber bands around them instead of one. "I can't keep my mind on my work. How long does it take to ask Isaac about his feelings for me? Levi has to know that I'm on pins and needles. Do you think he's afraid to tell me that Isaac doesn't want to go out with me?"

Sarah slapped her bundle of flowers against the

countertop, sending petals everywhere. "That's the only reason I can see for stalling this long."

"Calm down," Laura Beth said softly. "The men have work to do. None of their cornfields have been cultivated. It's time to plant beans. They have horses and cattle to take care of, fences to repair, hay to put away, and all that work should be done before Levi can come trotting over here to put you out of your misery. You have been as cranky as Caleb was when his last tooth came in. Shall I get you a cold teething ring?"

"Is that your way of telling me that I'm acting like a child?"

"You took the words right out of my mouth."

Sarah crossed to the table, sat down and rested her chin on her hands. "I pray for patience, but I still don't seem to have any."

"Thankfully for the rest of us, you don't need any more patience."

"Why not?" Sarah didn't lift her chin off her hands.

"Because I see Levi Raber is coming up the lane."

"He is?" Sarah jumped to her feet and raced to the window. He was riding on the fender of Ernest's tractor. He climbed down as soon as Ernest brought the vehicle to a stop.

Sarah stood at the sink with her hands clasped tightly together and her eyes closed.

"Aren't you going to go speak to him?" Laura Beth asked.

"I'm afraid of what he has to say."

"You can't change it by wishing, so go hear the man out."

Her sister was right. Sarah went to the door and opened it. Levi, Ernest and Joshua were gathered around the front of the tractor. Levi stepped away from the group when he caught sight of her. "I wanted to get some lavender cream for *Mamm*. She says it soothes her headaches, but she is out of it. I was wondering if you might have something similar."

Sarah was aware of everyone watching them. "We do have some creams and lavender water that might do the trick. Follow me, and I'll show you."

Sarah led him to the drying shed that was built onto the side of the barn. She opened the door and stepped inside but left it open after he came in. She glanced outside and saw Ernest and Joshua were still standing beside the tractor. She turned to Levi. "What took you so long? I have been waiting for ages."

"Farming comes before your love life. I got here as soon as I could."

"Why did you bring Ernest?"

"I was walking this way. He happened by and offered me a ride."

"Did you tell him why you were coming here?"

"Will you take it easy? Of course I didn't. I told him I was coming to get something for Mother." He looked around at the bundles of lavender hanging on their drying racks. "This stuff smells really good. No wonder people buy it."

"I agree that it smells nice." She walked to the workbench and sat on one of the stools beside it. "Now, what did your brother say?"

"He thinks of you as a friend. You care about my

brother—it's easy to see that. He once cared about you a great deal. I think you can resurrect those feelings. He has agreed to ask you out and see where it leads."

She pressed both hands to her cheeks. "He has? I'm so glad."

"You will have the opportunity to show him what a good wife you will make, and how much you care about him and about our family. My brother needs someone like you."

Sarah choked back a laugh. "Someone who can't paddle a canoe without falling overboard?"

"*Nee*. He needs someone who can love him wholeheartedly in spite of his faults. Someone who is determined to do what is best for him without thinking of herself. Someone who's willing to crawl out a skylight and get help for a child when a man with a gun is waiting outside."

Sarah realized she was being conned. "That's laying it on a little thick."

His eyebrows shot up. "What?"

"You heard me."

He winced but then his eyes brightened with mischief. "The part about the skylight was too much?"

"Definitely." She folded her arms across her chest. "What else did Isaac say?"

"Nothing important," Levi said quickly. Too quickly.

"Tell me."

He sighed. "He isn't excited about the idea, but he is going to ask you out of consideration for remaining his friend all these years."

"Because he feels sorry for me."

"Not at all."

"Wonderful. I think we're done. Thank you for being my go-bctwccn. Does your mother really need something for her headaches?"

"She does and that's the truth."

Sarah stood and opened one of the drawers of a side cabinet. Taking down a small jar of cream, she held it out to Levi. "Have your mother rub this on her temples and then lie down with a cool cloth over her eyes."

He took the jar from her. "*Danki.* Are you going to walk out with Isaac when he asks?"

"I'll think about it." She made to move past him.

He stepped in front of her. "I know you haven't stopped caring about Isaac just because he isn't eager to go out with you."

She didn't want to admit it, but he spoke the truth. "All right, I still care, but I'm not going to cry myself to sleep over him, and I don't need a pity date."

"I'm asking that you walk out with him a few times. What could it hurt?"

Her mouth dropped open with shock. "What could it hurt? It could hurt me!"

"You're overreacting."

"*Nee*, I'm not. I deserve a hardworking, devout man who believes I light up his life the way the moon and the stars light up the night sky. One who thanks *Gott* for bringing us together. I dream of raising my family here. I want that more than anything. What if…what if I fall in love with him and he doesn't love me in return? What then?"

Her raw nerves made her want to run and hide. Why

had she shared her deepest fear with Levi? She wished she could call the words back. Tears sprang to her eyes. Nothing was right. She pushed past him and ran out the door.

LEVI STEPPED OUTSIDE to follow Sarah, but she was already crossing the field of lavender toward a low stone wall. She looked back when she reached the wall, sat down on it, swung her legs over and disappeared down the other side. He had never felt more like a villain in his life.

Sarah Yoder wasn't simply a part of his plan to get Isaac married. She was a woman with deep emotions. He had just inflicted more pain than he had ever imagined he was capable of doing. He turned and saw Joshua and Ernest watching him. He considered offering an explanation for Sarah's behavior but realized comforting her was more important. He followed her trail through the crushed flowers until he reached the wall. She was sitting on the other side of it with her knees drawn up to her chest and her arms around them. He thought she was crying but he couldn't see her face.

"Sarah, I would like to apologize."

"Go away."

"Tell me if I'm laying this on too thick. I'm truly sorry that I made light of your feelings. They do matter. You deserve to be loved for who you are. My brother is a fool if he can't see that. I will cross the county on my knees so that you can believe how contrite I am. Please forgive me?"

He waited a long moment, afraid she wasn't going to speak to him after all.

"The part about crossing the county on your knees is a bit much." Her voice was muffled.

He slipped over the wall and sat down beside her with his back to it. "Should I shorten it to cross the road?"

She sniffled and wiped her nose with her sleeve. "Crawl a mile would be better." She tipped her head to look at him. "Do I get to choose the road?"

"Sure."

"Lincoln."

The name was familiar, but he couldn't place where he had seen it. "Okay. Is it pavement, dirt or gravel?"

"Gravel."

He deserved the punishment but he sincerely doubted that she would put him through the agony. "Am I forgiven?"

"My Amish faith says I must."

"If you weren't Amish, where would I stand?"

"On the edge of Lincoln Road, waiting to crawl a mile of it on your knees. Follow our lane over the creek and up the hill and you will be on it."

Lincoln was the rough and rocky road that rose and dipped through some rugged country between Cedar Grove and the King farm. "I'm sincerely glad you follow the teachings of our Amish faith."

"You're forgiven. Now go away."

"Are you sure you're okay?"

She glanced at him again. "Just go."

"Thanks for the lavender cream for my mother. I appreciate your kindness."

He stood up and hopped over the wall. She sprang to her feet. "Wait."

She scrambled over the wall, wiped her cheeks with her hands and brushed the wrinkles from her dress. "I need to speak to your brother."

He arched an eyebrow. "Are you sure?"

"There are things I need to know and things I want to say to him."

"I will be happy to relay the message."

She shook her head and squared her shoulders. "No more go-between, no more messages or letters. I must speak to him face-to-face."

"I can see it now."

Her eyes narrowed. "See what?"

"The determination that took you through a skylight and over the top of a barn with a gunman standing outside. I'm afraid my brother is in for a rude awakening. Come along. Can Ernest bring you home afterward?"

"I'll ask."

They walked back to the house together. Laura Beth was standing on the porch with her son in her arms. She glanced from Sarah's tearstained face to him. "Is everything okay?"

"Time will answer that," Sarah said as she climbed to the fender of Ernest's tractor. "I'll explain later. I need to speak to Isaac. Ernest, can you bring me home afterward?"

"Sure." Ernest frowned at Levi. "Then someone might

want to do some explaining to me. I don't like to see my friends upset."

Levi leveled his gaze at Ernest. "I don't like to see my family members upset either. You have some explaining to do as well."

Ernest nodded briefly. "I reckon I do at that. Climb on board. The sooner we get to your place, the sooner we can clear the air all around."

The trip home took only about twenty minutes. It was a rough, jarring ride. At his farm Levi looked around for Isaac but didn't see him. He hopped off the tractor. "I'll check inside."

Levi walked into the kitchen and immediately knew something was wrong. The coffeepot on the stove was boiling over and the smell of burnt coffee filled the air. He turned off the gas, grabbed an oven mitt and pulled the pot off the burner. He looked around. "*Mamm*, where are you?"

Isaac came up from the basement with two empty bushel baskets in his hands. "What's that stench?"

"*Mamm* let the coffee boil over. What were you doing?"

"Putting some jars of produce away for her in the cellar. How did things go with Sarah?"

"She's outside waiting to talk to you. Where's *Mamm*?"

"I don't know."

Levi stepped into the living room and saw his mother slumped in her chair. She was deathly pale. He rushed to her side. "*Mamm*, what's wrong?"

She didn't answer. He glanced at Isaac and pointed toward the front door. "Get Sarah in here."

Isaac bolted outside. Levi took his mother's hand and patted it. She didn't respond. He shook her shoulder. Her head slipped sideways. Fear gripped his heart.

Moments later Ernest and Sarah were at his side. "What happened?" she asked.

Levi shook his head. "I don't know. I just found her like this."

Sarah looked over her shoulder. "Isaac, call 9-1-1. Tell them to send an ambulance." She turned back to Levi. "Has she been sick?"

"She hasn't been herself for the last few weeks, but she hasn't done anything like this before."

Sarah stood up. "Let's move her to the sofa."

Ernest immediately stepped forward to gather Henrietta in his arms. He carried her to the sofa across the room and tenderly laid her down. Levi saw he was almost as pale as Henrietta.

Ernest knelt beside the sofa and took hold of her hand. "Don't do this to me, Henny. I can't lose you again."

CHAPTER SIX

LOSE HER AGAIN? What did Ernest mean by that? Sarah wanted to ask, but before she could, Isaac held his phone away from his ear. "The ambulance is on its way."

Ernest rose from his place beside Henrietta. He wiped his eyes with the back of his sleeve. "I should move my tractor so they can get close to the house." He quickly left the room.

Sarah prayed the ambulance would hurry. She had no idea what was wrong with Mrs. Raber, but her color didn't look good. Her lips had a bluish tinge to them. Sarah read the distress on Levi's face and wished she could do more to comfort him. She laid her fingers over his as he clutched his mother's hand. "It's going to be okay, Levi. *Gott* is merciful. We have faith in His goodness."

He looked at her and some of the fear left his eyes. "I pray you are right."

She nodded. "The doctors will want to know your mother's medical history. Does she take any medication? If she does, you will need to send it along with her."

"I don't think she takes anything. Isaac, do you know?"

"She takes something for her blood pressure and something for her heart. I'll get them. She keeps them in her room." He left and returned a few moments later with two prescription bottles.

Levi appeared stunned. "How is it that you know what pills she takes and I don't?"

"You and *Daed* were always busy with the horses. I'm the one that took her to her doctor's appointments every few months."

"Why didn't she tell me this?"

Isaac shrugged. "She didn't want to worry you."

"I should've known something was wrong. I should've asked. I could see she wasn't well lately. I wish you had told me." His gaze returned to his mother's pale face. "Why didn't I pay more attention? I promised *Daed* I'd take care of you."

Sarah's heart went out to Levi. She recognized the guilt underlying his words. The wailing of a siren in the distance claimed her attention. "I hear them coming. I'll go direct them here. Our farms are sometimes difficult for the EMS to find." She ran out of the house and down the lane toward the county road. She waved her arms when she saw the ambulance approaching. They turned in and stopped.

The driver rolled down his window. "Are you the person who called with a medical emergency?"

"My friend called. It's his mother. We found her unconscious. Go straight ahead. She is in the house. Her family is with her." Sarah stepped aside as the ambulance drove away. She walked slowly back to the house.

Ernest was standing on the porch with his hat in his hands. "She's got to be all right. She has got to be."

Sarah sought to comfort him. "She is in *Gott*'s hands."

"As are we all. It is His will that must be done and none of mine. I just hope I didn't leave it too late."

"Leave what too late?" Sarah asked.

"Forgiveness," he said, staring at the front door. He looked to Sarah. "Shall I take you home? I want to let the bishop know what has happened, and then I'll go to the hospital."

The front door opened, and the ambulance crew came out with Henrietta on the stretcher. Levi went to the front of the vehicle and got in. Isaac stopped beside Sarah as he waited for his mother to be loaded into the back of the vehicle.

"I have something I want to ask you, Sarah," Isaac said in a low tone.

"Don't worry about that now. Go take care of your mother and your brother."

"Me? Take care of Levi? *Nee*. He would laugh to hear you suggest it."

"He's frightened, and he's blaming himself for not knowing she has a heart condition."

"He would have known if he had paid more attention to his mother and less to his horses."

"I think he realizes that now. Don't hold it against him. You could have shared what you knew as well."

"I guess I could have. Maybe I enjoyed knowing something that he didn't. Levi thinks he knows everything and that he's always right. He holds others to impossible standards. He isn't the easiest fellow to get along with, never has been, but he's gotten worse since *Daed* was killed."

"I'm sorry to hear you two have differences, but you

must forgive Levi's past hurts. It is what your mother would want."

His gaze softened. "Wise Sarah, always helping others. Even this poor excuse for a friend."

He did care about her. A weight lifted from her chest. "Talk to your brother and make amends."

"I'm not sure I know how."

She smiled at him gently. "Saying you're sorry is always a good place to start."

The brothers needed to put aside their differences and join forces to support their mother. Hopefully, Henrietta's illness would provide the prodding they needed. "I pray for all of you."

One of the ambulance crew got out of the back. "You're welcome to ride along, Mr. Raber. Your mother is asking for you."

"Danki." Isaac tipped his head to Sarah and got in.

"She's awake. That's *goot*," Ernest said, coming to Sarah's side. He held his hat in his hands, twisting it around by the brim.

"Let me know if I can do anything for you or your mother," Sarah said to Isaac before they closed the doors. She wasn't sure if he heard her or not. The ambulance pulled away with its red lights flashing. Ernest strode toward his tractor, and Sarah hurried to keep up with him.

"I WISH WE would hear something." Levi paced back and forth in the hospital's small waiting room.

Isaac leaned forward in his chair with his elbows on his knees. "I'm sorry."

Levi stopped pacing to look at him. "What for?"

"A lot of things, but mostly for not telling you about Mom's illness. That was wrong of me."

Levi sat down beside him. "You were respecting her wishes."

"That was part of it, but another part of me wanted to punish you."

Levi bowed his head. "I don't blame you. *Daed*'s death was my fault. I never should've let him take that horse out."

"That was an accident."

"One I could've prevented."

"*Daed* knew what he was doing. He loved getting behind a fast horse."

"I'm the one who should've been exercising that animal. I was the one responsible for his training. His owner hired me, not *Daed*."

"You might not want to hear this, but *Daed* was a much better driver than you are."

Levi chuckled. "You are right. He was."

"You couldn't know a balloon would come out of nowhere to spook the horse. I never blamed you. *Mamm* doesn't blame you."

The new gelding their father had been driving had panicked when a deflating helium balloon drifted out of the sky straight toward his face. A shiny purple Happy 5th Birthday balloon lost by some unknown child caused the horse to bolt in fright. The sulky cart overturned. His father's broken ribs had punctured his lung. He died in Levi's arms.

Tears stung Levi's eyes. "*Mamm* hates the horses."

"She doesn't hate them. It's that she's always been

afraid one of us would get hurt doing something she felt went against the Amish teaching she was raised with. *Daed* being killed cemented her belief that our business wasn't acceptable to *Gott*."

Levi glanced at his brother. "We've never talked about this before."

"There are a lot of things we haven't discussed."

"There are. If I haven't mentioned it before, I happen to love you, little *brudder*."

A crooked smile lifted one side of Isaac's mouth. "Even if I don't like your horses?"

"*Daed* and I always hoped you would come around to our way of thinking and share our passion."

"I thought you didn't want me underfoot. I thought you liked being *Daed*'s favorite."

Levi shook his head in disbelief. "I was never his favorite. He spent more time talking about how smart you were and how he hoped we could raise a winner so that he could buy you your own farm than he did talking racing with me."

Isaac sat up straight. "*Daed* wanted me to have my own farm?"

Levi pulled back a little. "Didn't you know that?"

Isaac shook his head. "When did he tell you this?"

"When you returned from your summer out here. All you talked about was going back and farming with *Daadi*. *Daed* wanted you closer to home. He took a chance on a couple of high-priced mares already in foal. They didn't produce the winners he had hoped for. I resented the way you turned your back on our business after he went into debt for you."

"I had no idea. Reckon Sarah was right. Saying I'm sorry has opened up some long-overdue conversations."

"When did she say that?"

"While we were waiting for them to get Mother settled in the ambulance."

Sarah was a wiser woman than he had given her credit for. "She was pretty upset with me when I talked to her earlier." It seemed like days had gone by, not simply hours.

Isaac smiled softly. "Sarah has a good heart. I don't think she'll hold a grudge."

Perhaps his brother would end up with Sarah after all. Levi looked down at his boots. Not that it mattered now. There was no way he could go back to Pennsylvania knowing his mother was ill.

The door to the waiting room opened and a young woman in a white lab coat and wearing a stethoscope around her neck stepped inside. "Are you the family of Henrietta Raber?"

Levi shot to his feet. "We are her sons. I am Levi. This is Isaac. How is she?"

"Please sit down." The doctor took a seat across from them.

Levi and Isaac exchanged worried glances before sinking back onto their chairs.

The doctor smiled. "I'm Dr. Megan Black. Your mother is resting quietly. I have had an opportunity to speak on the phone with her physician in Lancaster and I'm still waiting for some test results before I can give you a definitive diagnosis. It appears your mother suffered a fainting episode brought on by her A-fib."

"I don't know what that is." Levi was familiar with illness in horses but not in people.

"Atrial fibrillation. It's an abnormal heart rhythm. She is also suffering from dehydration and low blood pressure. I believe those things played a role in her fainting episode today. Her physician tells me her husband passed away less than a year ago. Has your mother been depressed?"

Levi glanced at Isaac, who nodded. "We've noticed some changes. She hasn't been doing the things she used to enjoy. She rarely left the house before we came here," Levi said.

"She eats like a bird," Isaac added. "I know she has lost weight."

Dr. Black nodded and glanced at her notes. "Forty pounds, according to her records from Pennsylvania. That's quite a bit for a woman her size. I want to keep her here for a few days. We need to adjust her medications, get her fluid levels back up to normal and see if we can't improve her nutritional status. You may go see her now. She'll be moved to our cardiac unit as soon as there is a bed available. Do you have any questions?"

"Is she going to be okay?" Isaac asked.

"She'll need to be monitored and I will want home health to follow up, but her chances of making a complete recovery are excellent."

Levi sagged with relief as he thanked God for sparing her.

"Try to eliminate or limit any stress she has been under. I have no doubt that your Amish community will rally around to help get her back on her feet. I've seen it happen with every Amish patient I have taken care of. Would you give the staff the phone number for your telephone booth or your nearest non-Amish neighbor in case we need to contact you?"

"I have a cell phone," Isaac said.

"Excellent. Make sure the nurse has that number." The doctor rose and opened the door. Isaac and Levi followed her down a short hall to the emergency room. She pulled aside the curtain and Levi saw his mother lying on the white sheets of a hospital bed. She had a bag of fluid dripping into an IV needle in her arm. There was an oxygen mask over her face. On the wall above her head, a TV-like screen showed red and green blips moving across it. He had no idea what he was seeing, but he assumed the doctor would tell him if there was something wrong.

He stepped up close to his mother. "*Mamm?* Can you hear me?"

Her eyes fluttered open. "I'm happy to see your face one last time, my dear son."

"You will see him many more times," the doctor said, holding her chart in her arms.

Henrietta turned her face away. "It's *Gott*'s will that I go to be with my Walter."

The doctor laid a hand on Henrietta's shoulder. "Nothing can deter the will of God, but I doubt you will see Him today."

Levi's mother looked past him. "Where is Isaac?"

Levi glanced over his shoulder. He was sure Isaac had been right behind him. "I will get him for you."

He stepped out in the hall and saw that Isaac was

talking on his phone. "I can't tell her I'm serious about a woman who isn't Amish. She's in the hospital... We'll have to wait... You don't mean that... Look, I can't talk now."

The outside doors slid open and a tall Amish man with a gray beard down to the middle of his chest came inside followed by a tiny elderly Amish woman leaning on a cane. Levi's cousin Mary Jane and her daughter Angela came in behind them.

Mary Jane rushed forward. "How is she?"

"The doctor thinks she will make a full recovery. My mother believes she is on her way to see my *daed*. How did you know she was here?"

The tall man beside Mary Jane smiled. "A lack of telephones doesn't prevent news from traveling fast on our Amish telegraph. I am Bishop Weaver. This is my mother, Martha Weaver. Ernest Mast was kind enough to spread the word to me and to your family. I have not had a chance to welcome you to the community yet. I'm sorry we must meet under these circumstances. I will go and speak with Henrietta. I knew her as a young girl. We are blessed that she has returned to the community where she was born."

The bishop and his mother stepped around Levi and went into the cubicle behind the curtain. Mary Jane followed him. Angela lingered. "We have already arranged for several women in our congregation to sit with your mother tonight and for as long as needed."

"*Danki*. I hate to think of leaving her here."

"She won't be alone. Mother and I will stay with her until eight o'clock. After that, Sarah Yoder will sit with her through the night. Our *Englisch* neighbor is waiting outside to drive you home whenever you are ready. He claims he doesn't mind waiting because it gives him a chance to catch up on his reading."

Isaac came walking back to the exam room. His face was grim. "Is it all right if I go in?"

Levi nodded. "She was asking for you. Is everything okay? I overheard part of your phone conversation."

"I was letting a friend back in Lancaster know what's going on. I'll be fine."

"We have a ride back to the farm whenever you're ready."

"I would like to stay for a while, unless you need me at home."

Levi shook his head. "I can manage the evening chores by myself."

Isaac nodded to Angela. "Thank you for coming so quickly."

"We take care of our own. That is our way."

A nurse came out of the exam room. "Mr. Raber, the unit has a bed ready for your mother now. We're going to be moving her. I'll ask all of you to step into the waiting room until we get her settled. Visitation is restricted in the cardiac unit, so please be aware we allow no more than two visitors at a time in the room. Do you have any questions?"

None of them did. Levi waited until his mother was settled in her room in the cardiac unit. Then he assured her he would be back later. He left her room, glad that Isaac had stepped up to stay behind. It made it easier for Levi to leave, and he knew his mother was glad to have Isaac close.

The forecasted rain had arrived. A steady drizzle greeted him when he stepped outside the hospital doors. It would help the corn, but it didn't do anything for his mood. As his driver was about to pull out of the hospital parking lot, Levi leaned forward. "Could you take me by Joshua King's farm first?"

"Sure can."

Levi sat back and stared out the rain-speckled window. There was no reason to see Sarah, but he felt the need to speak to her again. To let her know how his mother was getting along and simply to see her. Something about being with Sarah smoothed out the rough places in his life.

She and her family came out onto the porch when the car stopped in front of the house. She was holding Caleb on her hip. With everyone waiting for news, Levi realized he wouldn't have a chance to speak to Sarah alone. He stepped out of the car and climbed the steps of their porch.

"How is your mother?" Laura Beth asked.

"The doctor thinks she will be fine, but she does want to keep her in the hospital for several days just to be sure. She advised us to try and limit Mother's stress."

Joshua slipped his arm around his wife's shoulders. "Then our prayers have been answered."

"That's all I came to say, except I'm grateful to you, Sarah, for your help today. My brother and I talked about a lot of things that we should have discussed long before now."

He was unprepared for the way her gentle smile tugged at his heartstrings. "I'm glad for both of you. God comes first, but our family is the second most important part of our time here on earth." She dropped her gaze to the babe she was holding. "Isn't that right, Caleb?" The blond-haired, blue-eyed chubby boy shyly turned his face into her shoulder.

"Do you need any help with your farm chores?" Joshua asked.

"I can manage." Levi tore his gaze away from the appealing sight of Sarah holding a toddler. Knowing there was nothing else to say, he tipped his hat and got back in the car. As the driver pulled away, Levi looked out the rain-streaked window to see Sarah was still on the porch watching him. She lifted Caleb's hand to wave at him.

She had such a good heart. His brother was nuts if he didn't do all he could to gain her affection.

Levi turned back around. If that happened and his mother made a full recovery, he might be able to return to Pennsylvania with a clear conscience.

Only for some reason the idea was less appealing than it used to be.

SARAH WAITED UNTIL the car disappeared from sight before going back into the house. She set Caleb on the floor with his favorite pull toy. It was a wooden horse on wheels that made *clickety-clack* sounds as if the pony was running when he pulled it.

The rain was keeping Laura Beth and Sarah from harvesting the last of the lavender and it was keep-

ing Joshua stuck inside as well. Laura Beth set up the
cream separator in the kitchen. Sarah was going to help
her sister but saw Joshua was ahead of her. The two of
them shared a speaking glance as he closed his fingers
over her hand and together they turned the crank. Sarah
knew there was some special meaning in the gesture,
but she didn't ask what. She left them alone. Would
she have that kind of relationship with Isaac? Would
some shared memory make them smile at each other
with tenderness?

She got a dust rag out of the closet along with some
furniture polish and began to clean all the wooden sur-
faces in the room. After finishing in the living room and
guest bedroom, she went up the stairs, cleaning each
spindle of the railing until she reached the top. She sat
down on the step and tried to get her mind off Levi
and the sadness she had seen in his eyes. She should be
thinking about Isaac. Henrietta was his mother, too, but
somehow she knew Levi was taking his mother's illness
to heart more than his little brother was.

"Daydreaming?" Joshua asked from the bottom of
the stairs.

"Remembering. Every time it rains, I think about
how much you looked like a drowned cat when my sister brought you in the door that first night you showed
up here."

He came up the steps and sat one tread lower than
her. "I imagine that was a pretty good description of
me. Your sister saved my life when she pulled me out of
the rain-swollen creek, but she saved something much
more important when she rescued Caleb from his car

seat before my car was swept away by the flooding. I still have nightmares about it sometimes. God was good to me that night, although I had been sure He'd forgotten all about me when I left my Amish community for the outside world."

"He didn't."

"I know that now, but sitting in a jail cell for selling stolen goods reinforced that feeling. When I got out I found my wife was dying and I had a son she hadn't bothered to tell me about. Her last wish was for me to take Caleb to her parents to be raised in an Amish home. It felt like God was playing the ultimate bad joke on me. It was your sister's kindness and the welcome I received in this community that showed me how wrong I was. God was always looking after me, even when I had turned my back on Him."

Sarah weighed her next words carefully. "When did you know you were in love with my sister?"

"Probably the first time I saw her eyes light up when I entered the room and I wasn't holding the baby. She fell for Caleb first, you know. How are things between you and Isaac?"

"I haven't decided how I feel about him. On one hand, I'm angry with him for ignoring me when he first arrived."

"And on the other hand?"

"On the other hand, I pray we can rediscover the affection we once held for each other. We are older now and we can look at each other with new eyes. I'm not the same person I was five years ago, and neither is he. Levi said Isaac intends to walk out with me."

"How do you feel about that?"

"I still care for Isaac a lot. If I do go out with him, it will be because he has convinced me that he cares about who I am now, not who I used to be or because he feels sorry for me."

"Do you remember when I said I wouldn't call you sensible? I may have to change that opinion."

Sarah grinned as she pressed her palm against his forehead. "Are you feeling all right?"

"I'm sure it's just a twenty-four-hour bug. I'll be back to my skeptical self by tomorrow." He rose to his feet. "How about a game of checkers?"

"As long as we can keep Caleb from eating them, you're on."

He went down the stairs, and Sarah followed more slowly. Finding a path forward with Isaac might not be easy, but to have a chance at the kind of love her sister and Joshua shared would be worth it.

She stopped and tried to recall if Isaac's eyes lit up when he looked upon her, but all she could remember was the sparkle in Levi's gaze when he was about to say something outrageous.

She dismissed the thought. Isaac was the one who mattered.

LEVI COULDN'T SLEEP. A little before midnight he gave up trying and drove the tractor twenty miles through the pouring rain until he reached the hospital. He didn't care for tractors, but he knew how to handle one. He had learned at Arnold Diehl's stables as a youngster prepping the track before the day's workouts.

Inside the hospital, he walked down the empty corridor to the cardiac unit. His footsteps sounded unnaturally loud in the silence, tempting him to tiptoe. A nurse buzzed him into the unit. Ahead of him he saw an Amish fellow turn into his mother's room. Levi found the door slightly ajar. He eased it open, not wanting to wake his mother if she was asleep.

To his surprise, Ernest sat in a chair beside his mother's hospital bed. Sarah sat across the room. Her head was tilted back and to the side in her chair. He could see she had fallen asleep.

Neither his mother nor Ernest noticed him. His mother turned her head toward her new visitor. "Ernest? What are you doing here?"

"That's a foolish question, Henny. Where else would I be, knowing you were here. It took five good years off my life seeing you loaded into that ambulance."

"I'm sorry."

Ernest reached over and took her hand. "Don't worry your head about it. I suspect I have more than a few good years left in me."

She closed her eyes and turned her head away from him. "I don't have much time left," she whispered.

"What kind of *narrisch* talk is that?"

She looked at him again. "It's not crazy talk. It's why I had to come back. I wanted to be where I was happiest when I was young. I needed to see you. Before I face my judgment, I have to know that you forgive me."

Levi knew he shouldn't listen in, but he couldn't seem to back out of the doorway.

Ernest let go of Henrietta's hand and crossed his

arms over his chest. "I reckon you'll have to put off dying for a while, then, because you'll get no forgiveness from me."

"Oh, Ernie, you don't mean that."

"I've lived thirty years with your betrayal, Henny. Do you think I'd say that was okay just so you can die in peace? Nope. You're gonna have to ask me again when you get out of this hospital. When you're standing on your own two feet in the exact same place where you wrecked my life instead of lying there trying to make me feel sorry for you."

"Oh, go away and let me die in peace," she snapped in a much stronger voice.

"I'll go away, but you'd be better off living the life *Gott* has given you rather than courting an early death. What would Walter say to such nonsense?"

She turned away in a huff and drew the covers over her shoulders.

Ernest rose to his feet and headed for the door. Levi stepped out into the hall as Ernest closed the door softly and turned to him. The older man's shoulders slumped. "Was that too harsh, do you think?"

Levi struggled to control the anger burning hotly inside of him. "To deny a woman on her deathbed some comfort and forgiveness? *Ja*, I'm thinking that was too harsh."

"Your *mamm* is not on her deathbed. She's been wallowing in pity and maybe wanting to die, but she's a lot stronger than you think. It very nearly broke my heart to say such things to her, but I'm not giving her an excuse to waste away in bed and neither should you."

"Are you a doctor now?"

"*Nee*, but I spoke with Granny Weaver. She says your mother will get stronger if she puts her mind to it."

"Who is Granny Weaver?"

Before Ernest could answer, a small, dark-haired nurse came hurrying down the hall pushing a piece of equipment. "I need to check Mrs. Raber's vital signs."

The men stepped apart to allow her to enter the room. A few seconds later Sarah came out. She pulled the door shut and turned to Ernest, her eyes snapping with anger. "Ernest Mast, are you out of your mind? Do you know what you've done?"

CHAPTER SEVEN

LEVI TOOK A step away from the fury in Sarah's eyes. Her gaze was pinned on Ernest, but Levi didn't want to chance her turning it his way.

Ernest stood wide-eyed with astonishment. "I was doing what I thought was best and why did you pretend to be sleeping?"

"I was asleep until I heard your voice." She took a deep breath and seemed to calm down. "I intended to speak, but I was so flabbergasted by your cruelty that I was struck dumb."

Ernest turned his hat in his hands as he looked from her to Levi. "I meant no harm. And if I stirred the old gal up a little, well, *goot.*"

"Her heartbeat is irregular and much too fast, thanks to you," Sarah said.

A second nurse came rushing down the hall and entered the room.

Ernest looked uncertain. "Granny Weaver said—"

"Who is Granny Weaver?" Levi demanded.

Sarah switched her gaze to Levi. "The bishop's mother. She is our healer, but this is beyond her skills."

Ernest glanced from one to the other. "Is she really so sick?"

Levi shook his head in disbelief. "She's in the cardiac care unit at a hospital. *Ja*, she is pretty sick."

"I didn't intend to be unkind. I only meant to sit with her for a while, but then she started talking about dying. It made me angry. She has a lot of life left to lead, *Gott* willing, and it's a sin to wish herself in the grave. If she returned to Cedar Grove just to make me watch her die, I'm not having it."

Levi threw his hands up in the air. "I don't know what's going on with the two of you. When you first showed up at our place, she was cool toward you, but it wasn't until you invited her to go fishing with us that she ordered you off the place. Explain to me why going fishing would make her angry."

"It wasn't that I invited her to go fishing. It was where I said I was taking you."

"To the lake?"

Ernest shook his head. "To a special spot on the lake that was important to me and her." He jerked his thumb toward her door. "Should I go back in?"

"Nee," Levi and Sarah said together.

Sarah took Ernest by the arm. Levi followed as she led him to a small waiting room at the end of the hall. It was furnished with a red vinyl sofa, a small round table, four white chairs and a television overhead on the wall opposite the sofa. Sarah closed the door. Levi took a seat at the table. Ernest pulled out a chair across from him and sat down. Sarah stood beside the table with her hands clasped together. Levi felt like he was back in the schoolroom facing the teacher after one of his pranks had gone awry.

"Ernest, I have known you since I was a babe and I don't remember you being angry with anyone. If someone should ask me who is the jolliest man I know, I would say you. You have some explaining to do."

Levi propped his arms on the table. "What is your history with my mother?"

Ernest leaned back with his hands clasped together on his stomach. He stayed silent for a long moment. "I would like to answer that, but it involves both of us and I can't speak for Henrietta. I can only tell you that I once loved her very much and I still do."

"You said my father was your best friend."

"He was."

"Your best friend married the woman you loved?"

"That's true. He was the man she wanted. It's hard to admit that even now, but I never begrudged them their happiness."

"That was a long time ago, Ernest," Sarah said gently.

"There's no time limit on loving someone. Sure, she and I have spent a lifetime apart, but my heart knows hers."

He pushed back from the table. "I should go before I say too much." He rose and started for the door. He opened it but stopped and looked back. "You can tell her I forgave her a long time ago if you need to, but I'd rather tell her myself. Do you understand? Both of you?"

Levi glanced at Sarah. She pressed her lips together and nodded. "I will keep you informed of her condition."

"Danki."

"I'm sorry I got so angry with you," Sarah said.

He managed a wry smile. "You're forgiven. I haven't had a scolding in a while. It might do me some *goot*."

The small, dark-haired nurse pushed open the door. "Mrs. Raber is resting now. Her heartbeat is back to normal. She has asked us not to allow visitors in until morning. I'm sorry."

Ernest nodded. "Just as well. I'm on my way home anyhow."

The nurse grinned at him. "How's the fishing been? I haven't heard a good fishing story in a month."

He jerked his thumb over his shoulder. "Ask that young fellow. He tossed in his line and pulled out a pretty gal."

She laughed. "I can't wait to hear the whole story. You'll be by again next Saturday, won't you? Gramps put twenty-pound test on his reel."

"Thinks he can outfish me with heavier line, does he? I'll show him. Tell him I'll be by if it ain't raining and maybe if it is." He settled his hat on his head and left the room.

The nurse smiled at Sarah and Levi. "Ernest takes my grandpa fishing every other Saturday. Grandpa is blind, and in a wheelchair, but they never fail to bring home a mess of catfish for us to fry. Ernest claims Grandpa landed all the little ones and he caught all the big ones. It's a running joke they never tire of arguing over."

She was chuckling to herself as she left the room. Levi leaned back in his chair. "Ernest is an unusual man."

Sarah sank onto the sofa. "Calling Ernest unusual is

a bit like calling the sun bright. It doesn't quite describe him. I'm sorry your mother doesn't want visitors now. Maybe if you had the nurse explain that you are here, she might change her mind."

"I don't want to do anything to upset her. I will let her have her way in this. The hospital can call Isaac if anything changes. What about you? Do you have a way home?"

She pulled a cell phone out of her pocket. "I can call someone. I had given up using my phone, but I still had it at home. I'm glad now I didn't get rid of it."

"Don't bother calling someone. I'll take you."

"Our place is out of your way."

"What's another ten miles on a rainy night for a friend?"

She giggled and put her phone away. "It will only be eight and a half miles out of your way."

"Exactly. No trouble at all." He stood up and offered his hand. She took it and he helped her to her feet. They stood only inches apart. The smile on her face faded and his heart began hammering in his chest. The desire to pull her into his arms took his breath away. She wasn't for him, no matter how attractive he found her. Being this close to her, touching her, was a mistake.

SARAH WAS SURPRISED that the calloused strength of Levi's touch was so incredibly gentle. Electricity seemed to fill the air around them. She was afraid to look into his eyes. She didn't want him to see her reaction. This was the brother of the man she hoped to marry. She pulled her hand away and shoved it into the pocket of her apron, where she curled her fingers into a tight ball.

Levi cleared his throat. "Do you have a cloak? The damp will make it a chilly ride."

"I'm not made of sugar. I won't melt in the rain." She tried for a light tone to dispel the strange tenseness in her body.

"I guess that's true. You didn't dissolve in the lake."

She looked at him then, expecting to see laughter in his eyes, but his expression held warmth and some emotion she couldn't read. "You'll never let me live that down, will you?"

"Ernest brought it up first." He walked to the door and held it open for her.

She scooted past him, hoping to avoid touching him. Any contact with Levi seemed to turn her brain to mush. If he noticed her quick maneuver, he didn't say anything.

Outside it was raining more heavily than it had been when Joshua delivered her to the hospital earlier. She stared out into the parking lot from the cover of the awning over the entrance. "At least your tractor has a canopy and a big windshield."

"The canopy will keep the rain off that is coming straight down, but it won't do any good against what blows in from the side or the back." A gust of wind sent a spray of rain in under the overhang. The splash and splattering of the water off the roof were the only sounds in the quiet town.

"We won't get home any quicker if we stand here discussing the weather." She took off at a run across the parking lot and quickly climbed to the tractor seat.

He came up behind her, standing on the power take-off shaft cover, a ten-inch by ten-inch plate of steel.

"Do you want to drive?" he asked.

She looked over her shoulder. "You don't mind?"

"Not at all. I'm not particularly fond of tractors. They are loud, smelly and much uglier than a horse."

She held her hand palm up. "Key?"

He handed it over. She started the engine with fingers that trembled slightly. It rumbled to life and filled the air around them with the smell of diesel smoke. He coughed a couple of times. "See what I mean?"

"*Glawwa, glawwa.* Complain, complain." She put the tractor in gear.

"It's not complaining if it's the truth."

"Watch your footing back there. The PTO shield can be slick if it's wet. It's a quick way to get a broken leg."

"Or worse."

"That's right." She turned on the windshield wipers, pulled out the switch for the headlights and the flashing amber slow-moving vehicle lights on the front and rear of the tractor that were meant to alert other drivers. After checking carefully around her, she drove out of the lot.

On the highway she increased her speed. It wasn't long before they left the lights of the town behind. Sarah tried to concentrate on driving and not on the feel of Levi's body hovering close behind her. She drove as fast as she dared. When she turned off the pavement onto Lincoln Road, she had to slow down unless she wished to bounce him off the back. At one sharp turn, he wrapped his arm around her to keep his balance. Just as quickly he jerked it away. "Sorry."

"No problem," she said, wishing it were true.

She had never been so glad to see the turnoff to her family farm. She slowed down at the low-water bridge over the creek. An inch or two of water was already spilling over the top of it, but she had no problem crossing it. She had to gun the engine to climb the last steep hill above the creek. As she pulled up to the house, a light came on upstairs. Joshua or Laura Beth must've heard them coming.

She left the engine running and turned to get down. It was then she noticed that Levi was soaking wet from the water that poured off the back side of the canopy. He had been huddled over her so the water wouldn't blow in on her. His teeth were starting to chatter. She had been rushing to get home, not suspecting that he was getting chilled in the process. Wearing wet clothes while a person was standing still was uncomfortable enough, but wearing them while traveling in the open at forty miles an hour was another thing altogether. And he was just foolish enough not to complain.

"Levi Raber, get down and go into the house this minute. I am not letting you drive off until you get dry and warm."

He stepped off the tractor and rubbed his hands up and down his arms. "Has anyone told you that you are a bossy woman?"

She heard Joshua's chuckle from the porch. "Bossiness runs in the family. I can attest to that. Come in. I'll find you something to wear."

Laura Beth came out with a bathrobe over her nightgown and holding a lantern in her hand. "Stop laughing and go get the man some dry clothes."

"See what I mean?" Joshua skirted away from his wife's reach, took Levi's arm and led him into the house.

Sarah turned the tractor off, climbed down and hurried to the cover of the porch. "I'm sorry we woke you."

"What are you doing home already? I thought you were staying at the hospital until seven in the morning."

"Ernest came to visit and upset Mrs. Raber. She decided she didn't want anyone with her. The nurse asked us to leave."

Laura Beth's eyebrows shot up. "Ernest upset her? I can't imagine that."

"I was shocked, too. He said he was in love with her before she married Levi's father. Do you know anything about it?"

"I don't but that isn't surprising. Most Amish couples keep their courtships a secret. I would have been too young to pay much attention. I do vaguely remember the wedding. There wasn't anything odd about it. I wonder if that's why Ernest never married." She led the way into the house and into the kitchen. "Do you want some hot tea or cocoa?"

"I do but I'll fix something for Levi and myself. You go back to bed."

"I believe I will." Laura Beth left the kitchen and went upstairs. Sarah heard Joshua's footsteps going that way a short time later.

The kettle was whistling when Levi walked in. "I appreciate the loan of the clothes."

Sarah turned around and started giggling. Joshua's pants were too long. Levi had rolled them up. Joshua's jacket sleeves hung over Levi's knuckles. She pressed a hand to her lips. "You and I are going to have to find a way to stay dry when we get together or at least take along an extra set of clothing."

He held his arms wide. "I thought staying out of a canoe and away from the lake would do it. Reckon I was wrong."

"Lavender tea or hot cocoa?" She turned back to take the kettle off the heat.

"I've never had lavender tea. I would like to try some." He took a seat at the table.

"With the lavender tea you must try my lavender cookies." She opened the cookie jar on the counter and pulled out a handful. She divided them up onto two saucers and carried them to the table. She returned to the counter and put her homemade tea bags into two mugs. She poured in the hot water to allow them to steep and carried the mugs to the table.

He pulled one toward him and wrapped his fingers around it. "It smells good."

"Try a cookie."

He picked one up and looked at it closely. "Are those real flowers in the icing?"

"Lavender buds. It's okay—you can eat them."

He took a small bite. "Not bad."

"Not bad? I'm overwhelmed by your praise."

"Are you fishing for compliments?"

She held her index finger and thumb close together. "A tiny one wouldn't hurt."

"Okay, they are actually *goot*. Which surprises me because I don't think about eating flowers very often."

"Many flowers have edible parts. I will spare you the botanical lecture about lavender that my sister loves to give. Unless you are dying to know more. I've heard it so many times I can recite it by heart."

"Do you like the flower business?"

She checked to see if he was teasing but he looked serious. "I love the flowers almost as much as my sister does. I particularly enjoy taking our baked goods to the farmers' market and visiting with people who don't know anything about lavender or about the Amish. Many of them have some funny ideas about us."

"I love it when they ask if it's true that we don't pay taxes. I always wanted to whip out my property tax bill and tell them it's just a donation to the county."

She giggled. "I know. We don't pay Social Security taxes or Medicare because we don't use them. The government gets enough from us in income taxes, sales taxes and the gasoline taxes we pay to run our tractors. My favorite is the one about the blue door."

"What's that one?"

"If an Amish man has a daughter of marriageable age, he paints the door of the house blue. I've never been to an Amish house with a blue door. Have you?"

"*Nee*, and I've been to more than a few homes with marriage-aged daughters."

"Are you trying to tell me that you're on the hunt for a wife?"

"*Nee*. Not me. I'm usually delivering a trotter for

a family's marriage-aged sons. Nothing looks better pulling a courting buggy than a high-stepping horse."

"I thought you only raised racing horses?"

"Less than two percent of standardbred horses will ever make it into a race. Some aren't fast enough or won't hold their gait. Sometimes the young horses get injured and their competitive racing days are over, but they can still pull a buggy. Those are the kind of animals that wind up pulling Amish buggies all around Lancaster, as do the horses that are too old for racing but can easily take the Amish family to church and back on Sundays."

They sat sipping their tea in silence. Finally he stood up. "I should head home and try to get a little sleep. Would you do me a favor and call the hospital to see how she is before I go?"

"Of course." Sarah pulled her phone out of her apron pocket and dialed the number. She handed the phone to him when it started ringing. She could tell by his expression that the news was good.

He closed the phone and handed it back to her. "She's resting well and hasn't had any more episodes of irregular heartbeats."

"That's *goot* news."

They walked together out to the front porch. The rain had all but stopped. She looked up at him, trying to read the emotion in his eyes. He took a step away from her. "*Guten nacht*, Sarah."

"*Goot* night, Levi. Thanks for keeping the rain off my back."

He settled his hat on his head. "It's what any friend would do." He climbed on the tractor and drove away.

"Then *danki, mei freind*," she said softly, knowing that was exactly how she had to look upon Levi. As a friend and nothing else.

LEVI TRIED TO put his feelings about Sarah in perspective as he drove home. He was more attracted to her than he had a right to be. She had her eye on Isaac. They might enjoy each other's company and find shared humor in life, but that was all it was.

It was a little after five in the morning when Levi pulled up in front of the house. There was a predawn lightness in the eastern sky. He was surprised to see Isaac coming out of the barn with a feed bucket in his hand.

"Morning. Where have you been?" Isaac asked.

"I couldn't sleep last night. I went to see *Mamm*. Sarah was sitting with her, and Ernest stopped in. He and *Mamm* got into an argument and her heart went into an irregular beat again."

"Is she okay?"

"It went back to normal. She told the nurses she didn't want anybody else in her room, so I took Sarah home." He got down from the tractor.

"Ernest and *Mamm* were fighting? What about?"

"Something that happened before *Mamm* and *Daed* got married. Apparently Ernest was in love with her back then. He wouldn't answer my questions when I pressed him about it later. He said it was up to *Mamm* to tell us about it."

"That's mighty odd."

"So is seeing you up before the crack of dawn."

"I wanted to get the chores done early so I could spend the day at the hospital. I'm glad you're back. I wasn't looking forward to a long buggy ride."

"You could've called one of our *Englisch* neighbors to take you."

"I thought about it. I would've done that if the hospital had called and said there was a problem, since you weren't here. But I don't want to put anyone out. It's a little early to be making phone calls."

"True. The tractor is all yours. What chores are left to be done?"

"Nothing. I fed the chickens and gathered the eggs. I left them on the kitchen counter. I fed the hogs, the cattle and the horses, and I turned the horses out into the pasture and cleaned the stalls. The horses will probably be muddy soon, if they aren't already. I'll help you brush them down when I get home this afternoon."

Levi was surprised by his brother's industriousness. "I appreciate the offer."

"I realize I've been letting you do the bulk of the work around here and I figured it was time I started doing my share. This place needs a lot of fixing up. I don't want *Mamm* to be ashamed of the place where she lives."

"You talked about living here and farming with our grandparents after the summer you spent here. You loved this place. Do you still feel the same about it?"

Isaac let his gaze rove over the buildings and fields. "I guess I do."

"We will work on fixing the place up together after *Mamm* gets home."

"I'd like that idea. I'm sorry for the trouble I've caused you in the past, Levi. I'd better go wash up. I don't want the nurses to think I smell like a pigpen." He smiled broadly.

"You can always stop by Sarah's place and roll around in her flowers. That would make you smell *goot*."

Isaac's smile faded. "I'm not sure what I'm going to say to her."

"Sarah is a kind woman. Talk to her like you would any friend."

"You mean tell her I'm only going out with her so you and *Mamm* will stop bugging me about it? I don't want to hurt her feelings."

Levi stared at his brother's mulish expression. Should he continue to encourage Isaac to start seeing her? He pushed his own feelings for her to the back of his mind, determined to keep them there. "She's a sweet woman. Maybe that's why God brought you here."

Isaac took a deep breath. "I'm still hoping Brittany will change her mind and come out here. We could make a good life together. *Mamm* will grow to love her and it won't matter that she isn't Amish."

Until this moment Levi hadn't realized how much his brother was like their father. Isaac put too much heart and not enough thought into his plans. If Isaac's new work ethics continued, he could make a good life on the farm. It would please their mother if he joined the church and married an Amish woman instead of leaving the Amish to marry an *Englisch* one. Levi dreaded to think what that would do to her ailing heart. Isaac had blinders on.

If that Amish woman was Sarah, it would be even better for everyone. Sarah would get her heart's desire, and Levi could head back to Lancaster knowing his mother and his brother were in good hands. He would keep his promise to his father and earn back their brood-mares and stables. Isaac might not know what was best for him, but Levi did. "When are you going to speak to Sarah?"

"Soon." Isaac's eyes narrowed. He tipped his head slightly. "When she realizes we aren't meant for each other, are you going to ask her out?"

Levi could see the spark of conflict growing in Isaac's brain. He decided to toss a little kerosene on it. "Of course."

"Because this farm will go to you if you marry first?"

"That's my plan. I'm sure you'll be able to find work around here after I sell it. Ernest will know of someone who needs a hired man. Brittany won't care what you do for a living, will she?"

He turned and walked into the house, leaving Isaac to stew over his words.

CHAPTER EIGHT

HENRIETTA WAS RELEASED from the hospital three days later. Levi and Isaac arranged for a hired car and driver to bring her home in comfort. She walked with Isaac's help from the car to the house and sank into her favorite chair in the living room with a deep sigh. Levi exchanged a worried glance with his brother. She was not in any shape to take over the running of the household. Would she ever be?

Isaac knelt beside her. "Can I get you anything?"

She cupped his cheek and managed a weak smile. "Having my sons with me in my own home is all I need."

The sound of a tractor arriving sent Levi to the front door. Joshua King brought his big blue tractor to a stop by the front steps. There were eight women seated in the trailer he had hitched on behind. Sarah was among them. Levi stepped out to greet them. They all got out by themselves except for the bishop's mother. She got down with the help of a stepladder and several of the women. Most were Amish women, but two of them wore *Englisch* clothing. They unloaded cleaning materials and baskets before they trooped up his porch into the house, greeting him as they walked by.

Sarah was the last in line. She stopped beside him. "How is your mother doing?"

"She's happy to be home."

"I'm glad to hear it." She followed the other women inside.

Joshua stayed on his vehicle. "I'm delivering some help for the day. I'll be back to collect them around supper time." He tipped his hat and drove off.

Feeling slightly bemused, Levi went into the house and stood in the doorway of the living room. All the older women were gathered around his mother, chatting happily. She caught sight of him and waved him and Isaac over. "These are some of the girls I went to school with. Wasn't it wonderful of Sarah to think to bring them here?" She introduced them all. The only one he knew was her cousin Mary Jane. The smile on his mother's face cheered him. This was more interest from her than he had seen in months. Sarah stood outside the group. He caught her eye and mouthed his thanks. Her sweet smile warmed his heart.

Martha Weaver, the bishop's mother, raised a hand to still the chatter. "I'm going to put your sons to work, Henrietta. We don't want you going up and down the stairs until you are fit. Your young men need to move your bed down here. Where would you like it?"

Instead of objecting as he expected, his mother pointed to the windows on the south side of the room. "There so I can keep an eye on my *kinder* while they are outside."

"Spoken like a *goot mudder*," Martha said. The women with her immediately began rearranging the furniture.

Levi looked at Isaac and tipped his head toward the stairs. "We have our orders."

It didn't take him and his brother long to disassemble and bring her bed downstairs. They had barely finished getting it back together and stepping out of the way before the women were stripping the sheets and replacing them with fresh ones.

His mother moved from the chair to her freshly made bed under her own power and settled back with a sigh on the pillows piled against the headboard. "This is much better than that hospital bed."

The women set about cleaning the house, mopping the floors and dusting. Levi and Isaac got out of their way at Sarah's urging. They stayed outside doing chores and fixing the fence of the small corral beside the barn where they would be close by if they were needed. He saw Sarah come out with several rugs in her arms. She laid them over the clothesline and began to beat them.

He nudged his brother. "It looks like Sarah is free. You should go speak to her."

"I will when there aren't a bunch of gossiping women watching us."

"I'm not worried about what people will say. I reckon it won't hurt to show Sarah which brother is the most helpful." He put down his hammer and walked toward her. Instead of following as he hoped, Isaac went back to fixing the fence.

Levi took the rug-beating paddle from Sarah's hand and began whacking the large oval blue rag rug from his mother's bedroom. "I tried to get Isaac to come over, but I'm afraid my brother is feeling shy today. If he is looking this way, give me a big smile."

She glanced to where Isaac was working. He was looking at them. She smiled brightly at Levi. "Why am I grinning at you like a fool?"

"To make Isaac a little jealous. What's he doing now?"

"Pulling out a nail he bent over with his hammer."

"That sounds promising." He glanced over his shoulder. Isaac glared at him and went back to work, pointedly ignoring Levi.

"How are the two of you getting along?" Sarah asked.

"Better."

"This is better?"

He laughed loudly and bent toward her. "Much."

Concern filled her pretty blue eyes. "He's going in the barn. He looks upset."

"He'll get over it. I want to thank you for thinking to entertain *Mamm* today. Having so many old friends show up is doing wonders for her. It was a *goot* idea."

"I remembered when I had my appendix out. My friends came to see me once I was home. Visiting with them made me laugh and forget how much I hurt. It was Ernest who gave me the names of your mother's school friends and helped me contact them. Have you learned anything more about their feud?"

"I haven't mentioned it to *Mamm*."

"That might be best for a while."

"I know. I'm afraid to upset her and risk another episode with her heart becoming irregular." He handed the rug beater back to Sarah. "That's the best I can do."

"Danki."

He touched the brim of his hat. "My pleasure."

Late in the afternoon, Isaac paused to watch the women file out of the house when Joshua returned. He gave a loud sigh. "How are we going to take care of her when they all go home?"

"We'll manage," Levi mumbled around the nail he held in his mouth. He pulled it out and hammered it into the last board that needed replacing.

"Wish we had a couple of sisters," Isaac said, half in jest.

"Or wives," Levi added.

Isaac frowned at him. "Wives? Speak for yourself. What do you think about hiring a housekeeper? *Mamm* may never get stronger. I've read a lot about her condition and talked to her doctor back home."

"I thought the doctor said she could make a full recovery."

Isaac picked up the rotted board to add to the burn pile. "Most people with A-fib live normal lives with treatment, but some are so affected they become bedridden. You saw her this morning. She could barely walk across the room to her chair."

"She just got out of the hospital. Give her a few days." Levi heard Mary Jane calling to them. He walked up to the house.

Mary Jane waited for him on the porch. "We have set out some food when you are ready. Your mother claims she's not hungry, but a few spoonfuls of my beef broth will bring her appetite back. I've put some on the back burner of your stove to stay warm. The rest is in the refrigerator."

"We appreciate everyone's help and prayers," Levi said.

Mary Jane patted his arm. "It's nothing. I'm sure she will be back to her old self in no time."

"Laura Beth and I will be over tomorrow to finish the laundry and make your meals," Sarah added.

Granny Weaver handed her basket to Sarah. "It's a shame your mother refused a home health nurse, but I understand not wanting to burden her family with extra costs. A hospital stay is never cheap. Whatever your family can't cover, our congregation will take care of."

Levi knew his mother didn't have to worry about the hospital bills. The money from the sale of his father's farm, even after paying off his debts, was more than enough to cover her needs. He had already stopped by the local bank to make sure he could have access to the monies if his mother wasn't able to come in. It turned out that his mother had made sure both he and Isaac could withdraw needed funds.

He waved to the women as Joshua drove off and went into the house. He found his mother dozing in her bed. She woke with a start. "Has everyone gone?"

"They have."

"It was kind of them to be so generous with their time."

"It's no more than you have done when someone in the community back home was in need."

"It's easy to offer charity, but it's harder to accept it. The bishop's mother reminded me that we must be humble in all things, and that includes accepting assistance. Did...did Ernest come by today?"

"*Nee*, but I can send him a message if you'd like to see him."

"Not yet. I will abide by his wishes for now."

"Can't you please tell me what's going on between the two of you?"

She turned her gaze out the window. "One day I will. Until then, I ask you to respect my wishes for a little longer." She looked at Levi. "He and I must settle things first. I believe I would like some of that broth now."

Knowing his curiosity was defeated by her stubbornness, he went to fetch the soup.

Late the next morning, Laura Beth and Sarah arrived along with Caleb. Isaac went out the back door, leaving Levi to greet them alone. The sight of Sarah's bright smile lifted his spirits. His mother had had a restless night. He had spent most of it dozing on the sofa in case she needed anything.

Laura Beth and Caleb were soon entertaining his mother in the living room while Sarah set to work in the kitchen. Levi was tempted to stay and visit with her, but he went outside looking for his brother instead. He found Isaac working on the cultivator, replacing a lost shovel.

"Sarah is in the kitchen." Levi wanted to nudge his brother toward the house. Why was he dragging his feet about spending even a little time with her?

"I know. I'm getting up my nerve to speak to her."

"You are going to ask her out, right? You told *Mamm* you would. I told Sarah you would." Sarah deserved a chance to find happiness with his brother if that was what she wanted.

"Okay, but if she's smart she'll say no." Isaac walked away.

For Levi it was easy to imagine asking Sarah to go for a buggy ride with him or to a picnic. She was a remarkable young woman. He didn't understand why his brother couldn't see that.

SARAH WAS PEELING potatoes at the kitchen sink when Isaac came through the door. Her heart quickened. Were they finally going to get the chance to talk? He took off his hat and hung it on a peg by the door. "Sarah, do you have a few minutes?"

She dropped the freshly peeled potato into a pan of water and laid her paring knife aside. "I have plenty of time as long as your mother doesn't need something. Laura Beth is with her, so I'm free for a while."

"Goot." He took a seat at the table.

"Would you like some coffee?" She dried her hands on her apron and turned toward the stove. "I made some fresh."

"Sure." He nervously rubbed his hands on his pant legs.

She poured them both a cup of coffee and sat at the table across from him.

He cleared his throat. "We appreciate your kindness."

He looked so worried that she reached across the table and patted his hand. "That's just what friends do for each other."

He closed his eyes. "Would you consider walking out with me?"

She opened her mouth and closed it again. It was what she wanted. Why was she hesitating now? Why not say yes?

Because they had grown apart. Time had dimmed the feelings they once had for each other. If they renewed their acquaintance, would those emotions grow again? She had faith that they would. She remembered her sister's advice that all good marriages were based on true friendship.

"Isaac, I suggest that we try being friends first before we make an actual date. What do you think?" She saw his relief.

A half smile replaced the grim look on his face. "I like the sound of that."

"And, Isaac, you don't have to pretend to like me."

His lopsided smile reminded her how charming he could be. "I'm not good at pretending. What would two old friends do on a nice day like today?"

"We might hunt for wild morel mushrooms since the woods on this farm have been known to produce a good crop. I've always wanted to search for them here."

His grin vanished. "Go mushroom hunting? I don't think so."

"You'll enjoy it. I promise. It's like hunting for treasure." Her attempt to cajole him into joining her worked.

He nodded. "If that's what you want to do."

"*Wunderbar*. Do you have a couple of burlap bags we can use?"

"I'm sure we do. I'll ask Levi where he keeps them."

She stood up. "Let me tell my sister where we'll be."

"Sure." He followed her into the living room.

Laura Beth looked up from the book she was reading to Henrietta when Sarah and Isaac came in the room. Caleb was in her lap listening to the story.

Sarah found herself suddenly tongue-tied when she realized she was about to tell her sister and Isaac's mother that they were going off on a walk together. Mushroom hunting with the other young people she knew wouldn't embarrass her this way. This was different. This might be the start of a new future for her.

"I'm going to show Isaac where the morel mushrooms grow around here."

Laura Beth smiled knowingly. "Enjoy yourselves and I hope you bring home lots of delicious fungus."

Henrietta turned and pointed out the window. "Just beyond the pasture fence is a wooded ravine. Follow the creek for about a quarter of a mile and you will find where it spreads out into a marshy area. The mushrooms used to be plentiful along the bottom of the ravine and around the edges of the bog. When I was young, we had so much fun looking for them every spring. Have a good time, you two, and watch out for the thorny vines."

"We'll do that," Sarah assured her. "I finished the potatoes and left them in the pan."

"I'll take care of them." Laura Beth waved them away with one hand. "Have fun."

Out in the barn they found Levi laying out fresh straw in the horse stalls. Sarah waited till he looked up. "We are going mushroom hunting. Would you like to come along?" She held her breath as she waited for his reply.

"Thanks for the invite, but I have enough work to keep me busy today. You kids run along."

Kids? Did he think of her as a child? He wasn't that much older than she was. "Could we trouble you for a pair of burlap sacks?"

He nodded toward the back of the barn. "I keep a few empty ones in the feed room."

"I'll get them," Isaac said and headed to the back of the barn. He returned with two bags a minute later.

Sarah knew she should go but she was reluctant to leave Levi behind. "Last chance. It can be lots of fun."

"Another time. *Danki.*" He began spreading the straw again. Sarah was forced to turn away. She tried to tell herself that she really didn't want him to come. Her goal was to spend time getting to know Isaac again. It shouldn't matter that Levi had turned down her invitation, but the sense of loss she felt as she left the barn without him proved it did.

LEVI STOPPED RAKING out the straw as soon as Isaac and Sarah were gone. He jammed the hay fork into the rest of the bale and started after them. The desire to join them was foolish. He should leave the two of them alone, but for some reason he didn't want to do it.

He stepped to the open door and glanced out. Isaac was staring at his cell phone. He gave Sarah an apologetic look. "I'm sorry, Sarah. I should answer this. I don't really want to go traipsing through the woods. You go ahead."

"Are you sure? It isn't fun hunting alone."

Levi ran a hand over his chin. Sarah had endured too many disappointments at his brother's hand. He thought he knew how to persuade Isaac to change his mind. He walked out and caught up with them outside. "Wait for me."

Isaac looked mildly surprised, but Sarah looked delighted. "You changed your mind. *Wunderbar*."

"I can finish the stalls later. Go ahead and take your call, little brother." Levi stepped between the couple. He smiled and winked at Sarah while ignoring his brother. "I've never been mushroom hunting. What does it entail?"

Her eyes grew wide, but she quickly followed his lead. "You have honestly never been mushroom hunting? You have no idea the fun you're missing. First we have to find an area where the mushrooms like to grow. They like rotting wood on the forest floor and damp areas with lots of leaves. They can sometimes be hard to spot, but once you see them and know what you're looking for, it will be easy."

Levi leaned close to her. "This does sound like fun. Where are we going?"

"To a ravine on the other side of the pasture. We'll climb down to the creek and start searching."

Isaac regarded them with a frown. "Something tells me it will be more work than she makes it out to be."

"It's a walk through the woods. What's difficult about that?" She smiled brightly but her chin was up as if daring him to disagree.

Levi grinned but didn't take his eyes off Sarah's expressive face. "You heard her. It's just a stroll through the woodlands…together. I'm sure I'll enjoy it."

He switched his gaze to Isaac. "I thought you were going to answer your phone, little brother. You don't want the person on the other end to think you're ignoring him or her. I mean, you always jump to answer it when your phone buzzes. Almost like a trained pup."

Isaac glared at him. He put his phone away. "It can wait."

Sarah's eyes sparkled with happiness and unspoken thanks when she glanced his way. Levi was almost sorry he had goaded Isaac into not taking the call. She spun around and headed for her buggy parked beside the house. She rummaged for something in the back seat. "You should wear a long-sleeved jacket and you should bring gloves and a knife, and a walking stick is helpful."

"You'd like me to stay here, wouldn't you?" Isaac asked under his breath.

Levi had trouble controlling his mirth. "Nonsense. I simply want to see Sarah have a nice time. Does it matter if it's you or if it's me hunting mushrooms with her?"

Sarah turned to face them with a bundle in her arms. "You've never tasted anything more delicious than a morel mushroom fried up the same day you plucked it off the ground. It makes it all worthwhile. I have to get changed first."

One side of Levi's mouth lifted in a grin. "You brought a change of clothes? Will this involve getting us soaked again?"

"*Nee*, only slightly muddy." She met his gaze and chuckled. "I hope."

She took her bundle of clothes into the house.

Isaac faced Levi. "What are you doing?"

"You want Sarah to realize the two of you aren't made for each other, remember? I'm helping you out. If she sees another man is interested in spending time with her, she'll forget about you all the quicker. There's no reason I can't go mushroom hunting with her, is there?"

"I guess not. I just wonder if you're doing this to help me or to help yourself."

Levi hoped he hadn't overplayed his interest. Isaac didn't like coming in second behind Levi. At anything.

Sarah came out a few minutes later wearing a pair of denim pants under her dress. She looked down, following his amused gaze. "The briars and thorny shrubs can be murder on bare legs and arms. I'm not baptized yet, so I can bend the rules about clothing."

Isaac rocked back on his heels. "I've changed my mind. I'm coming with you."

"You won't regret it." Her smile was so bright Levi wished it was for him and not for Isaac.

She slipped into a long-sleeved homemade denim jacket. "This farm has a reputation for having a lot of morels in the woods, but Mr. Helmuth never let anyone hunt for them. All we need now is a few sturdy walking sticks."

"I think I can find something." Levi went in the barn and came out with the wooden handles from several brooms. "Will these work?"

Sarah took one. "Perfect."

She started across the pasture and the two men followed behind her. Wing and a Prayer came trotting toward them, tossing her head and arching her tail as she pranced happily across the fresh green grass.

Levi noticed Sarah admiring her. "She's as pretty as she is fast," he said, holding out his hand to her. The filly immediately came and stood for him as he ran his hand down her sleek neck and patted her sturdy shoulder.

Sarah raised her hand to the mare's face, stroked her nose and then scratched her just behind the ear. Wing leaned into her hand in horsey bliss before nipping at the sack Sarah held. She laughed and pushed the filly's nose away. "I see now. You're just looking for a treat."

Isaac started walking. "I thought we were hunting mushrooms, not playing with his horse."

Levi met Sarah's amused gaze and shrugged. "If it was a tractor, he'd be over to inspect it in a second."

Sarah laughed. "Joshua is the same way."

Levi was glad he'd given in to the impulse to go with her.

They both walked faster to catch up with Isaac at the far end of the pasture.

After slipping through a gate and making sure it was fastened tightly behind them, Sarah led the way toward a wooded ravine. The path leading down into it was no more than a deer trail. Levi had to hold on to nearby saplings to keep from slipping down the embankment. Sarah seemed to float along without any need to steady herself. He looked back. Isaac was having as much trouble as he was.

At the bottom of the ravine, Sarah crossed the shallow creek by hopping across several stones. Levi didn't bother. It wasn't deep enough to worry about because he was still wearing his boots. Dappled light filtered through the overhanging trees, making the area cool and damp. The woodsy smell of old leaves and decay filled the air. The chatter of squirrels and birds quieted with the presence of intruders.

"Exactly what are we looking for?" Isaac asked.

Sarah crouched near a fallen tree. She pulled aside some leaves and exposed a spongy-looking yellow cone-shaped mushroom about three inches tall. She grinned up at Isaac. "This is what we seek."

SARAH KNEW ISAAC would enjoy searching for the prized mushrooms once he got started and he did. He was like a kid searching for Easter eggs, soon crisscrossing the creek to search each side of the banks. Levi went slowly and methodically down the edge of the water, searching by moving aside some of the leaves with his boot. Since he didn't have a knife to cut them or a burlap sack to carry, he would call out to Sarah. "Found some."

His words usually brought Isaac back to his side of the creek looking for more. Sarah was a little surprised by the competition that seemed to develop between the brothers. Isaac began keeping his eyes on Levi more than on the ground. When he noticed Levi's interest, he would slip ahead to search the area himself.

"I found a bunch," Isaac said, looking triumphantly at Levi.

Sarah came to search in the general area and uncovered three more large mushrooms. She grinned at Isaac. "I knew you would enjoy this."

He yanked his out of the ground. "It is fun."

"Oh, don't pull them up like that. It can destroy the plant roots. Always cut them off so there will be more next year."

Levi seemed indifferent to his brother's gloating. "I thought that's why you put them in burlap sacks, so that their spores will spread and grow new ones."

Sarah peered at him closely. "I thought this was your first time hunting mushrooms."

"It is, but I've heard others talk about it."

"At the racetrack?" Isaac scoffed.

Levi shrugged. "Drivers and owners have lives outside of the horse barns."

"You and *Daed* never did." Isaac jumped across the stream and went ahead of them.

Levi took Sarah by the elbow and helped her to her feet. She brushed off her hands. "Do you miss it?"

"Every day, all day long."

She sensed his deep unhappiness. They began walking slowly. She stopped looking for mushrooms and focused on him. "Are you still planning to return to Lancaster?"

"My mother's health makes that impossible for now."

"She will get well."

"That is my deepest desire, but there's no way to know if that's true."

"You can train horses here. New buggy horses are always needed. The *Englisch* pay good money to have their horses trained by us."

He chuckled softly. "Someday I will show you the difference between riding behind your buggy horse and driving Wing and a Prayer."

"You just walked by a whole mess of them." Isaac leaped across the creek and stopped beside a fallen log a few yards behind Sarah. He was grinning from ear to ear.

"I was merely checking to see if you were paying attention," Sarah said.

"We should see how many each of us has found." He sat on the log, opened his sack and began counting. He looked up. "I have twenty."

Sarah dutifully counted hers. "Twenty-two."

"Ach, I can't let a girl beat me." He stood up and moved ahead.

Sarah heard a rumble of thunder in the distance. A ravine was never a good place to be in a rainstorm. "We should head back, Isaac."

"Not until I find two more. Three more." He walked on, searching the ground.

"We're leaving," she shouted, hoping to change his mind.

All he did was wave his hand as he rounded a curve up ahead. She turned to Levi with a beseeching look. He lifted his hat and raked his hand through his hair before settling the hat in place once more. "He's a grown man. He can take care of himself."

"He is your little *brudder*. You must watch out for him."

He gave a disgusted sigh. "I reckon I must. Start back. We'll catch up with you." He walked off after his brother.

A sprinkle of rain hit her *kapp* and shoulders. She should head toward the house, but she waited until she saw Isaac and Levi returning. As soon as she caught sight of them, she hurried back the way they had come.

The sprinkles stopped but she could hear heavier rain closing in on them. Sarah spotted a rocky overhang and took refuge under it seconds before the downpour started. The men pressed in beside her. She looked at Isaac. "Did you find some more?"

His sour expression told the whole tale. "I would have if my brother had let me keep looking."

Levi surveyed their situation. "If the creek starts rising, I'll boost you and Isaac on top of these rocks and you can climb out that way."

"What about you?" She wasn't going to leave him in a flooding ravine.

His mouth turned up at one corner. "Don't worry. Isaac can pull me up and we'll all hike out."

"That's a much better plan."

The downpour lasted less than five minutes. Thankfully the creek didn't rise, but Sarah soon discovered the rain had turned the leaves and damp ground underfoot into a treacherous, slick mess. She kept her balance using her walking stick and was thankful she had thought to bring one. When they reached the deer trail, Sarah saw it had a rivulet of water running down the center. She paused to glance back at Isaac. "Keep to one side. This looks slippery."

"Who cares about a little water." He went to step around her, slipped on the wet leaves and fell to his knees.

"Women first," Levi said, climbing past his brother and holding his hand out to Sarah.

She gladly accepted his help over the slimy ground but looked back at Isaac. "Don't be mean, Levi. Help him up."

"Okay. Take my hand, little man."

Satisfied, Sarah took two more steps upward with the help of a small tree growing beside the path. The branch she pulled on snapped. She flailed a second and fell against Levi. Her impact sent him over backward. He held on to her as they both went sliding down the steep slope.

CHAPTER NINE

WHEN THEY CAME to a stop, Sarah opened her eyes. The arching branches of the trees overhead swayed in the wind and sent a sprinkle of raindrops to hit her face. She assessed herself. Nothing hurt.

She was lying on her back on top of Levi. She turned her head. He was sprawled on his back in the stream with her clasped against his chest, his strong arms holding her safe. The water was only a few inches deep. She sat up and started laughing. His hat was missing and there was a smear of mud across his cheek. "You poor thing. Are you hurt? You're all wet again."

He raised his head and shook the water from his hair. She blocked the spray with her hand. He glared at her. "If I hang out with you much more, I'm going to grow gills," he muttered.

She choked back a laugh. "I'm sorry. It was an accident."

"Didn't you get wet?" he asked.

Sitting on top of him, she realized she was still dry and mud-free. "Nope."

"Is that so." He rolled over and dropped her in the pool beside him. She shrieked and shot to her feet, shaking the water off. The back of her was soaked from the waist down.

Isaac laughed uproariously from his spot on the bank. Sarah started giggling and looked at Levi. "At least you have dry clothes at the house."

He struggled to his feet. "Small consolation." He stomped up the hill past his brother. He was coated with mud from the back of his neck to his feet. Sarah stifled another giggle as he disappeared from sight through the trees.

Isaac held out his hand to help her up the bank. "You were right. Mushroom hunting is loads of fun. You should have seen the look on his face when you hit him. It was priceless."

"He held on to me and tried to keep me from getting hurt. We were blessed there weren't any big rocks in our way."

Isaac held her hand to the top of the ravine. When they came out into the open, he released her. She saw a new warmth in his eyes when he turned toward her. "I want to thank you, Sarah."

"For what?"

"For reminding me of how much fun we used to have together." He slipped an arm over her shoulder and gave her a quick hug.

"You're welcome." Suddenly self-conscious, she stepped away from him. Over his shoulder she noticed Levi watching them from the pasture gate. Wing stood close beside him nuzzling his arm. He turned around and walked toward the barn, leaving them alone.

Isaac took her hand. "I'm not ready to go back. Let's go hunt for some more."

That was what she wanted, wasn't it? To spend time with Isaac. She looked toward the barn. So why did she feel compelled to follow Levi? Sarah gave Isaac's fingers a squeeze before she pulled her hand from his. She gestured to her wet pants. "Let's go to the house. I'd like to find something dry to wear."

"Sorry. I didn't think about that. We'll leave the rest of the mushrooms for another day."

They crossed the pasture together. Isaac glanced her way. "I'm going to depend on you to let me know what kind of fun the kids around here are up to."

"You mean parties and singings and the like?"

"Sure. I've been bored half to death since I arrived. That is, until today." He smiled at her and her heart grew lighter.

"There are always picnics and parties. The county fair is held the last week of July."

"What about this week?"

"Tomorrow is church Sunday. There is always volley-ball after services."

"That wasn't exactly what I had in mind."

"You used to love volleyball. It can be fun."

"As much fun as mushroom hunting?" He started chuckling.

She laughed with him. "Maybe not that much." This was what she had missed about Isaac. The feeling that they could laugh about anything.

LEVI CLEANED UP at the outside faucet next to the barn. He could see Isaac and Sarah standing at the edge of the woods. They were laughing about something. It didn't even matter if they were laughing at him. He had done what he'd set out to do. He had persuaded Isaac to spend time with Sarah. Maybe he had tricked Isaac, but he was doing them both a favor. So why did it feel like a mistake?

Because he liked Sarah. He liked her a lot. He had never met anyone quite like her. Something about her made the day brighter. Even when she was with Isaac. He tried to imagine them together for a lifetime. He couldn't. Was that because they didn't belong together or was it because he didn't want them to be together?

He groaned. He had a crush on his brother's girl.

If she thought about him at all, it was because he was Isaac's brother, not because he was someone who interested her. She was made for the family life. It was easy to imagine her with children, visiting with her sister and her friends and making quilts. Perhaps Isaac could fit into that life if he became a little less self-centered. Isaac had been making improvements lately. He was getting work done instead of stalling. He had been diligent in caring for their mother. And yet Levi didn't want to see him with Sarah. She deserved more.

She deserved a hardworking, devout man who believed she brightened his life the way the moon and the stars brightened the night sky.

He went around to the back of the house and made it upstairs without being spotted by his mother or Sarah's sister. He didn't feel like explaining one more set of wet clothing. He came downstairs a few minutes later to find Caleb attempting to crawl up them.

He stopped beside the little one, bent down and

picked him up. "I'm not sure you should be doing this. You might fall on your noggin."

Caleb scowled. "Want down."

He tried to wiggle out of Levi's grip. Levi could see the boy was determined to try again. He carried Caleb into the living room. Laura Beth was helping his mother back into bed. She glanced at him. "Thank you. Where was he off to?"

"Up the stairs."

She winced. "He goes up pretty well. It's coming down that gives him a problem."

His mother pulled the covers up to her shoulders. "Did Sarah find any mushrooms?"

"Enough to fix us some for supper and to take home a dozen or more."

"That's *wunderbar.*"

Laura Beth tucked the sheet around his mother. "Why don't you try taking a nap. I'll see that Caleb doesn't disturb you."

His mother smiled at the toddler he held. "He doesn't disturb me."

"He wears me out," Laura Beth said.

"I can watch him for a little while," Levi said.

"Would you? That would be great. Try to see that he doesn't eat dirt."

Levi chuckled as he carried the little fellow outside and put him down on the lawn beside the house. "You heard your *mudder.* No dirt."

Caleb proceeded to tell him about the grass and the flowers and the trees. Levi had to concentrate on what the child was saying but he was able to get the gist of most things. "Do you want to go see my horse?"

Caleb patted his hands together. "See horse."

"I take that as a yes. She's out in the pasture. Her name is Wing and a Prayer. She's very fast."

"Fass," Caleb said.

"That's right. Very fass." He picked up the boy and carried him out to the pasture fence.

Wing came trotting over when he called her name. Caleb happily patted Wing's nose. "Pretty horse."

"Shall I tell you what her good points are? She's only two but she's big for her age. That means I'm not gonna start racing until she's two and a half. I want her bones to be strong enough to take the strain. She's a wonderful, easygoing horse. She never breaks stride. That's important."

Caleb seemed to be taking in Levi's every word. The idea that he might tell his own son the story of Wing someday sent a shiver of anticipation across Levi's nerves. It was why he wanted the farm back. It had been passed from father to son for generations. He didn't want it to stop with him.

"Fass horse."

"That's right. She has speed I've never even seen. I can feel it in her. She's going to be a champion and I want Sarah to watch her first race with me." It was true and he had never imagined having a woman beside him cheering Wing on.

He looked at the little boy in his arms. "Don't you dare tell anyone I said that. If you repeat that, I'm going to tell your mother that you ate dirt."

"Dirt." Caleb laughed and clapped his hands. "Dirt."

"I see you think that was a hollow threat." He turned and walked to the house. He would take Wing out for a long drive so that he wouldn't be here when Sarah and her family left. So he wouldn't have to watch Isaac and Sarah together saying good-night.

ON SUNDAY MORNING Sarah helped get Caleb ready for church while Laura Beth finished packing the food that would be served after the meeting was over. Although Caleb was a well-behaved little boy, she had a struggle getting him into clean clothes. When she finally did up the hooks and eyes on his vest, she smiled at him. "You look like a grown-up little man."

Caleb clapped. "Fass. Dirt."

"I have no idea what fass dirt is, but stay away from it."

Caleb was wearing dark pants with suspenders over his white shirt and a small black vest. The only thing he lacked was a hat. Sarah carried him down the stairway. "Laura Beth, where is Caleb's hat?"

"He doesn't like keeping one on yet. Leave it off today."

Sarah held Caleb's hand as they walked out the front door. Joshua brought up Freckles harnessed to the freshly washed buggy. He dusted off the seats while waiting for his wife to come out. By the time Laura Beth finally hurried down the steps with her basket of food, even he was becoming impatient. However, her quick smooch on his cheek erased his frown lines.

Sarah took her place in the back seat with Caleb on

her lap. On the short trip to the Troyer farm, he happily played with a string of large colored beads, alternating between chewing on them and trying to hang them around her neck. She had to straighten her *kapp* more than once.

The Troyers were the King family's closest neighbors, but they were still two miles away. The gravel road rose over hills and fell into deep gullies through a section of rough country they had nicknamed the Stumbling Blocks. The land was too steep and rocky to farm. Some of it was fenced off for pasturing cattle, but most of it was simply unused land home to the area's white-tailed deer, pheasants, turkey and the occasional bobcat. Past the Stumbling Blocks, the land opened out to a broad flat plain dotted with farms.

Sarah and her family arrived early, but there was already a line of black buggies coming from the direction of Cedar Grove. The procession was only as fast as the slowest horse in line. It would be unthinkably rude to pass anyone on the way to Sunday service. Even the few boys driving open courting buggies held their prancing horses to the sedate pace. It would be a different story at the end of the afternoon.

Thomas and his sons were unloading the large gray box-shaped wagon that held the backless wooden benches the congregation would sit on. The bishop and Ernest were carrying the benches into a large metal machine shed where the service would be held. The Troyer house was too small to accommodate the entire congregation at once.

One of the Zook brothers came to take Freckles and

lead her to where they were lining up the empty buggies. After she was unhitched, she was led to the corral fence where the other horses, still wearing their harnesses, waited patiently in the shade to make the trip home.

Sarah looked for the Raber family but didn't see them. She wondered if Henrietta was feeling well enough to attend the service. If she wasn't, Isaac or Levi would have to remain at home with her. Sarah was eager to see Isaac again. Their last afternoon together had ended with a definite improvement in their relationship.

She lifted Caleb out of the back seat and settled him on her hip, knowing that was the only way to keep him clean. He would make a beeline for the tire swing hanging from the tree beside the house as he always did when they visited the family.

The inside of the Troyers' building was spotlessly clean. Family and friends, including Joshua and Laura Beth, had spent hours making sure every surface was cleaned inside and out, not only the shed but inside the house and barn, too. The work of hosting a service was such that no family was expected to host more than once a year.

Sarah followed Laura Beth inside the house, where a swarm of women were unpacking hampers and boxes of food that they arranged on the counters to be served later. Sarah greeted many of the women she knew, including Ruth Mast. Ruth was the mother of Sarah's dear friend Ella. Little Grace came scooting between the group of women to hold up her arms for Caleb. "I can take him."

Sarah put him down and Grace led him away to a group of small children being watched over by two teenage girls. Sarah chuckled and looked at Ruth. "Grace is becoming quite the little mother."

Ruth smiled fondly at the child. "You have no idea. This time of year the house is full of baby lambs that need bottle-feeding, a new litter of kittens and a very large puppy. I expect to trip over something or someone and break a leg any day now."

A commotion outside drew Sarah to the kitchen window over the sink. She recognized Ruth's son Faron trying to control his buggy horse. The brown gelding was rearing and flailing his front hooves. Everyone backed away except for one person. Levi stepped out of the group of men and took off his coat. He managed to catch the frantic horse by the bridle and cover the animal's eyes in one easy, fluid movement. The horse quieted almost immediately.

Ruth was standing beside Sarah. "That gelding was a poor bargain. He seems to have forgotten everything he was trained to do. Is that Henrietta Raber's son?"

"Her oldest. His name is Levi. His younger brother is Isaac."

"Levi certainly knows his way around a skittish horse."

"The family owned a broodmare farm back in Pennsylvania. Levi raised and trained racehorses there."

"Perhaps he can give my son some tips on how to train that one. It used to be a racehorse."

Sarah saw Isaac standing beside his mother and went

outside. She greeted Henrietta. "It's good to see you felt well enough to come."

"I tried to make her stay home," Isaac said.

"There's no difference between sitting in a chair at home and sitting here."

"Except that one is a soft cushioned seat and the other is a hard wooden bench," he said.

"She will have a soft seat here." Ernest and his nephew Owen walked by carrying an overstuffed chair from the Troyer living room.

Sarah expected a protest from Henrietta, but she was surprised. Henrietta nodded toward Ernest. "*Danki* for your thoughtfulness."

"It's the least I could do." He and Owen took the chair inside the machine shop.

Henrietta watched them walk away and then turned to Sarah. "I understand the baptism classes are starting today."

"They are."

"I have urged Isaac to join this class, but he says he isn't ready. It is my heart's desire to see both my sons join our faith before I die. My heart is nearly worn out. I hope you know that, *sohn*."

"You're exaggerating," he said, looking annoyed.

Baptism was the biggest decision an Amish person could make, but their faith wasn't for everyone. If she joined the church and he didn't, they wouldn't be able to marry unless she was prepared to be shunned by her family and friends. That was unthinkable.

"Attending the class is not a commitment to be baptized, Isaac. It's more about learning if being Amish is something you truly want."

"Sarah is right. Make your poor old mother happy and go to the first class."

"I guess it won't hurt." He led his smiling mother inside the building. Sarah was ready to clap her hands with delight.

She looked around to see what Levi thought of the exchange. He was still with Faron and his meddlesome horse. They were conferring with Thomas Troyer. Levi led the horse to a corral away from the other horses and turned the animal loose. The sleek brown gelding immediately began trotting around the perimeter, tossing his head in agitation. Levi slipped his coat back on and spoke to Thomas. Thomas nodded and led Levi's buggy horse over to him. Levi put Jasper in with Faron's horse. After the two got to know each other, they galloped playfully around the pen a few times and then settled down to eat the hay Faron put over the fence for them.

Laura Beth came by carrying Caleb. "The bishop says the prayer meeting is ready to start."

The instructional classes would take place during the first thirty minutes of the church service. Sarah along with the other applicants and several of the church elders retired to a room set aside for their instructions. Today they were using the Troyer living room.

Sarah sat beside Angela on a wooden backless bench. Thaddeus Weaver and Isaac took their places on a separate bench beside the women. Across from them were several elders of the church, including the bishop.

Out in the shop, the *volsinger*, the hymn leader, began

the first song and the rest of the congregation joined in. The slow and mournful chanting rose in the still morning air as members blended their voices together in praise. For Sarah it was the most moving part of the service. It filled her with a desire to please God. It made her happy to be a part of something rare and cherished. All Amish hymns were sung without musical accompaniment and learned without a musical score. The songs in the *Ausbund* had been passed down through the generations for more than seven hundred years.

The chanting voices of the churchgoers drifted to Sarah through the open windows and provided a solemn background for learning about her faith.

One by one, the elders took turns asking the students questions about the faith and about their understanding of the eighteen articles of the Dordrecht Confession. Sarah had read them before starting her preparation classes, but the German words carried little meaning when she was trying to memorize them. Joshua had given her an English translation and that left her with a clearer understanding of the founding document of Amish beliefs and the Ordnung, the rules of each individual church group. The more she learned about the traditions of the Amish church, the greater her respect grew. Her ancestors had endured great hardships and remained true to their faith. She prayed she could do the same. She glanced at Isaac and wondered what he was feeling.

The bishop rose and stood before them. "We are pleased that you have chosen to receive baptismal instructions. This week we will review the first two articles of the Dordrecht Confession."

Sarah heard the second song begin outside. It was always the same hymn. *"Das Loblied,"* a song of love and praise. The bishop read the text of Article 1 and then the elders quizzed each of the students about their understanding of it.

Toward the end of the session, the bishop spoke about the church's Ordnung. Sarah and Angela had spent the previous evening reciting the unwritten church rules for each other. Sarah stumbled when she began to list them, but Bishop Weaver smiled to reassure her.

"It's important to know them, but it's more important to follow them. We are each of us responsible for other members. It is our duty to guide anyone who goes astray from our teaching back to the path. Isaac, you have not had a chance to learn our rules for yourself. Seek the counsel of church members and our elders if you are ever in doubt."

"I can help you learn them," Sarah offered and then blushed when two of the elders scowled at her. She hadn't been confident enough in her own answers to guide someone else.

One of the elders leaned forward. "If a member of our congregation goes astray and refuses to repent, do you feel you could vote to put this person under the *Meidung*?"

The baptized members of the congregation had to vote unanimously to shun an individual. Sarah couldn't remember it having been done in her community, but it had been done in the neighboring church.

She glanced at Isaac, imagining how hard it would be to shun someone she knew. She tried to convey her feelings. "I understand that it is done out of love, not malice, and the aim is not to punish but to bring about a change of heart. I think I could if I believed that person was in the wrong."

Thaddeus leaned forward. "Our fervent desire must be to make the shunned person see they have sinned against all. If it is painful to be separated from their friends and family, how much more painful must it be to be separated from God?"

The bishop looked pleased with his grandson. "*Goot.* Now let us join the others."

When they were finished, they all went out together. Sarah leaned close to Isaac as they walked toward the building housing the meeting. "That wasn't so bad, was it?"

"I guess not."

"I know every Amish church district is different, so if you have any questions about our group, feel free to ask."

"Do you think you could shun someone? I'm not sure I could."

"Then you should talk to the bishop about it."

"I guess I could but not now."

The large garage doors of the shop were open to the morning sun. Backless wooden benches were lined up either side of the center aisle down the middle of the building. Men and boys sat on one side while women and girls sat on the other. Around the perimeter, some of the elderly members, including Henrietta, were seated in more comfortable chairs.

The room was a sea of black on the men's side. Black

coats and pants were the standard Sunday dress. Identical black hats hung from a long row of pegs on the back wall. The women in their long dresses and white aprons were more colorful, wearing an assortment of solid colors mostly in blue but also in mauve and dark green.

Sarah and Angela took their places behind the married women. Isaac and Thaddeus sat on the opposite side among the single men. The younger boys took up the last row so they could make the quickest escape when the meeting was over. Sarah glanced over several times to try to catch Isaac's eye, but it was Levi she always found looking her way.

LEVI COULD BARELY believe it. Sarah had actually convinced his brother to start baptism classes. Isaac might say he was in love with an *Englisch* woman but a desire to wed an Amish woman was a common reason for questioning young Amish guys to move forward with baptism. Levi had chosen baptism because he valued and believed in the religion he had been brought up in.

Several times he caught Sarah looking his way, but he knew she wasn't trying to catch his attention. Finally he nudged his brother with his elbow. "Sarah has her eye on you."

Isaac smiled at her and went back to staring at the floor. Any conversation between the brothers would have to wait until after the service.

When it was over, Levi helped his mother from her chair. Once she was on her feet and leaning on her cane, she waved him away. "I'm fine. I can get about under my own power."

Ernest came up to her. "Where would you like me to put your chair?"

"In the shade of that nice tree with the tire swing. That way I can enjoy watching other people's grandbabies play."

Levi and Isaac shared an amused look. Their mother was not very subtle. They began helping to carry the benches into the house, where they would be stacked together to create tables. Not everyone could eat at once, so the elders went first. Most of the children were already playing together and didn't seem to be worried about getting a bite to eat.

A group of women her age gathered around Henrietta to visit. His mother looked happy at the attention. Levi was surprised when Ernest came out of the house with a cup of coffee for Henrietta. She thanked him and he went back inside, returning a short time later with a plate of food and utensils. Sarah followed him. He took a seat on the ground beside Henrietta and accepted a plate from Sarah.

"Have the two of you made up?" Sarah asked. That was exactly what Levi was thinking.

Ernest and Henrietta looked at each other and shook their heads. "We have not," Ernest said. "But we can't bring our differences to church."

"Right." Sarah rolled her eyes, and Levi had to choke back his laughter.

The loud cry of a child made Sarah run to rescue Caleb from the tire swing. He had somehow managed to stand on top of the tire but he couldn't get down. Sarah plucked him off his unsteady perch and sent him to play with Grace.

"I see you have found another child that needs rescuing," Ernest said. "How many is that now?"

A sweet smile lifted a corner of her pretty mouth. "Do I count the time I saved you from a horde of bees?"

"You didn't save me. You assisted me in vacating the area much faster than my own legs could travel."

"And how did she do that?" Henrietta asked.

"It wasn't a pretty sight," Sarah said sadly. "He was at the corner of our rock wall when he disturbed the honeybees, which he had assured us he knew how to handle. He was beating them away from his face with his hat. All I had was an empty wheelbarrow I was about to put in the barn. I ran up to him, shoved him into my wheelbarrow and went careening down the hill to the creek, where I dumped him in the mud."

Levi caught her eye. "I know how that feels. Minus the bee stings."

Sarah chuckled but shook her head. "You were only muddy on one side. Ernest was coated better than a caramel apple on a stick." She looked around. "Where did Isaac go?"

"I saw him talking to Faron a few minutes ago," Ernest said. "Tell them about your other rescue of a child in trouble."

She turned bright pink and shook her head.

"What were you rescuing the *kinder* from?" Levi asked.

She wrapped her arms across her middle and stared at her feet. "It was one little boy, and it happened a long time ago."

"Sarah is being modest, as she should." Ernest turned

to Henrietta. "The Troyers' barn caught fire two years ago. Their youngest son, Melvin, was trapped in the hayloft. The poor child was crouched in the loft door, too afraid to jump. There wasn't a ladder, so the men fighting the fire made a pyramid by standing on each other's shoulders, but they weren't tall enough to reach the child. Sarah scampered up those men like a squirrel. She grabbed the boy and brought him down safe to his mother's arms."

Levi listened to the story with growing respect for Sarah. She could be fearless when she needed to be. If he were ever to marry, he'd want his wife to be like Sarah. He nodded toward her. "Impressive. Do you have a fondness for adventures?"

She lifted her chin and scowled at him. "*Nee*, but I don't shy away when I'm confronted with one."

"I can believe that." In his mind's eye he could see her behind one of his fast horses, urging the animal to even greater speed. He couldn't see her cowering from the dangers in his sport.

Something of what he was thinking must have shone in his eyes because she blushed and jumped to her feet. "I should help with the cleanup."

Levi watched her go into the house. "She's a very interesting young woman."

"She would make someone a *goot* wife," his mother said.

"Now, who would you be thinking might suit her?" Ernest asked.

"Why, Isaac, perhaps," Henrietta said wistfully.

He shook his head. "I don't see it. I suspect another fellow has an interest in her."

Levi glanced at the older man and found Ernest was staring at him. No matter what Ernest thought, Levi knew better. Sarah had her heart set on Isaac.

He spied his brother helping several of the boys set up a volleyball net. Isaac wasn't as interested in Sarah as she was in him. Levi rubbed his chin. How could he change that?

"I think I would like to go home now," Henrietta said. Levi helped her to her feet.

"I'll take you," Ernest said. "Let your sons stay and get acquainted with the folks in our community."

She nodded. "All right." The two walked off together. If they were still angry with each other, it didn't show.

One of the women gathered up Henrietta's plate and utensils. "You should get your mother some help at home for a while. Have you thought about hiring a helper or housekeeper?"

Levi glanced at his brother across the way. Sarah was beside him. She hooked her arm through his and pulled him away from the other boys. The two of them walked off toward the flower gardens at the side of the house. He saw his brother take his phone out and begin talking on it. He soon walked away from Sarah.

"I haven't considered a housekeeper but it's a fine idea." Maybe what Isaac needed was more exposure to Sarah.

Levi walked over to her as she was getting ready to leave later that afternoon. She had a hamper and another box under her arm. Levi opened her buggy door for her. "I see you and Isaac spent some time together today."

"We went for a walk after his phone call. The bishop

wasn't happy to see he'd brought his phone to the service."

"And you talked about?"

"We talked and we spent some time getting to know each other again."

"That's *goot*. Are you going to see more of him?"

"I guess that depends."

"What does that mean?"

"It means we've decided to focus on getting to know each other as friends. Then we'll see if we want to take our relationship to the next step."

"I hope things work out for the two of you. I have an idea to move things forward. My mother needs help with the housework and cooking until she is feeling better. You've seen how frail she is. Our garden is a mess and so is the rest of the house. Would you be willing to become Mother's helper? I'd pay you a salary and you would be able to see my brother daily. What do you say?"

"What's the catch?"

"There isn't one. Are you interested?"

"Maybe."

"My brother isn't exactly breaking down your door to see you. I think this might help with that, and I have another idea as well."

She regarded him with suspicion. "What do you mean?"

"Did you notice how quickly he changed his mind about hunting for mushrooms when I said I wanted to go along?"

"I did."

"Isaac doesn't like competition. If you and I were

to pretend an interest in each other, it might spur him into paying more attention to you. Think it over. Let me know soon about the job and if you want to go along with my idea. You can leave a message on our answering machine in the phone booth. Isaac never checks it because he has his own phone. Mother really does need the help."

As Levi walked off, Sarah caught sight of Isaac watching them with a faint frown on his face. He was standing with Thaddeus and several other young men. He started toward her, but Thaddeus sidetracked him with a comment. Sarah's family arrived at the buggy and she left without speaking to Isaac again.

She mulled over Levi's offer on the trip home. The extra income would certainly come in handy and she would be helping someone who truly needed it.

She then faced the biggest plus head-on. She would have a reason to be near Isaac on a daily basis. He wouldn't be able to ignore her if she was around constantly. It would give her a way to impress him with her cooking skills. She could show him she knew how to darn socks, make soap, take care of the garden and the house. Why, it would almost be like giving a prospective wife a trial run. She liked Henrietta. She adored Isaac, and she could tolerate Levi.

She leaned forward to speak to Joshua. "Can you let me off by the phone? I need to make a call."

After he dropped her by the phone hut near the end of their lane, she called the Rabers' number. To her surprise, Levi answered. "Raber Farms."

She stuttered for a second and then said, "This is Sarah. Were you so sure I would call that you were waiting by the phone?"

"Of course not. I was checking our messages. Someone in Delaware offered me a position as his head trainer. The man who bought our farm in Pennsylvania gave him my number. I was about to return his call and tell him I can't take the job. What did you decide?"

"I'll do it. When should I start?"

"I may need some time to persuade Mother she needs help and to convince Isaac you aren't out to snare him into matrimony."

She clenched the phone tightly in her hand. "I'm not out to snare him. I simply want to encourage him to consider me as a spouse."

"Then why not pretend you are interested in me? I know that will get his attention."

"Are you sure that will work? It doesn't feel right." But she had seen for herself that Isaac paid more attention if she was with Levi.

"Sarah, we both have Isaac's welfare at heart. You are the prefect woman for him. Sometimes he's too hardheaded to see what's right in front of his face."

"You really think I'm right for him?"

"I do. I wouldn't suggest this bit of playacting if I didn't."

Sarah couldn't believe she was about to agree to such a questionable scheme. "Okay, I'm willing to give it a try."

"You are? Great. Come over Tuesday, then, and *danki.*" He hung up before she could say anything else.

This was going to backfire worse than her canoe plan. She was almost sure of it.

CHAPTER TEN

THE FOLLOWING MORNING Levi worked Wing on the lunge line for half an hour and then walked her for another half to cool her down. Training the filly lifted his spirits and yet it made him miss the life he used to have. Wing was special. She would race one day and prove his father had been right about her potential. Levi couldn't give up that dream. He had a promise to keep.

When he finally went in the house, he found his mother asleep in her rocking chair. He touched her shoulder. "*Mamm*, I need to talk to you."

"I'm listening," she said in a drowsy voice. Her trip to church the previous day had worn her out.

"I have hired someone to help you out around the house."

Her eyes popped open. "You did what?"

"Don't tell me you don't need help. You need rest. You don't need to worry if the housework is done or dinner gets made."

She was silent for a long moment. Then she nodded. "What you say is true. Who did you hire?"

He had expected more of an objection. "You're giving in just like that?"

"I may seem like a foolish woman sometimes, but I know my limits."

"He hired me."

Levi swung his head around. Sarah was standing in the doorway with a large basket in her hands.

His mother smiled at him. "I didn't know you had such good sense, Levi. Come in, Sarah, and sit down. What have you brought me?"

"I've brought you some lavender oils, some dried flowers and some fresh ones. The scent is said to be calming. A few sprigs inside your pillowcase can help you relax and get to sleep more quickly. If you like, I'll make you some lavender tea now."

"That would be lovely. Levi, give the girl a hand."

"She's here to give *you* a hand," he reminded her.

"Don't be snippy. Make him some tea, too, Sarah. He needs to relax as much as I do."

Sarah chuckled. "Where is Isaac? Perhaps he'd like some tea or maybe one of my lavender cookies."

Henrietta waved a hand toward the window. "I believe he is out working on our tractor. He is interested in engines. Levi only likes things with four feet."

Sarah smiled so sweetly at his mother that Levi almost wished she would smile at him that way.

She went into the kitchen and began unloading her basket. He followed her and stepped close to keep his voice low. "I thought you were going to give me a day to break the news to *Mamm* and Isaac."

She opened a jar and the heady fragrance of lavender filled the kitchen. "I'm not here to work. I'm here to deliver something I believe will help your mother. I won't stay long."

She pulled a plastic bag out of her basket. It was

full of iced cookies with flower petals on top of them. "Would you like a cookie?" When he declined, she shrugged and took a bite.

He breathed in the fresh floral scent all around him and knew he would forever associate the smell of lavender with Sarah. His brother was worse than a fool if he continued to ignore the pearl right in front of his eyes. She was smart, a little sassy, perhaps, but she cared about her family and the people around her. She would make any man a fine wife.

His gaze was drawn to her full lips, half parted in a smile. Would they taste like the lavender cookie she was nibbling?

Levi realized where his thoughts were leading him. "This is kind of you. I'll let Isaac know you're here."

"Don't bother. I'm leaving in a few minutes. I don't want him to think I'm chasing after him."

"Aren't you?"

A tiny grin played at the corner of her mouth. Her eyes sparkled as she leaned toward him. "I am, but we don't want him to know that, do we?"

This Sarah was far more tempting than he could resist. He turned on his heels and abruptly left the house before he said or did something stupid. Sarah wanted Isaac. Isaac was the one who needed a wife.

He didn't.

SARAH ARRIVED AT the Raber farm early the following morning. She saw Levi working with a new horse and stopped her buggy on the lane to watch. She recognized the gelding as the one Faron Mast had had trouble with on Sunday. Levi had the horse on a long lead, taking it from a walk to a trot, back to a walk and then to a stop, all with soft spoken commands.

He made it look easy. The horse had all his attention on Levi as he approached him with his head low. The animal accepted the praise Levi lavished on him and allowed Levi to run his hand across his back and down his legs. She knew that Levi missed the horses he had once raised with his father. Perhaps training buggy horses for Amish customers would ease some of his loss.

She urged Freckles to go on down the lane. Isaac came out of the house and took hold of the mare's bridle with a welcoming smile. "*Guder mariye*, Sarah."

"Good morning to you, too." She got out and cast a sidelong glance at him from beneath her lashes. He was so amazingly handsome with his straw-blond hair and bright blue eyes that matched the sky overhead.

"Ready for more mushroom hunting?" he asked with a chuckle.

As much as she wanted to say yes and spend the day with him, she had agreed to do a job, and she wasn't going to shirk her duty. "Nope. I'm working today."

"I saw you watching Levi just now. You should know he's much more interested in horses than in any girl."

She raised one eyebrow. "That sounds like a warning."

"Maybe it is."

Was Levi's plan working already? "How is your mother? She certainly seemed happy to be the center of attention among her friends."

"Levi and I thought so, too. Can I help you with anything?"

"You can stay out of my way and let me get my work done."

He held up both hands in surrender. "I know when I'm not wanted. Mother is supposed to see her doctor tomorrow. Would you be able to come along with us?"

"Of course. I have been hired to do whatever your mother needs."

"I need the company more than she does. I'm not fond of waiting rooms with boring magazines to read. At least this way I'll have someone to talk to besides *Mamm*."

Sarah walked away smiling. Isaac was happy to see her. She hoped that wouldn't wear off with daily visits.

Inside the house she set her baskets on the table. The kitchen was clean. If the men had made themselves breakfast, they had cleaned up admirably.

"Sarah, is that you?" Henrietta inquired from the other room.

Taking off her traveling bonnet, Sarah went to the doorway. "How are you this beautiful morning?"

"Not bad for an old bag of bones."

Sarah smiled. "I have the cure for that."

Henrietta looked doubtful. "How so?"

"The only way to put some weight on you is for you to eat more than a few crumbs. What did you have for breakfast?"

Henrietta turned her head to stare out the window. "I had toast."

Sarah walked over and sat on the side of her bed. "Just toast?"

"I had coffee with it. I'm not hungry."

Rather than upsetting Henrietta by scolding her, Sarah stood up. "What are your orders for today?"

Henrietta looked at her. "Orders? What do you mean?"

Sarah folded her hands in front of her. "What would you like me to do first? I can sweep the floors. I can wash the windows. I can do mending if you need that. You are in charge of the house. I'm simply here to follow your instructions."

"I haven't thought about what needs to be done. The ladies from the church did most of the dusting and unpacking things when they were here last week."

"Then I'll just sweep the floors. Did you have something in mind for lunch?"

Henrietta made a face. "I can't think about eating yet."

"All right. What do you think your sons would like?"

"Isaac is the picky eater. Check with him. Levi eats anything that's put in front of him."

Sarah chuckled. "That's good to know. If I burn anything, I'll make sure I serve it to Levi."

Henrietta laughed. "He is so much like his father. I worry about him sometimes."

"About Levi? Why? Because of the horse racing?"

"Because he seems to prefer horses over people. He should be married already. He needs a woman to make a home for him. A horse can't do that."

"Levi seems capable of taking care of himself," Sarah said and realized that she meant it. But it wasn't Levi she was interested in. "What about Isaac? What kind of woman would suit him?"

"Someone who doesn't take the world too seriously but knows how to work hard and care for a home. Perhaps someone like you."

Blushing, Sarah muttered a denial. "I'm sure he can do much better than me."

"Spoken like a demure Amish maid."

Sarah took a step back. "I should get busy."

It was flattering that Henrietta thought she might be the right kind of woman for Isaac. After all, who knew him better than his mother? She would have to remember to thank Levi for offering her this job.

Sarah swept the floors upstairs, taking note of one messy bedroom and one neat and tidy room. She assumed Levi was the occupant of the tidy room. When she came downstairs, she was surprised to see Henrietta sitting at the kitchen table.

"Look at you. You must be feeling better." Sarah washed her hands at the kitchen sink.

"I was feeling guilty making you work so hard."

"It's good for me. I need to build up my muscles. Caleb is getting so heavy I have a hard time picking him up."

"He's a beautiful child. Your sister is blessed." While they talked, Sarah got started making a chicken-and-vegetable soup from the ingredients in her basket. When she had the stock and chicken simmering, she began chopping up her vegetables.

"I can do some of that," Henrietta said, reaching for the carrots.

Sarah happily handed over her knife and started on making bread. It wouldn't be ready for lunch, but by supper time there would be piping-hot loaves to be served with the pork roast she had planned.

Once the vegetables were chopped, Henrietta transferred them to the simmering liquid. Sarah kept a close eye on her unsteady steps but she didn't interfere. The more Henrietta could do for herself, the better it was for her. Sarah continued kneading her dough but happened to glance at the stove. Henrietta had taken a spoon and dipped out a bit of the stock. She sipped the sample.

"What do you think?" Sarah asked. "Does it need more salt?"

"Maybe a touch."

Hiding a grin, Sarah bent over her dough. "Add some, will you?" Sampling the soup was as good a way as any of getting a few extra calories into someone who professed not to be hungry.

Henrietta stepped over to the spice rack. "It could use a little paprika. Isaac enjoys it seasoned that way."

"Add some, by all means." She might as well learn how to prepare the dishes that Isaac liked.

The outside door opened, and Levi came in. "Something smells good."

"Sarah is making soup for lunch," his mother said, taking another sip of the broth.

He grinned as he walked to the sink and washed up. "That's funny because you are the one stirring the pot, *Mudder*. It's good to see you working in the kitchen again. Isaac is getting mighty tired of my cooking."

"Why doesn't Isaac cook?" Sarah asked.

"Because I never learned to boil water," Isaac declared as he came in the door. "I might not like what Levi makes, but it's better than anything I can turn out."

"All you need is a little practice," Sarah suggested.

"And a willing guinea pig," Levi added. "Which I am not. I'm fine with fried eggs morning, noon and night."

Isaac moved to put his arm around his mother. "Do you hear that? I need you to get well and stay well. I can't live on his cooking."

Levi dried his hands on a kitchen towel. "We have Sarah to make sure you don't starve."

"No matter how *goot* Sarah's cooking is, it will never rival *Mamm*'s."

Sarah parked one flour-coated fist on her hip. "You can say that without tasting a single bite of something I've prepared?"

"Oh, I remember that look." Isaac playfully hid behind his mother. "Sarah's temper is about to come out."

"I am long past the age of pitching a temper tantrum. If you have come in simply to annoy me, please leave." She resumed kneading her bread, but she didn't mind his teasing.

"You don't have to tell me twice." Isaac snagged a carrot from her basket and went out the door.

She pinned her gaze on Levi. "And what about you?"

LEVI LOOKED HER up and down. "I came in to check if you needed any assistance. I'm happy to see you have things well in hand."

She was adorable with a smear of flour across her cheek and that challenging expression on her face. At least Isaac was paying some attention to her. Their teasing attitudes toward each other boded well for the friendship Sarah claimed was important. If she was content with nothing more than that from Isaac, then who was Levi to disagree.

His mother moved to sit on one of the chairs at the table. She was smiling at Sarah. "It's good to see Isaac talking to a friend in person instead of talking on his foolish phone. He will need to give that up soon."

"It's handy to have just now," Levi said.

"Because I'm sick?"

He nodded. "It's a long run to the phone hut."

"I don't know why everyone is concerned about me. I am ready to go when the Lord calls me."

He stepped over and dropped a kiss on the top of her head. "Maybe we aren't ready to let you go."

"As if you have any say in it."

"Henrietta, would you check the soup again?" Sarah asked. "The vegetables should be done soon. And check if the chicken is tender enough."

It was clear she was trying to change the direction of their conversation. His mother got up and went to the stove. She dipped a ladle into the pot and poured a small amount into a bowl. After sampling the vegetables and the chicken, she turned to Sarah. "Another twenty minutes should do it."

"Did the paprika help?"

"It's just the way Isaac likes it. I believe I will go and rest until it's ready. I may be able to enjoy some of your soup later." She walked with unsteady steps into the other room.

Levi leaned against the counter. "That was clever, Sarah."

She looked toward the doorway to make sure his mother wasn't listening. Then she smiled at him. "Chicken broth can soothe a queasy stomach and increase a person's appetite. I thought if I had her sample it enough times, she would get a little added benefit. I saw her sneak a few bites of carrot while she was chopping them."

"Every little bit helps."

She plopped her dough into a large glass bowl and covered it with a kitchen towel. "I watched you working with Faron's horse this morning. Do you think you'll be able to overcome the animal's bad habits?"

"Horses are funny creatures. They can behave for months and then one day they act up. The driver lets them get away with it and the horse has learned the human may not be the herd leader after all. The horse has to respect a person in order to follow directions without question. You seem to be doing okay with Isaac."

She smiled softly, and he wished the smile was for him and not for his brother. He quickly dismissed the idea. Isaac was the one she wanted. Sharing her attention in the cozy kitchen was much too tempting. He pushed away from the counter. He needed some space between them. "Call me when lunch is ready."

Outside he found Isaac sitting on a large stump they used as a chopping block when they were cutting wood. He was on his phone. As soon as he saw Levi looking his way, he said goodbye and hung up.

"Your friend from back home?" Levi asked, suspecting by Isaac's reaction that it had been the girl he had been seeing.

"Is there anything wrong with that?" Isaac demanded, his tone defiant.

"Don't ruffle your feathers. There are times when I wish the horses knew how to use phones. I'd sure like to hear how Biscuits and Gravy is getting along. He had a nagging cough the week we left. Sunny Sophia should've had her foal by now. I was hoping for another filly. Stormy Seas Sailor should be ready for the track. He's a half brother to Wing and a Prayer. I'm hoping he has half her talent and heart."

"Why don't you call Arnold Diehl and ask about them. You know he'd tell you everything you wanted to know."

"I could, but I think a clean break is better. I'd want to discuss which antibiotics Biscuits and Gravy should be on. I'd want to be there for Sunny Sophia's birthing. Taking Stormy Seas Sailor around the track is the only way I could see just how good he is. It's hard to take someone else's word for that. Maybe I'd want to tweak his training. *Nee*, I won't call Arnold."

"I guess you left some friends behind, too. I'm sorry."

"We must live the life *Gott* gives us."

"Even when it's not easy."

"Even then. How are things between you and Sarah?" Levi held his breath waiting for his brother's answer.

"Am I going to propose marriage anytime soon? Not a chance. Do I enjoy hanging out with her? Sure. What's not to like?"

"And how does Sarah feel about it?"

"I think you're right. She still likes me a lot. Crazy, isn't it? One woman can remain a true friend for years without seeing me in person while another woman is finished with me the moment I'm out of her sight."

He wasn't sure what Isaac was talking about, but he seemed to need someone to listen. "Perhaps that's because one woman knows how valuable true friendship is and the other woman doesn't."

Sadness filled his eyes. "That's really the only explanation, isn't it?"

Levi sat down beside him. "I have a lot more experience with horses than I do with women, but it seems to me some women believe loyalty is more than a word. It's a commitment. It goes both ways, of course. A man has to believe in loyalty, too. The promise to love, honor and obey is made by two people. If only one is willing to do the work, the marriage will fail."

"I reckon a fella is better off learning that before he says 'I do,' but how can he be sure the woman he marries will be willing to put forth the effort?"

Levi looked toward the house when he heard the screen door open. Sarah stepped out and cupped her hands around her mouth. "Lunch is ready."

He waved to let her know they had heard and stood up. "It would be wise to know a woman well before you propose, but some things, like the goodness of a woman's heart, have to be taken on faith. Let's go eat. And try not to insult Sarah's cooking. We do want her to come back."

SARAH WATCHED THE men walk toward her. It was hard not to compare the brothers to each other. Isaac's blond good looks drew her eyes, but there was something about Levi that made her take a second look. He was dark where his brother was fair, but he had a quiet strength about him. She could see it in his walk and in the way he held his shoulders back, as if he was capable of carrying the weight of his family easily.

His dark eyes were framed with thick eyelashes. She couldn't always tell what he was thinking, but when he smiled, his eyes glinted with humor as they crinkled at the corners. He didn't smile often enough.

She went back into the house and began dishing up bowls of soup. She carried them to the table one by one while the men washed up. After that she went into the living room. Henrietta was lying down with her eyes closed. Sarah touched her gently on the shoulder. Her eyes came open immediately. "Is it ready? It smells yummy."

Sarah offered a hand to help Henrietta sit up. "Don't stand too quickly. It can make you dizzy."

"Don't tell my sons I said this, but I rather enjoy being fussed over."

Sarah grinned. "It will be our secret."

"I believe the lavender in my pillowcase is helping me sleep."

"I'm glad. Now, if I can just find something that will spark your appetite, I'll consider my job here a success."

Henrietta stood. "I'm not dizzy at all." She seemed mildly surprised.

"That means your blood pressure is getting back to normal. Which is a very *goot* thing."

The two women walked into the kitchen together. Levi, as the head of the family, was seated at the head of the table with Isaac on his right side. Henrietta took a seat at the foot and Sarah sat across from Isaac. Everyone folded their hands, closed their eyes and said grace silently. Levi cleared his throat to signal the end of the prayer and everyone began to eat. As with most Amish families, there was no chatter at the table other than a request to pass the biscuits or the butter. Henrietta ate slowly, but Sarah was pleased to see she finished most of her soup and half of a biscuit.

When everyone was done, Sarah stood and began to clear the table. Henrietta gathered together the bowls, but Sarah took them from her and carried them to the sink. "I've got these. You should go out and enjoy the nice weather for a little while."

"The meal was *goot*," Levi said, getting to his feet. "We'll be working on the porch roof this afternoon. I hope the hammering won't disturb you, *Mamm*."

She waved away his concern. "Work comes first."

"I'll get those shingles out of the barn." Isaac rose and left the house.

He hadn't even mentioned if her cooking was good or not. Part of the reason for her taking the job was to impress him with her wifely skills. Sarah tried not to let her disappointment show. If the way to a man's heart was through his stomach, it was clear it would take more than chicken soup to bring Isaac around.

"What was that look for?" Levi asked.

"I was merely trying to decide what to bake this afternoon. Does Isaac have some special treat that he likes?"

"He's always been fond of shoofly pie."

She smiled at him. "Good to know. What about you?"

"I'm partial to those lavender cookies you brought yesterday. Are there any left?"

Sarah chuckled. "I put them in the cookie jar. Help yourself."

He lifted the lid of the barrel-shaped canister and pulled out three cookies. "I think these are my new favorites."

She couldn't help but smile. "They're my favorites, too, but I think that's because it's the first cookie I remember making with my mother. I was insisting that I wanted to make flower cookies. She sent me to the garden, and I brought in a handful of lavender. She made the icing so the flower petals had something to stick to. We made them every summer."

"Memories of our loved ones are what keep them close to us."

"What's your favorite memory of your *daed*? I'm sure it has something to do with horses."

"Actually, it doesn't. It was fall. I must've been three or four years old. *Daed* and I went to the orchard to pick apples. I remember the smell of the apples and the crunch of fallen leaves underfoot. I couldn't reach any of the fruit except the ones that had already fallen on the ground. I think I started to cry. *Daed* put his hat on the fence post and set me up on his shoulders. It made me feel like a giant. I could reach higher than he could.

I remember thinking that it must be how *Gott* felt looking down on us."

"What a wonderful memory," Henrietta said, coming into the room. "What is your first memory of me?"

Levi opened the cookie jar and pulled out another cookie. He handed it to her. "I remember being scolded because I had used a chair to climb onto the counter and get into your fresh-made peach pie. I didn't have a spoon or fork, but my fingers worked beautifully. It was worth the scolding. I love peach pie to this day."

"I remember so many things you boys did together." Henrietta sat at the table and nibbled on her cookie.

Sarah quickly got a small glass of milk and set it by her elbow. "Tell me what they were like when they were little."

"Levi was the adventuresome one. The first one to go too high in a tree or to climb up onto the barn roof."

He pointed his cookie at Sarah. "See, we have something in common."

Sarah grinned. "It seems we do. I had to jump. Fortunately into a hay feeder half-filled with hay. How did you get down?"

"The same way minus the hay."

"He sprained his ankle. His father was mighty upset with him."

"Isaac had pushed the ladder over so I couldn't get down, and he wouldn't put it back up. Actually, I think he was too small to manage it, but I chose to believe he wanted to leave me up there on purpose."

"You never told me that Isaac was the one who left

you up there. You told us the ladder accidentally fell over."

"I didn't want to get him in trouble. He felt bad enough." Levi dusted cookie crumbs off the front of his shirt.

"I think you took the blame for a lot of things that Isaac did," Henrietta said quietly. The sound of hammering could be heard outside.

"He's my little *brudder*. I'm supposed to take care of him. Which reminds me—I need to go help him replace the shingles on the porch."

Sarah returned to the sink and began filling it with hot water. Henrietta set the empty glass of milk on the cabinet beside her. "The adventures of my children are more entertaining now than when they were occurring. Boys can give their *mudder* some frightening moments. But I wouldn't trade those days for anything."

"I'm glad to hear that." Sarah handed Henrietta a kitchen towel. "I'll wash and you can dry."

Henrietta chuckled. "Are you done fussing over me?"

"For the time being. I don't think drying a few dishes will wear you out."

"You are good company, Sarah. I'm glad Levi thought to bring you here. He is a *goot sohn*."

"I'm sure Isaac is, too." Sarah had hoped to learn more about Isaac, but it was Levi she was learning to know better. Surprisingly she had enjoyed the moments of shared memories. He was an interesting and complex man. It sounded as if he had spent his life looking out for Isaac. Was that what he was doing now by offering her this job? She had assumed it was because he wanted his brother settled so he could return to Pennsylvania. Maybe she had judged him too harshly.

"Isaac is a wonderful boy, but he lacks the desire to settle down, and that worries me."

"According to my brother-in-law, Joshua, all young men resist settling down until the right woman comes into the picture."

Henrietta dried the last bowl. "I don't know if that's true or not, but I pray the right woman for Isaac comes along soon."

Sarah wanted to be that woman.

CHAPTER ELEVEN

THE DRIVER LEVI had hired over the phone showed up right on time the next day. Sarah's happy squeal of delight startled him as she rushed outside to embrace the woman getting out of her car. He assumed the woman was a member of the Mennonite faith. She wore a long-sleeved modest blue dress and had a small black *kapp* pinned to her gray hair.

Sarah took her arm and led her toward the porch steps. "Levi, this is Miss Julie Temple, one of the teachers at our school."

"Public school," Julie said, correctly reading his surprise. "There aren't enough Amish students in Cedar Grove to make having their own school cost-effective. Our little country school doesn't have enough non-Amish students in this area to stay open. Combined, we can keep the school operating. We have two teachers for all eight grades. I have fourteen students in the upper grades, and my coworker has seventeen students in grades one through four."

"I was Miss Julie's class pet for all four years that she had me," Sarah said with a chuckle.

Levi grinned. "And yet you have remained so humble. How is that even possible?" He wanted to ask her teacher a great many things about Sarah as a child, but he refrained.

Julie laughed and patted Sarah's arm. "I like him."

He stepped back to let the women enter the house. "Do you know my mother?"

"I don't believe so. The name Henrietta is unusual. I don't recall a student by that name."

Levi's mother came in from the living room leaning heavily on her cane. "I was a student at Cedar Grove Elementary before your time."

Julie nodded toward her. "I'm pleased to meet you, Mrs. Raber."

"This is my son Isaac," Henrietta said, gesturing behind her where Isaac stood with her shawl and bag in his arms.

"We should go," Isaac said. "Her appointment is at ten."

"It won't take long to get there," Julie said. "Sarah, are you coming with us?"

"I am."

"Wonderful. You must tell me how Joshua and Laura Beth are getting along. I look forward to seeing them at the father-and-son baseball game again this year. Joshua is a fine coach for those little boys."

Sarah took Henrietta's belongings from Isaac so he could help his mother down the steps. "Joshua's looking forward to the day that Caleb can pick up a bat."

"So many parents suffer from an impatience to see their little ones grow up quickly. The Amish aren't as guilty of it as our non-Amish parents are, but I still see it."

Sarah opened the car door. "Not Laura Beth. She would keep Caleb little forever if she could find a way."

"I don't blame her a bit. She waited a long time for a child."

After Henrietta was situated, Sarah got in. "Henrietta, I almost forgot to tell you Angela and Mary Jane will be over this afternoon. I must help my sister make soap today. It's her bestselling item at the farmers' market and we are running low. I hope you don't mind, Levi."

"Not at all. I knew we couldn't have you every day." Mary Jane and Angela were wonderful women but, in his opinion, they were a poor substitute for Sarah's cheerfulness.

The ride to the doctor's office took less than half an hour. The clinic was a single-story blond brick building attached to the hospital. Julie parked under the awning. Levi got out and entered the building. He returned with a wheelchair.

Henrietta gave him a sour look. "What is that for?"

"It's to save my back."

"You don't have a bad back."

"I will if I have to pick you up off the floor. Sit like a *goot frau* and do as you're told."

Henrietta turned to Sarah. "See how they treat me? Like a *bobbli*. I'm perfectly capable of walking."

"As much as I hate to agree with Levi, sit in the wheelchair, *Mudder*," Isaac said.

Sarah took Henrietta's arm. "I know you don't need a wheelchair, but these two will not stop harping at you unless you let them take care of you. This way you don't get worn out and they get to feel like they have done something special for you."

"For goodness' sakes, I've never seen such a fussy bunch." She sat down in the chair with a huff and stared straight ahead.

The clinic was at the far end of the building. Levi was glad his mother hadn't forced the issue and tried to walk all that way. The Heart Clinic had a cheerful waiting room with bright pictures on the walls and magazines scattered on small tables beside overstuffed chairs. A children's play area filled one corner. They waited only a few minutes before Henrietta's name was called. Levi laid his magazine aside and stood up.

Henrietta looked at him. "I don't need anyone to go in with me."

"Your sons want to hear what the doctor has to say," Sarah said gently.

"I can tell them later."

"Fine." Levi sat down and picked up his magazine again. He didn't read a word of it. Isaac walked out into the hall to speak on his phone twice during the wait. Each time he came back in, he seemed more impatient and edgy. Only Sarah waited patiently, looking calm and serene. He forced himself not to stare at her. He glanced at his brother putting his phone away.

"How are you keeping that thing charged?" Levi asked, knowing there was no electricity on the farm.

"I use the battery in the tractor. A friend gave me an adapter," Isaac said.

Sarah nodded. "That's what I used, too, when I had my phone."

Levi got to his feet. "Have they been in there a long

time?" The waiting room had no clock on the pale gray walls.

Isaac glanced at his cell phone. "Twenty minutes is all."

"Your *mamm* seems stronger to me. Don't you think so?" Sarah asked.

"A little." Levi hoped he wasn't imagining it because that was what he wanted to see. If Sarah had noticed, she must be doing better.

Isaac sat in the chair beside her. "I think so, too. At least she's eating better, even if it's not that much yet. She seems to like your cooking, Sarah. It is *goot*."

She blushed at his praise. "I'm glad you think so."

If his brother suspected Sarah was being dangled in front of him, he didn't seem to mind.

A nurse came out from a short hallway that led to the exam rooms. "Dr. Black would like to speak with all of you."

Levi shared a worried glance with his brother as they followed her. Inside the room the two men stood against the wall. Sarah sat on a chair beside the doctor. Their mother was sitting on the exam table looking annoyed.

The doctor took a seat at a small desk with a chart open in front of her. She turned to look at Levi and Isaac. "I understand your mother refused a home health nurse."

Their mother crossed her arms over her chest. "I don't need one. It's a frivolous expense."

"It's important that I have accurate information in order to adjust your medications. I will have the nurse teach both of you how to take her blood pressure and check her pulse twice a day. If she is having any symptoms of A-fib, such as shortness of breath, a fluttering sensation in her chest or a fainting episode, I need to know about it right away."

"I know how to check her blood pressure and pulse," Sarah said. "I don't have a blood pressure cuff, but I know that we can get one at the pharmacy."

The doctor looked mollified. "Excellent. Are you a daughter or daughter-in-law?"

"A temporary helper, but I'm there every day except Sunday."

Henrietta lifted her chin. "See, I didn't need a nurse."

"How is she?" Levi asked the doctor.

"She's getting better. Her blood pressure and pulse are both normal today. She has gained five pounds, which is a good start. I won't have the results of her lab work until tomorrow, but all in all, I'm pleased."

Levi felt a weight lift off his chest. He hadn't realized how worried he was until now.

They left the doctor's office a short time later. Isaac walked ahead, pushing their mother in a wheelchair. Levi walked beside Sarah. He'd never known a woman as resourceful as she seemed to be. "How do you happen to know how to take a blood pressure reading?"

"My sister's first husband was ill for many weeks. He had a visiting hospice nurse, and I learned from her."

"That must've been a difficult time for you."

"You learn to do what you have to do. A person never really knows what they are capable of doing until the need arises."

"I think having you in the house has made a wonderful difference for her."

"I try to keep her busy doing little things, so she has less time to fret about her situation. I think I will have Laura Beth bring Caleb over to visit. His antics will entertain anyone."

Levi left the doctor's office feeling more hopeful than he had expected. His mother was making progress and Sarah seemed happy to help. Her kindness toward his mother touched him deeply. He held the car door open for her. "I appreciate all you have done," he said softly.

"So do I," Isaac added as he got in beside her.

SARAH SUFFERED A pang of guilt as she sat between Levi and Isaac in the back seat of Julie's car. Her motive in taking the job had been a selfish one. She wanted to spend time with Isaac and perhaps impress him with her wifely skills. Caring for his mother had almost been an afterthought. Now she was being praised for it and that left her feeling uncomfortable. She kept her head down and avoided talking to either brother.

The ride back to the farm seemed to take forever, but Julie finally turned in the drive. "Look, Ernest is here. I do enjoy that man," she said.

Sarah tried to gauge Henrietta's reaction, but she was sitting up front and Sarah couldn't see her face.

"I wonder what he wants." Henrietta's sour tone proved she was displeased.

Julie chuckled as she stopped the car. "Unless I miss my guess, he's here to share some new fishing story."

Sarah saw Ernest was on a stepladder at the end of the porch. There were two long chains hanging down from the ceiling. On the floor by his feet was a red porch swing with thick slats and bright cushions piled on it. As soon as they all got out of the car, Ernest waved them over. "Isaac, Levi, give me a hand here."

Sarah met Levi's gaze. "I'll take your mother inside."

"Not so fast. I want to see what that old speckled toad is doing."

"I'm putting up your porch swing, you dried-up old hen. What does it look like I'm doing?"

"It's red, you fool. That's not a color for an Amish home. How dare you."

"I know what color it is." He pointed his finger at her. "And you know exactly why I painted it like this, you old bat."

"There's no reason to insult each other," Sarah said firmly, giving each of them a stern look.

"Ha! Do you feel insulted, you old hunk of fish bait?" Henrietta demanded.

He got down off the stepladder. "Not in the least. Sarah, we're only sharing a bit of baby talk between… nonfriends."

Julie looked from Ernest to Sarah. "Am I missing something?"

Sarah rolled her eyes. "We're all missing something, but these two won't fill us in."

Julie shrugged. "Alrighty, then. I guess I'll go home. Ernest, I cooked the last piece of fish in my freezer."

"I'll try to bring ya some on Saturday."

"Appreciate it." Julie waved as she got in her car and drove away.

Henrietta moved toward the front door of the house. Ernest scurried to open it for her. She walked by him with her nose in the air. "Don't let the flies in."

He winked at Sarah. "She still got it. What did the doctor say?"

"She's getting better."

He let the screen door slam shut. "I don't reckon we'll get to bury her anytime soon, then." He shouted to make sure that she heard him. Somewhere in the house, another door slammed.

He walked to where Isaac and Levi were hanging the swing from the chains. Levi pushed the swing back and forth. It made a faint creaking sound.

Ernest leaned toward Levi. "If I had a swing like that…"

"I'd paint it red and hang it on my front porch." The two men burst out laughing.

Sarah was still at a loss. "What are you two talking about?"

Isaac shook his head. "Don't look at me."

Levi folded up the stepladder. "It was something *Daed* used to say."

Ernest hooked his thumbs through his suspenders and rocked back on his heels. "I said it first, but we were both right. I just wanted to remind Henrietta of that. She ain't dead yet, and neither am I."

Sarah pointed to the swing. "Levi, are you going to explain this?"

He looked like a boy caught with his hand in the cookie jar. "As long as you don't get mad at me."

She planted her hands on her hips. "We'll see."

"It's not something an Amish fellow should say about his girl, but I've heard a few *Englisch* fellows say it. It means the girl has a nice…sway to her hips when she walks."

Sarah's mouth dropped open. "What? Are you joking?"

He held up both hands. "You asked… I'm only explaining."

She glared at each of them in turn. "You men should be ashamed of yourselves. What matters is what's on the inside of a woman, not her outside appearance."

Sarah spun around and marched away with her back ramrod straight. She wasn't about to give them the satisfaction of judging her sway.

LEVI WATCHED SARAH leave showing her outrage in every step. She would be more upset if she knew that was one of the first things he'd noticed about her. He turned to Ernest. "I think we have fallen into Sarah's bad graces." He nodded toward the swing. "You were taking a big chance bringing that thing here."

"I was aiming to remind Henrietta that I'm a long way from calling it quits on life."

"I hope I have as much gumption as you do when I'm your age," Isaac said. He sat down in the swing and gave himself a push.

"At a certain age, a fellow feels it's easier to speak his mind and not worry what other folks think."

Levi settled beside Isaac and scooted over to let Ernest sit in between them. "What age would that be?"

"A couple of decades older than the two of you."

"Are you going to tell us why you and *Mamm* are still at odds?" Isaac asked.

"Nope."

Isaac sighed. "I didn't figure you would. Just thought I'd ask. How's the fishing been?"

"I've never had a bad day fishing."

Isaac leaned forward to look at Ernest's face. "Do you mean to tell us that you have never gotten skunked?"

"Oh, there have been days when I never caught so much as a nibble, but that's not why I go fishing. There's nothing better than enjoying the splendor of God's creations while you're waiting for the next bite."

Levi heard a buzzing sound and realized it was Isaac's phone set on vibrate. His brother took it out of his boot and walked away to answer it.

Ernest watched him go. "That youngster is having a hard time giving up the *Englisch* ways."

"He is, but now I have some hope that he'll stay with us."

"A pretty Amish girl or *Englisch* girl is often how a fellow makes up his mind about what faith to follow."

"Don't you think that's a poor way for a man to decide his religion?"

"Of course I do. But then again, it's hard to argue that God doesn't use women to His advantage when it comes to getting a man into church. Once he's in the church with a helpmate by his side, the Lord may find it easier to steer him along the path of righteousness."

"I never looked at it that way."

"You haven't been fishing often enough. It gives you lots of time to contemplate the ways of the world and the workings of *Gott*. I might have it all wrong, but women do seem to be what makes the world go round."

"Coming from a man who never married, that's a bold statement."

Ernest laughed and slapped Levi's knee. "You got me there. So why haven't you brought home a bride? Haven't met the right one?"

"Catching a wife is a lot like fishing, Ernest."

"How so?"

"If you don't put your hook in the water, you're not going to catch anything."

"You make a good point. So you haven't been looking for a wife."

"The business *Daed* and I ran didn't leave me much time to think about courting. It didn't bring many women, Amish or otherwise, into my circle. Once I get Wing into the racing circuit and start winning, I hope to earn enough money with what I have saved to buy back our farm. Then I'll think about having a family."

"Getting the farm back is important to you, isn't it?"

"Very important. *Daed* poured his blood, sweat and tears into bettering the land and animals his father left him. I want to do the same. I know that's what he would want me to do."

Ernest rose to his feet. "You have to be mighty careful living a life to please someone else. You might miss out on what's best for yourself. I'll be around after Henny has had time to cool down."

"That might take a while. Shall we rig up a signal? I can tie a red rag around the fence post at the end of the lane if she's still mad and a white one if she's over it."

Ernest contemplated Levi's offer for a few seconds. "That's a fine idea but don't bother. I'll take my chances. I like a little spat now and again."

Ernest walked away as Isaac returned and sat down on the swing. His glum expression made Levi suspect that it hadn't been a friendly phone call.

"Do you want to talk about it?"

"About what?"

"About what seems to ruin your day every time you get a phone call. Was it Brittany? I know it's none of my business, but I do worry about you."

"I'm fine. Everything's fine."

"You're not very convincing but I'll leave you be. Between Ernest, *Mamm* and you, everyone has secrets around here."

"What would you say if I told you I want to go back to Lancaster?"

Levi turned to look at his brother. Isaac was serious. If his brother went back, Levi never would. His mother wouldn't leave Kansas. He'd be stuck here. He'd never fulfill his promise to recover his father's legacy. "Have you thought it through? How would you earn a living? Where would you stay? Since you asked, I'd say it sounds like a rash decision on your part."

"It probably wouldn't do any good anyway."

"It would worry *Mamm*, and she doesn't need that right now," Levi added for good measure.

Isaac nodded slowly. "I reckon you're right. I think I'll see if Sarah wants to go for a walk."

Levi gave a silent sigh of relief. "Okay. I can sit with *Mamm* for a while."

"Great." Isaac got up and went to the house.

Levi continued rocking in the swing until Isaac and Sarah came out of the house. Sarah looked his way, but then turned her back to him. "Your mother is lying down."

Was the swing making her uncomfortable? He almost laughed at the idea, but he got up and went to stand beside her. The rosy color of her cheeks proved she was embarrassed. "I'll go in and sit with her in case she needs anything."

"We won't be long," she said. She walked down the steps, turned around suddenly to glare at him and then walked stiffly toward the lane.

"You're right, Sarah. It's what's on the inside of a person that counts," he called out. "Mostly," he said softly to himself.

LEVI WAS LAUGHING at her again. Sometimes he could be very annoying.

"Is something wrong?" Isaac asked.

Sarah glanced at him sheepishly. She wasn't about to admit she was thinking about Levi when she had Isaac by her side. "Of course not. Go on with what you were saying."

"You know what I like about you, Sarah? You're uncomplicated."

"If that's a compliment, *danki*." Her life was getting more complicated by the day, but if it didn't show, that meant she was doing a good job at hiding it.

"Some women say one thing and mean another. They make a fellow guess what they want and then they change their minds. You aren't like that. It's refreshing."

"You need to hang around more Amish women. I'm not that special. What has you upset?"

He shot her a quick glance. "What makes you think I'm upset?"

"I don't know. This scowl on your face is one hint."

"Sorry. I didn't realize I was doing that. How is this?" He beamed a smile her way.

"Better. But why don't you tell me what's wrong and maybe we can figure out a way to fix it."

"I'd rather not talk about it. Let's just enjoy the day."

"Okay. Have you noticed that the wheat is heading out?"

He looked toward the waving green field on his left. "I had not, but you're right. The grain heads are forming."

"It won't be long before you'll have to start combining. A month, maybe, if the weather turns hot."

"I remember cutting wheat with my grandfather. I know everyone thought it was hard work, but I just thought it was fun."

"I remember." She smiled at the wistful expression on his face.

He blew out a slow breath. "It seems like a very long time ago."

She tipped her head to look at his face. "And yet sometimes it feels like it was only yesterday. A couple of my friends are planning a get-together at the lake later this week. Would you be interested in going?"

He managed to look interested. "Sure."

"We'll meet at Connor's Cove. Don't worry about

bringing food. We're going to cook hot dogs and hamburgers on the grill."

"Should I bring my fishing pole?" he asked.

"You can if you like. Lots of times we simply end up sitting around a campfire and telling stories. They'll be excited to have you there."

He looked skeptical. "Why is that?"

"Because you haven't heard any of our stories and we haven't heard any of yours. That makes you the perfect guest."

He chuckled. "I like that you can make me laugh."

She blushed and looked down. "I'm glad."

"I've never really had a girl as a friend before. I've had a lot of girlfriends, but that's not quite the same."

Sarah wasn't quite sure how to take that. She was glad he considered her a friend, but she was hoping to slip into the girlfriend category. She looked back at Levi standing on the porch watching them. Getting closer to Isaac was the reason she had taken this job, so why wasn't she happier that he was finally showing an interest in her?

Because she was starting to like Levi. A man who didn't want to live in Cedar Grove. One who was doing everything in his power to get back to Pennsylvania, including pretending to be interested in her. She had to remember that.

She turned her attention to Isaac. "What were some of the girls you dated like?" Sarah couldn't believe she was bold enough to ask that question. Did she really want to hear the answer?

"A couple of them were Amish girls, but for the most part, I dated *Englisch* girls. They were all different. They just liked having a good time. We'd hang out with other kids at a local burger joint and complain about how our parents didn't understand us, or in my case, I'd grumble about Levi."

Sarah giggled. "That sounds a lot like how some Amish kids I know talk about their folks."

He chuckled. "It must be a universal trait of teenagers."

"But you and I aren't teenagers anymore," she reminded him. "We'll have to find more serious things to discuss."

"We can always follow Ernest's lead. We can talk about the weather and about fishing."

She forced a smile. "We could, but I doubt we'd make it sound as funny as he does."

"What did my mother say about the swing when you two went inside?"

"Nothing. I think she intends to ignore it." Sarah wished he would ask about her life and what she wanted in the future.

"I'm really curious about those two. It's odd to think someone besides my father was in love with my mother."

"According to Ernest, he is still in love with her. At the hospital he said there's no time limit on love. It's wonderful to think that's true. I believe it is. Don't you?"

"I'm not sure I believe in love, let alone a love that lasts a lifetime."

She stopped walking and he paused to look at her. "Did I upset you?" he asked.

A pang of pity stirred her heart. "Telling me what you think won't upset me, but I was struck by how sad it is to hear you say that." How was it possible not to believe in love when it was everywhere?

Would it be up to her to show Isaac that true love did exist?

"We should head back," he said without looking at her.

"Okay." Neither of them spoke on the walk back. The silence felt strained, but she didn't have anything to say to him.

At the house, he tipped his hat to her. "See you tomorrow."

Freckles had been hitched to her buggy and was waiting by the front gate. Isaac went toward the corral and Sarah went into the house. A quick glance into the living room showed her that Henrietta was sleeping peacefully. Levi sat by her side in a brown leather wing-backed chair with his feet propped up on a matching ottoman. He closed the book in his hand, held one finger to his lips and got up.

They went out onto the porch. "Did you have a nice walk? You look happier."

Levi was always interested in her feelings and thoughts. She wished Isaac could be more like his brother.

She nodded and smiled at him. "We found we still have a few things in common."

A mischievous grin pulled at the corner of his mouth. "Is canoeing on the lake still one of them?"

SHE LAUGHED. It was a beautiful sound. Levi recognized his attraction to her was growing much too strong. He hardened his heart. He had no business flirting with

Isaac's girl. He needed to put some emotional distance between them and keep it that way.

"That subject of canoeing did not come up." She leaned toward him. "And shame on you for mentioning it."

Levi opened the door of the buggy for her. "I don't intend to let you forget your foolishness. The memory may keep you from doing something equally stupid."

Doubt clouded her eyes at his tone. She climbed in the buggy. "There is nothing foolish about going for a canoe ride."

"Standing up in one isn't very smart. Use some common sense while you're throwing yourself at my brother."

Her eyes widened with disbelief. "I don't need you to tell me what is or isn't foolish, and I am not throwing myself at your brother. Remember this was your idea." She snapped the reins and drove away.

Levi watched until she was out of sight. He pushed his hands deep into his pant pockets. "The foolish part isn't falling out of a canoe. It's falling for the girl who's in love with my brother."

CHAPTER TWELVE

LEVI MANAGED TO avoid Sarah over the next two days by being out of the house before she arrived and staying out until she left in the evenings. He took Wing for long, easy workouts up and down the country roads or he planted soybeans. On the third day he left early for the local cattle auction, hoping to acquire a milk cow. He purchased a young Guernsey with a calf at her side for a reasonable price and got home just as Sarah was leaving. By the fourth day he was running out of excuses.

"Where are you off to today?" his mother asked at the breakfast table.

"I'm going to cultivate the corn one more time before it gets too tall and then I'll bale the last of this hay crop."

Isaac stirred a spoonful of sugar into his coffee. "I never thought you'd embrace farming."

His mother frowned at him. "Farming is a wonderful way of life. I'm happy to see Levi putting horse racing behind him. Together you boys can make a *goot* living here." She smiled at both her sons.

Isaac took a sip of his coffee and leaned back in his chair. "I have to admit that I like farming a lot better than I thought I would. Levi might be doing all the work this week, but his heart isn't in it."

"Why do you say that?" she asked with a quick frown.

"Because he still trains Wing and a Prayer every day. If he was ready to take up farming full-time, he would sell her to somebody who could race her. I'm sure Arnold Diehl would give you a fair price and cover the cost of shipping her to his stable."

Levi kept quiet. It didn't matter what his family thought. He wasn't going anywhere yet, not until his mother was well and Isaac was settled, but when the time was right he would say goodbye to Cedar Grove and head back to Lancaster to reacquire Raber Stables.

His mother waved aside Isaac's comment. "Once Levi finds the right woman, he will forget all about racing standardbreds."

It was time to turn the conversation away from himself. "How are you and Sarah getting along, Isaac?"

"Fine, I guess."

"I was wondering if things were getting serious between the two of you." Levi tried to sound casual.

"Why? Are you planning to ask her out?" Isaac chuckled at the idea.

"The thought has crossed my mind. She doesn't seem all that taken with you. You had your chance." Levi was happy to see Isaac's grin fade. If Isaac believed he had competition for Sarah's affection, he might get serious.

"Sorry, *brudder*. She seems pretty taken with me. In fact, she invited me to a cookout with some of her friends this evening. We're going over to Connor's Cove at the lake."

"Sarah is a lovely woman," his mother said, eyeing Isaac closely.

He shifted uncomfortably in his chair. "I know that."

"Sounds like fun. I hope you have a good time. Tell Sarah I said hello." Levi needed to get out of the house before she arrived. He rose, put on his hat and opened the door.

She was standing on the other side of the screen door. "Good morning, Levi. I was beginning to wonder if you still lived here."

There wasn't a hint of warmth in her eyes. She opened the screen door.

His heart thudded against his ribs. His palms grew sweaty. How did she have this effect on him without even trying? She came inside. The scent of lavender drifted in with her.

Amish women never used perfume or scented soaps, but the sweet, clean fragrance seemed to follow her around. It was easy to imagine her standing in the sunshine with an armful of flowers. This was his chance to slip out the door, but he let it close behind her.

"Good morning, Henrietta. Isaac, are you still planning to come to the cookout with me this evening?"

"I was just telling Levi about it."

She finally met Levi's eyes. He noted a hint of defiance in hers. "I would ask if you wanted to come along, but I know how busy you have been. I assume you have been busy, since I haven't seen much of you lately."

He should leave but he couldn't pass up a chance to spar with her. He leaned his shoulder against the doorjamb and crossed his arms. "Are you saying you missed me?"

Her eyes opened wide then quickly narrowed. "Quite

the contrary. Henrietta and I have had a few very enjoyable days without you underfoot. She's doing much better, in case you haven't noticed."

"I have noticed a lot of things. The house is clean. The laundry is done. The garden has been weeded. Filling meals have been cooked and left warming in the oven for me. Cakes and pies have been left for me to sample. The shoofly pie was mighty good. I imagine I would find Isaac has had his socks darned if I wanted to pull off his boots. Your housekeeping skills are impressive."

Her eyes shifted to Isaac's face and then back to his. "I'm glad I have lived up to your expectations."

He arched one eyebrow. "I didn't think impressing me was your goal."

She looked down as a wave of pink rushed up her neck. "I did not come here to impress anyone, only to help Henrietta with the things she is unable to do yet."

"Levi, stop giving Sarah a hard time." Isaac tossed back the last of his coffee.

Sarah smiled at him. "*Danki*, Isaac. Henrietta, I need to take your blood pressure. Stay right where you are while I get the cuff."

"I'm tired of having that thing squeeze my arm morning, noon and night. Can't we skip it today?"

"I am only following the doctor's orders. Have you had any dizziness?"

"I have not."

"What about when you got up this morning?" Isaac said. "You were unsteady on your feet."

She looked away. "You imagined it."

Sarah frowned. "You are a poor liar, Henrietta. How many dizzy episodes have you had since yesterday?"

"Three. Short ones."

Levi stood up straight. He thought she was getting better. What was going on?

"What about pain or fluttering in your chest?" Isaac asked.

"Once. It only lasted twenty minutes or so."

"When was this?" Levi demanded. "Why didn't you tell one of us?"

"You and Isaac had already gone to bed. I got up to get a drink of water. I sat in the chair until it passed, and I was fine."

Sarah shared a concerned look with Isaac. "I wonder if the doctor would want to see her."

He took out his phone and handed it to her. "Give her a call and find out what she says. *Mamm*, you have to tell us these things."

"I don't want to worry you."

Levi pulled out a chair and sat beside her. "It's not working. I'm more worried now than if you had told me when it happened. It seems I have to worry that you won't tell me when something's wrong."

His mother clasped her hands together on the table but didn't look at him. "I knew you would make a fuss."

Sarah wrapped the cuff around Henrietta's arm and squeezed the black bulb that pumped it up. The numbers showed Henrietta's blood pressure was higher than it should be. Sarah stood up. "I'm calling the doctor right now."

Isaac took his mother's elbow. "You are going to lie down and don't argue."

"I'm not arguing. Such a fuss for nothing." She rose to her feet, staggered a little and finally allowed him to lead her out of the kitchen.

SARAH DIALED THE clinic only to be put on hold. She walked out onto the porch with the phone pressed to her ear while she listened to music.

Levi followed her. "Do you think this is something serious?"

"I have no way of knowing."

"Sarah, I'm sorry I was abrupt with you the other day."

"Why were you angry with me?"

"I wasn't angry with you. I was angry with myself and I took it out on you."

The doctor came on the line and Sarah had to drop her conversation with Levi, but she was going to take it up with him later. He owed her more of an explanation.

Sarah recited Henrietta's vital signs.

She listened to the doctor's instructions and then ended the call. "Dr. Black wants us to bring her in."

Levi shook his head. "*Mamm*'s not going to like that."

"Do you think we should get hold of Ernest or wait until we know more?"

"If it was me, I'd want to know right away."

She nodded in agreement. "Okay. Go let him know what's going on."

"I'll take the tractor over to his place and we'll meet you at the clinic." He went down the steps and turned back to her. "And, Sarah, thank you. I don't know how we would have managed without you."

"I'm glad I could be here."

"So am I." The warmth of his tone made her realize how much she had come to care for him. She scolded herself for being foolish. Levi wasn't the man she wanted. Now wasn't the time to examine her feelings for him.

He jogged down to the machine shed. Sarah called her old teacher, praying she could drive them. Julie answered and promised to come right over.

Henrietta made the trip in angry silence. Sarah knew it wasn't good for the woman's blood pressure. She started to worry that her decision to have Levi fetch Ernest was only going to make things worse.

When Julie pulled up under the awning at the clinic, Levi and Ernest were already waiting for them. Ernest had a wheelchair ready.

Henrietta looked him up and down when she got out of the car. "This is a surprise. Did I interrupt your fishing?"

"There will always be more fish in the lake. I can't say that about my friends."

His answer seemed to soothe her. She sat in the wheelchair without another word. Ernest pushed her through the clinic doors. Isaac followed behind them. Sarah stared at Levi. "What just happened?"

He shook his head. "For the life of me, I can't figure those two out. I was sure she would be furious to see him here."

Sarah held her hands wide. "We must give thanks

for the small miracles that are sprinkled through our lives by God's grace."

"Amen," Julie said.

Sarah and Levi joined the others in the waiting room. When the nurse called Henrietta's name, her sons stood up. Henrietta raised her hand to stop them. "Ernest will come in with me. You *kinder* wait here."

Levi and Isaac sank onto their chairs on either side of Sarah. They looked at each other with puzzled expressions. Isaac scratched his head. "She makes me feel like I should go sit in the other corner and play with those toys."

Levi pushed his hat back with one finger. "I get the clown puppet."

Sarah sighed. "I want the doll with the pink dress."

The receptionist behind the tall counter chuckled but turned it into a cough. A half an hour later Ernest came out pushing Henrietta. He looked pleased. "We can go now."

Levi lunged to his feet. "What did the doctor say?"

Henrietta inclined her head. "I'm fine."

Ernest frowned at her. "Never met a woman with so much false pride. The doctor has made changes to her medicine and wants to see her again in a week."

Henrietta smiled triumphantly at her sons. "It is normal for these episodes to come and go until my medicine is regulated. I'm free to do whatever I want."

"As long as you are feeling good, the flutter thing in your chest isn't lasting for hours and you aren't getting tired easily," Ernest added.

She scowled at him. "That fluttering sensation is gone and I'm not a bit tired."

He pushed her toward the door. "You are going to go home and rest anyway."

"Old man, I don't know why you think you can order me around."

Ernest huffed. "That wasn't an order. It was merely a strong suggestion."

Once they had Henrietta in the car, Ernest and Levi shook hands.

"I appreciate you letting me know what's going on. Henrietta, I'll be over later to visit with you on that nice new porch swing."

"You can take it down, for all I care."

He chuckled to himself as he walked off.

WHEN THEY ARRIVED back at the house, Henrietta agreed to lie down for a while. Later that afternoon, Sarah was gathering the laundry off the clothesline when Ernest arrived. She was surprised to see Henrietta sitting on the porch swing waiting for him. He sat down beside her. Sarah put the clothes away and went to tell Henrietta she was leaving.

"Going home already?" Ernest asked.

"She's got to get ready to go to a cookout over at Connor's Cove. Isaac is going with her," Henrietta said.

"Is that so?" Ernest looked over Sarah's shoulder. "What about you, Levi?"

He had been in and out during the day to check on his mother. "I'm not going anywhere, and neither is Isaac."

Henrietta's eyebrows shot up. "What's this? Isaac, why aren't you going?"

"Because I'm staying home to look after you. And Levi is going to be here in case I need him."

"That's ridiculous. Ernest can stay with me." She looked at him out of the corner of her eye. "As long as he behaves himself and does what I tell him."

"No one gave you permission to boss me around." Ernest crossed his arms over his chest and looked the other way.

"It's all right," Sarah said. "There will be more cook-outs and singings where your sons can make new friends."

"You children are not missing this because of me. I insist you go."

"Insist all you want, ma'am," Levi said. "We're not going and that's that."

She turned to Ernest. "How is the fishing at Connor's Cove?"

He looked at her in surprise. "It's good if the wind is in the south like today. Evenings are the best time to catch something out there."

"The doctor said I could do anything I wanted to do as long as it didn't tire me. I want to go fishing tonight at Connor's Cove. What about you, Ernest?"

"I've never turned down an invitation to go fishing in my life. I'm not about to start now. I'll go get my poles and meet you back here at six."

She smiled at her children. "I reckon if you want to keep an eye on me, you'll have to go to the cookout."

Sarah caught Levi's scowl and agreed with him. She

shook her head. "I don't think this is a good idea, Henrietta."

"I think it's a fine idea." She stood up, wobbled slightly but righted herself, and using her cane, she headed toward the door. "I believe I'll take a rest until Ernest gets back."

Isaac threw his hands in the air. "She's impossible."

Levi shrugged. "It does solve one problem."

"What problem is that?" Sarah said.

"It solves the question of what's for supper." He chuckled as he walked away.

Sarah looked at Isaac. "I guess I will see you at Connor's Cove around six thirty." She shook one finger at him. "Don't let her bake anything to take along. There will be enough food there for everyone."

Isaac lifted his hat, raked his fingers through his hair and clapped his hat back on his head. "This should be an interesting evening. Let's hope she doesn't end up in the hospital or push Ernest in the lake. I can see it going either way."

Sarah started for her buggy and saw Levi was bringing it over to her. He patted her mare's shoulder. "I hope you and Isaac can manage some alone time tonight."

Right now it was Levi she wished she could be alone with. "*Danki.* Before I leave, I want to know why you were angry with me the other day. I haven't been doing anything that's foolish. If I have, I wish you would tell me what it is." She gazed into his eyes, waiting for his explanation.

He stared at the ground. "You aren't doing anything wrong or foolish. If you want to know the truth, I'm a bit jealous of Isaac. He has someone who thinks the world of him, who is kind and understanding even when he has sometimes been a real jerk."

She stepped forward and laid her hand on his chest. "You will find someone like that, Levi. God wants us to have a helpmate in this life."

He took a step back. She lowered her hand to her side. He cleared his throat. "You're right, and I don't begrudge Isaac his happiness. So pay no attention to me if I'm moody or grumpy sometimes."

Sarah nodded. "I'm glad you explained. I don't want to lose the friendship that you and I have."

He managed a half smile. "You never have to worry about that, Sarah. I'll always be your friend."

The warmth in his expression brought a flush to her skin. She turned away and got in her buggy, praying he hadn't noticed her reaction. There was more than friendship for Levi growing in her heart.

Sarah arrived at the Cove at six thirty that evening. She parked the tractor in the shade of a hackberry tree and turned off the engine. She got down and lifted a box out of the small trailer hooked on behind. Angela and Thaddeus came running up to her. "I'm glad you could make it," Angela said. "I was beginning to worry about you."

"Caleb was having a snack. I stopped to kiss him goodbye and he knocked his bowl of cherry applesauce onto my dress, so I had to change. Is everyone here?" She looked around for Isaac and Levi.

Angela gestured toward the lake. "Ernest and Henrietta are here. Did you know they were coming?"

"I did. Are Isaac and Levi around?"

"Levi is over talking to Faron Mast. Faron's really happy about the way Levi straightened his horse out. I'm not sure where Isaac went. I saw him talking on his phone a few minutes ago." She looked around and pointed down the shore. "I think that's him. How are things going between you two?"

"We're getting reacquainted," Sarah said. It was all she would admit to because nothing had changed. She was still waiting for him to realize that she was meant to be more than a friend. Only maybe she wasn't.

She handed her box of brownies and shoofly pie to Angela. "Would you put these on the table for me, please? I want to go say hello to Isaac."

She walked toward the place where she had last seen him among the trees along the edge of the lake. She heard his voice before she saw him. It was raised in anger. She stopped, and he stepped into her line of vision. He reared back and threw his phone as far out into the lake as he could. Sarah turned around to give him some privacy.

She went back to the picnic table where Angela was helping some of the other girls put out the food. "Did you find him?" Angela asked.

"I didn't want to interrupt his phone call." She glanced over her shoulder, but he wasn't in sight.

"Granny Weaver sent her wonderful chili along with us. I hope she gives me the recipe before she passes on to her reward. Thaddeus said she has told her children that they will have to wait until she decides who she wants to have it. If she dies before then, she knows her family will mourn her because they will never taste her chili again."

Sarah laughed. "She's a sharp gal for someone who's almost ninety."

"Isaac, can I use your phone?" Thaddeus asked.

Sarah turned around to see Isaac standing behind her.

"I lost it. Sorry."

Instead of staying with the group, he walked off by himself. He sat on a stump at the edge of the woods with his back to everyone. Sarah hesitated a few moments but decided as his friend she needed to offer her help. She approached and stood beside him. "What's wrong, Isaac?"

"Everything."

"Oh, that's too bad." She leaned down to see his face and smiled at him. "I was going to offer my help, but I don't think I have the time to fix *everything*. We're getting ready to eat and I want to get some of Granny Weaver's chili before it's all gone."

A hint of a smile brightened his somber expression. "Thanks for the offer."

She squatted in front of him. "Seriously, can I do anything to help?"

"I don't see how."

"I'm good at listening."

He remained silent. She wondered if she should leave him, but before she got up, he sighed loudly. "I have a girlfriend back home. Had a girlfriend."

Sarah had suspected something like that, but to hear him admit it was still painful. "Why do you say 'had'?"

He looked at her closely. "Aren't you mad?"

She stood and moved to sit beside him. "Disappointed, maybe, but not angry. We can't help the way we feel about someone." Just as she couldn't help but feel an attraction to Levi. It was acting or not acting on those feelings that mattered.

"It's over between us for good. I had hoped she and I could find a way to be together, but her family objects to me and she won't go against their wishes."

"Objects to you? Why?"

"Because I'm Amish. I'm uneducated. I don't have the ambition to better myself. Her parents are both doctors. One of them, her mother, was the cardiologist who took care of *Mamm* in Pennsylvania. That's how we met. I was waiting outside the doctor's office and this pretty girl with pink hair asked if she could pet the horse. I told her it would cost her one kiss. I figured that would spook her away. She didn't even bat an eye. She grabbed my shirt, kissed me and then stepped around me to pet Jasper."

Sarah tried not to show her astonishment. She couldn't imagine doing anything so daring or brazen. "She sounds like an unusual woman. Did you say pink hair?"

"It was pink that week. When I saw her again two weeks later, it was purple. She liked to shock her parents. I think that's why she asked me out the first time."

"It sounds like you still have feelings for her." Sarah didn't see how she could compete with such a rival for his affections.

"I do care about her. I imagine I always will, but we weren't meant to be together. I see that now. I was willing to leave the Amish for her. She wouldn't even agree to come visit me for a few weeks and meet my mother because her parents didn't think it was a good idea. They said she needs to focus on her studies, not on her boyfriend. So we're done. I'm glad now that I didn't tell my mother I was serious about Brittany. Maybe I knew it wasn't going to work out, but I just wasn't willing to admit it."

"They say that time heals all wounds, even a broken heart. I'm sorry." She stared down at her hands. "I can imagine how painful it is to love someone who doesn't love you back."

He slipped an arm over her shoulders. "I'm hoping you still want to be my friend. Are you disgusted with me?"

"I'm not," she said and realized it was true.

"What a mess. Where can we go from here?"

"We can be miserable together."

He tugged on her *kapp* ribbon. "It's very hard to be miserable around you, Sarah."

"Really? Why is that?"

"I don't know. There's just something about you that makes me glad to know you."

"*Danki.* If we aren't going to be miserable, can we go get some food? I'm starving."

He laughed. "*Ja*, we can go eat. It's nice to know my feelings come in second to Granny Weaver's chili."

She chuckled. "It's almost a tie."

"Hey. Please don't tell my brother about this," he pleaded in a low voice.

She looked up to see Levi heading toward them.

CHAPTER THIRTEEN

LEVI STOPPED A few feet away from Sarah and Isaac. Their serious expressions made him think he was interrupting an important conversation. "Angela wanted me to tell you they are cooking hot dogs now if you want some."

Sarah hopped up. "I was just saying how hungry I am, wasn't I, Isaac?"

"Sure were." He got up as well.

Levi glanced between the two of them. There was an air of secrecy about them. It didn't matter what was going on. It was none of his business. He had to remember that.

He walked back to where Thaddeus and Angela were handing out sticks to roast hot dogs with. Sarah and Isaac followed him. Levi stood shoulder to shoulder with Isaac and some of the younger kids. He soon had his charred hot dog on a bun and was adding ketchup from the table.

Sarah's hot dog was barely brown. She squeezed on some mustard as she frowned at his food. "That looks burnt."

Levi shrugged. "I like burnt."

"Oh. Then you should enjoy that. Yuck." She shivered with disgust.

He gestured toward her food. "How you can eat a cold, raw dog is beyond me."

She pointed to her bun. "This? This isn't raw."

He arched one eyebrow. "Because it passed *near* the fire?"

"We can agree to disagree about cooking methods, but if you want to taste something *goot*, put a little of Granny Weaver's chili on your hot dog." She lifted the lid from a large pot and spread a spoonful on hers.

Levi shook his head. "I don't care for chili."

"That means more for the rest of us." Faron slipped in between them and reached for the ladle. Sarah kept it away and spread some on Levi's dog.

"Hey." Levi scowled at her.

She ignored his displeasure. "Don't say you don't like it until you've tried it."

"You'll like it." Faron took the ladle from Sarah and poured a lavish amount over the three buns on his paper plate.

Sarah looked toward the lake, where Henrietta and Ernest were sitting on lawn chairs with their poles in hand. "Should we see if they want anything?"

Levi saw Isaac's hot dog had fallen off his stick into the fire. He was getting another one. "I'll check on them."

"I'll go with you."

He folded the bun around his hot dog and took a bite. His mouth lit up with amazing flavors. Sweet, spicy, savory, tangy. "Who did you say made this?"

"The bishop's mother. She hasn't given anyone in her family her recipe. They're afraid she'll die before she passes it on."

He took another bite. It was better than the first one. "How old did you say she was?"

"She will be ninety in a few weeks. You and your family are invited to her birthday party. It's being held at the Miller farm."

"I hope she lives to cook a lot longer."

Sarah chuckled. "I told you that you'd like it."

"I might have to start listening to you more often."

Levi walked down to where his mother was sitting. "Can I get you something to eat?"

"I'm hungry enough to eat a bear," Ernest said, turning to Levi.

Henrietta scoffed. "I'm sure they aren't serving bear."

"Just hot dogs, burgers and brats," Levi said. "And chili."

Both his mother and Ernest sat up straight. "Granny Weaver's chili?" his mother asked.

"Yup."

Ernest handed Levi his pole. "Keep an eye on my cork. We'll be back in a minute." He helped Henrietta to her feet and handed her pole to Levi. The two of them walked up to the tables.

Sarah came down with several hot dogs on her plate. "We're about to start some of the games. Are you going to be fishing?"

"That wasn't what I intended. I just asked Ernest and *Mamm* if they wanted something to eat. When they heard there was chili, they jumped up and told me to watch the poles. Whoa—I've got a bite."

He handed his mother's pole to Sarah. He jerked to set the hook and started reeling.

"Keep the tip of your pole up," Sarah said, setting her plate on the ground to hold the rod with both hands.

"I know how to fish. This is a big one."

The fish sped away from Levi. The reel squealed as the line was drawn out against the drag.

"Let him run. He'll get tired. Then you can work him back." She was bouncing up and down.

Levi looked her way. "Pay attention to your own fish."

"What? Oh!" She finally noticed that her bobber had gone under. She pulled back to set the hook and began reeling. "It's a big one."

Levi continued to play his fish, but watching Sarah's excitement was almost as much fun. They had both their fish close to shore when Sarah's took off toward Levi's line.

"Oh, he's gonna cross yours." She sidestepped away, still trying to pull the fish in another direction, but it was making a determined run for it along the edge of the lake.

Levi raised his pole to let her slip under. "Follow him."

Isaac came up beside Levi. "Looks like you've hooked a big one."

"Get the net," Sarah yelled. *"Nee, nee, nee."* She was still cranking as the fish went the other way. She came back toward Levi. "I think he's gone over your line."

He switched his pole from one hand to the other to let her cross in front of him without her having to step over his line.

Both fish were tiring. As Levi got his fish close to shore, he realized Sarah's line was tangled with his.

They stood almost shoulder to shoulder. Isaac squeezed in between them, leaned over the water and scooped both thrashing fish into the net. Levi and Sarah were laughing as they stepped back.

"I think mine is the bigger one," Sarah said.

"That one is mine," Levi insisted, just to see her outraged reaction.

She didn't disappoint him. "It is not. That's my hook in his mouth."

Isaac patted the air with one hand. "Calm down. I'll get them untangled and we'll see who has the biggest one."

The fish had thrashed so much in the shallows that there was no way to tell which line went to which pole. Isaac looked at Levi. "I'm never gonna be able to untangle this. I'm just gonna cut them loose."

"Don't do that," Sarah said, but it was too late. He had already cut the lines. She stomped her foot. "Now we'll never know who had the biggest fish."

"Are the lures the same?" Levi asked. "Ernest can tell us which one he was using."

Isaac finally held up both fish. "This one has a hook with worms." He looked in the other fish's mouth. "Same here."

"I hooked mine first, so I get to choose which one I want." Levi pointed to the largest one.

Sarah squeaked in protest. "That's not fair. I could tell I had a whale on my line. The big one belongs to me." He could see she was enjoying their squabble as much as he was.

Isaac was gingerly removing the hook from the first

fish's mouth. He laid it a few feet up the bank and began to work on the second fish. When he had it free, he picked them both up. "I declare the fish are the winners in this one."

He tossed them both back into the water.

"Oh no. Why did you do that?" Sarah demanded.

Levi laughed and patted his brother on the back. "So we will never be able to solve the mystery and we can argue about it for the rest of our lives."

Sarah's pout was adorable. "The poles belong to Ernest, so technically they were his fish. I still think mine was bigger. I had more trouble reeling it in."

"That's because you're a weakling," Levi said with a grin.

Her jaw dropped. "I can't believe you said that."

Ernest and Henrietta returned from the tables. She was holding on to his arm to steady herself while he carried both plates.

"Why aren't my poles in the water?" he asked.

Henrietta sat down and took her plate from him. Ernest frowned at the severed lines fluttering in the breeze. "You lost both hooks?"

Isaac produced both hooks. "They caught two fish at the same time, and they were so tangled up I had to cut the line."

Ernest looked around. "Did you put them on my stringer already? Were they good sized?"

"They were big—mine was the biggest. He threw them back," Sarah said in disgust.

Ernest looked at him in disbelief. "Why?"

Isaac grinned from ear to ear. "The fish were so tangled that I couldn't tell which one belonged to which pole. To stop Sarah and Levi from arguing about who got the biggest one, I let them both go. It doesn't seem to have worked."

"What do you mean you couldn't tell which line belonged to which pole?" Ernest demanded.

Levi handed the pole to Ernest. "Both fish had the same kind of lure in their mouth. There wasn't any way to tell them apart."

Sarah spun away with her nose in the air. "My fish was the biggest one."

Levi grinned. It was fun to tease her and know she could give back as good as she got. "I don't think so."

His mother rolled her eyes. "Of all the trivial things to argue about."

Ernest scowled at her. "Bragging rights to the biggest fish is not trivial, Henny."

She shook her head. "Childish. I believe I am ready to go home."

"I ain't done fishing!"

"Then enjoy the catfish's company because Levi is taking me home."

Ernest eyed her closely. "You feeling all right, Henny?"

"A mite tired is all. Thank you for a lovely afternoon."

"My pleasure. Reckon I'll see you at church on Sunday."

"If I live that long," she snapped.

Levi took his mother by the arm and helped her toward their tractor. Sarah brought along her chair, settled his mother in it and wrapped a quilt over her shoulders.

Levi turned to Isaac. "You don't have to come back with us if you can get a ride with someone else."

"I'll see that he gets home," Sarah said.

Levi smiled at her. "Can I trust you to take good care of my brother?"

She glanced at Isaac and then met Levi's gaze. "I always will. I promise."

SARAH ARRIVED AT the Raber farm a little before eight o'clock the next morning driving her brother-in-law's tractor, as Laura Beth needed their buggy. As soon as she walked in the door, she saw Isaac and Levi were still seated at the breakfast table. Levi looked up. "Mine was bigger."

She chose to ignore his comment for a whole three seconds. "Mine was bigger, and that is that."

"Will you two stop," Isaac pleaded. "I am not going to listen to this all day." He got up to refill his coffee cup.

Sarah pretended to ignore Levi, but she was always intensely aware of him. "How is your mother this morning?"

"She is upstairs sewing a new dress." He glanced at Isaac. *Bigger. Mine was*, he mouthed.

For some reason their fishing debacle seemed to have cleared the air between Sarah and Levi. Henrietta came in the room a few minutes later. It looked as though the fishing trip had done her good. She seemed relaxed and energetic. Sarah took her blood pressure and pronounced her fit.

Henrietta rubbed her hands together. "I have a hankering for pancakes this morning. Anyone else?"

Levi declined but Sarah and Isaac agreed to a short stack each. Levi headed for the door. "I've got chores to do. See you at lunch."

Sarah sat down across from Isaac. "What are your plans?"

He leaned close. "I'm going to the phone hut in a little while and cancel my cell phone service."

"Are you sure you don't want to get another phone?" she whispered.

He gave a quick shake of his head. "I'm done with them."

"I'm glad."

Henrietta turned around at the stove. "What are you two whispering about?"

"Nothing," Sarah and Isaac said at the same time. They looked at each other and laughed. It was as if they had slipped back in time to the days when they were always together and almost knew each other's thoughts.

"What are your plans for today?" he asked, still smiling at her.

She raised her head. "Henrietta, what are our plans for today?"

"I thought we could go through the attic and see what is usable and what can be discarded or given away."

"Sounds like fun."

Isaac cocked his head to the side. "Sounds like dust and spiders to me."

He was right about the dust. Thankfully they ran across only a few small spiders as they opened trunks and searched through dusty newspapers and magazines the previous renter had squirreled away.

Sarah walked outside of the house a little before noon. She didn't know where Isaac had gone off to. Henrietta was lying down after lunch. As Sarah opened the front gate, she saw Levi drive Wing out of the barn.

She pressed a hand to her lips to keep from laughing. Levi was looking at her as he drew to a stop. "What's so funny?"

"How do you keep from falling out of that thing?" He was balanced on a small cart with slender metal shafts hooked to Wing's harness and two wheels that looked like they had come off a bicycle. There was canvas stretched under it for the driver's feet. She wasn't sure if it was to keep debris kicked up by the horse's feet from hitting the driver or to catch him if he fell forward.

"Are you making fun of my jog cart?"

"It doesn't look comfortable. What did you call it?"

"A jog cart. It's what we use to exercise the horses. For racing we use a more streamlined version called a sulky. How is Mother?"

"She ate a good lunch, and we took a short walk. She seems determined to get better."

"That's good news."

She looked around. "Where is Isaac?"

"He's cultivating the corn in the south field. He wanted to get it done by this evening. The forecast is for rain tonight. I told him I would take over for him after I finished working Wing."

"Your brother seems to enjoy farming. Ernest says he has a knack for working with machines."

"I have to admit that I'm surprised by his continued interest."

The sound of the tractor drawing closer told her Isaac was returning. He pulled into the yard and turned off the engine. "Out playing around with that horse again, Levi? There's work to be done."

Sarah stepped up to stroke Wing's nose.

"Do you want to see how fast she is?" Levi had a challenging look in his eye.

She nodded. "Sure."

He moved over until he was half on, half off the small seat. He patted it. "Hop on."

Sarah shook her head. "I thought you meant watch as you get her up to speed."

"It takes at least a mile." He gave a slight nod toward Isaac. "Now is a good time to make him think you'd rather go with me," he said softly. "I never thought Sarah Yoder would be afraid to ride in a racing cart," he said loudly.

She planted her hands on her hips. "That's where you're wrong. I'm not afraid to ride on your cart. I'm afraid of falling off your cart. It doesn't look very safe to me."

He grinned. "I won't let you fall."

"Don't you need both hands on the reins? How are you gonna hold me on the seat? With your teeth?"

"I can drive with one arm." He held out his hand toward her. She did want to see how fast the animal could go. Was she as remarkable as Levi said she was?

Sarah narrowed her eyes. "Where is this run going to take place?"

"On that dirt road that leads back into Ernest's field. I have marked off a mile. It will be straight and not oval like a real training track, but she'll be able to show you what she's got. She has a beautiful turn of foot and more speed than she knows what to do with."

"If you want speed, Sarah, my tractor in road gear can go faster than his horse." Isaac stood a few feet away frowning at them.

Somehow Sarah knew she was going to regret this. "I want to see what this filly can do." She allowed Levi to help her onto the seat. She braced her feet against the bar that held the mud flap in place and wiggled on the seat to get comfortable without touching him.

He put his arm around her and pulled her tight against him. "Hold on to me."

It was exciting to put her arm around his waist and have every inch from her shoulder to her hip wedged against him.

Levi smiled at Isaac as he turned Wing around. "Don't worry. I'll have her back in twenty minutes."

"Don't look at him. Look at me," Levi said softly. "Let him think I'm trying to steal his girl."

"Are you sure?"

"Trust me."

She would have to trust him, and she prayed that her trust wasn't misplaced.

They traveled down the paved county road a half mile and turned off onto a dirt road.

Sarah glanced at Levi. His eagerness was almost tangible. She realized she was risking more than her neck. She might be risking her heart. Levi looked down at her with a big boyish grin on his face. She couldn't help but smile back. "Are you ready?"

"As I will ever be."

He handed her a stopwatch. "I want you to click it each time I tell you. I have marked the fence posts at a quarter mile, a half mile, three-quarters of a mile and the finish line."

Sarah gripped the stopwatch in her hand and tightened her hold on Levi. "I'm ready."

The words were barely out of her mouth before he sent Wing forward. Sarah couldn't say that this was any faster than what Jasper could've done. The wind was whistling past her ears and tugging at her *kapp* ribbons.

"Get ready to click the watch."

She saw a fence post with a red stripe around it coming up. He urged Wing to a faster trot. By the time they reached the pole, Wing was flying. Sarah had a death grip around Levi's waist.

"Click the watch."

She clicked the stopwatch and Wing surged forward with a burst of speed that nearly unseated Sarah.

Levi's filly wasn't just fast—she was flying. The horse didn't seem to be straining at all. She kept going faster and faster. They topped a slight rise in the road and Sarah realized there was a stop sign ahead of them. This road intersected another one.

"Is there anyone coming?" Levi wasn't slowing.

Sarah craned her neck to see if there were any vehicles on the road. She saw one white SUV parked a quarter mile away. It wasn't moving. "We're fine."

They flew past the stop sign across a gravel road

and onto a second dirt road. Wing was still accelerating toward the final pole when Sarah heard the shrill sound of a siren behind them. She and Levi looked back at the same time the red lights of a sheriff's car started flashing.

Levi eased Wing back before they reached the last marked fence post. He pulled over to the side of the road. Sarah saw it was the sheriff himself and not one of his deputies. She hid her face against Levi's shirt and prayed she hadn't been recognized. The sheriff was a good friend of her family and was sure to tell Joshua and Laura Beth what Sarah had been up to.

Sheriff McIntyre came up to the driver side. Levi's rib cage was shaking, and she knew he was trying not to laugh.

"Afternoon," the sheriff said.

"*Goot* afternoon," Levi replied.

The sheriff leaned forward. "Hello, Sarah."

She sat up feeling incredibly foolish. "Hello, Marty."

"You do know that horses and buggies are required to obey all the rules of the road just like automobiles?"

"*Ja,*" Levi said.

"Did you happen to see that stop sign back there?"

"We made sure no one was coming," Sarah offered as an excuse.

"Oh." The sheriff tipped his hat back on his head. "Is that one of the new stop signs that says only stop if no one is coming?"

She looked down at her feet and then realized she still had her arm around Levi. She quickly withdrew it and nearly tumbled off the seat. He caught and steadied her.

"Name?"

"Levi Raber."

The sheriff wrote in his notebook. "I'm afraid I'm going to have a couple of tickets for you, young man. You don't have an orange slow-moving vehicle triangle on the back of this thing. That is a requirement in this county for horse-drawn vehicles."

"We weren't actually going slow," Sarah said.

Marty cocked one eyebrow. "Don't make it worse, Sarah. Do Laura Beth and Joshua know you're out hot rodding around with this guy?"

She pressed her lips into a tight line. The sheriff nodded once. "I didn't think so. We're looking at failure to come to a complete stop at a stop sign. No slow-moving sign. I would love to give you a ticket for recklessness in transporting a passenger, but I'm not sure there is such a thing. Sarah." He nodded toward his vehicle. "Get in the car."

She looked at him in shock. "Am I under arrest?"

"If there was a law against acting like an idiot, I would arrest you for it. Get in the car. It's not safe to have the both of you perched on that postage stamp of a seat. Do you know how fast she was going before I stopped you?"

"How fast?" Levi asked eagerly.

"Thirty-five flat. I couldn't believe my radar gun."

Sarah climbed down. "Thanks for the ride, Levi." She started for the car but turned back to give him his watch. "It was fun."

It had been fun. She couldn't remember the last time

she had enjoyed someone's company as much as she enjoyed being with Levi. What did that mean for her friendship with Isaac?

The sheriff put his notebook in his pocket. "This is one fine piece of horseflesh."

"She's a two-year-old standardbred."

"Figured that." He walked up to examine Wing more closely.

Sarah sat in the front seat of the police car while the two men went over the horse point by point for the next ten minutes. They shook hands. Levi got back on the jog cart. He turned Wing around and walked her toward home. The sheriff climbed in the car beside Sarah.

"Levi Raber seems like a nice guy."

"He is."

"He tells me he's new to this area."

"He and his mother and brother just moved onto the Helmuth place."

"What's he going to do with that fancy racehorse in this state?"

"He's her trainer. His father owned a broodmare farm in Pennsylvania. Wing and a Prayer is one of the horses they raised."

"Amish and racehorses. I never would've put the two things together. I learn something new about you folks every day."

He followed Levi all the way back to the house with his red lights flashing. Two pickups went around them. Sarah realized the people in the community were always on the lookout for their Amish neighbors' large black buggies, but Levi's little cart could've easily been overlooked when somebody came barreling down the road toward them.

Their arrival at the Raber farm caused a stir. The bishop and his mother had come to visit Henrietta. Isaac ran down the steps to the sheriff's vehicle. "Are you okay, Sarah?"

She got out. "I'm fine. Thanks for bringing me back, Marty."

"Obey the traffic signs from now on."

"I will," she said.

"Levi, what's going on?" his mother demanded.

"I got a traffic ticket. Actually, a couple of traffic tickets, but the sheriff clocked Wing at thirty-five miles an hour in the last quarter mile. That's fantastic."

"I thought you were done with this racing nonsense." She turned away and went inside.

The bishop stared at Sarah, a scowl on his face. "Such behavior is not acceptable for an Amish woman. You may not be baptized yet, but a woman your age is expected to act with decorum."

"I'm sorry."

"It was my fault," Levi said.

"That is no excuse. A person is responsible for their own behavior." He went back in the house with Henrietta. Granny Weaver walked over to stroke Wing's sweaty neck. "Fast, is she? I had one like her when I was a girl. Nobody could catch me." She laughed half to herself. "A lot of boys tried. Don't keep her standing here all sweaty, Levi. Cool her off and give her a rubdown."

"I was just about to do that." He walked off leading Wing.

Granny leaned heavily on Sarah's shoulder. "Was it fun?"

"It was *wunderbar*. I'd love to try driving her by myself."

"Ha!" Granny cackled. "I thought so. Follow your heart, child. Many times we see only the path we want to be on instead of the path *Gott* needs us to follow." She walked away still chuckling and went into the house.

"What did she mean by that?" Isaac asked.

"I'm not sure."

"Was my brother trying to impress you with his fast horse?" There was an edge to Isaac's voice that she hadn't heard before. But then he smiled and she thought she had imagined it.

"He wanted to show me a bit of fun."

"Don't let him lead you into more trouble."

She bowed to him. "I will heed your warning."

"I have to finish cultivating my last three acres of corn and then you can tell me the whole story this evening. Okay?"

"That will give me time to embellish it."

He laughed. "Spoken like a true student of Ernest. I'll be back in an hour or so. Remember what I said about Levi." He waved as he walked away.

Sarah smiled as she realized how well Levi's plan was working. Isaac didn't like being outshone by his brother.

After the bishop and his mother left forty-five minutes later, Sarah found she didn't want to go in yet. She sat on the red swing and gave herself a push. The padded seat and cushioned back made it comfortable. The squeak of the chains wasn't too loud. It was a good spot to sit and think. And that was exactly what she needed.

She and Isaac were returning to the easy friendship they had known in the past. It was almost funny. There were times when it seemed like they hadn't been apart at all. He was growing to be a dear friend. Would that friendship blossom into love? She had to have faith in God's plan for her and Isaac.

And what about Levi? The stirring of feelings she had for him confused her. It was more than friendship, but how much more? Was it real? How could she care so much for two men?

"A penny for your thoughts," Levi said from behind her.

She tilted her head back as far as possible and saw he was standing with his hands in his pockets just staring at her. "I won't take less than a dollar."

He chuckled as he came around the edge of the swing and sat beside her. "You drive a hard bargain."

"I know my own worth."

He reached out, took hold of one of her ribbons and gave a gentle tug. "I wonder if you do." He dropped the ribbon and leaned away from her. "How goes the courtship of Isaac?"

"Slow. We are taking things slowly."

"Why?"

Because he's getting over a broken heart.

Isaac had begged her not to tell Levi about the girl he'd left behind. Sarah had to honor his request.

"Neither one of us wants to repeat our past mistakes by rushing into something we aren't ready for."

"That sounds so reasonable. Why don't I quite believe you?"

"Because you have a suspicious and devious nature."

"True. Maybe I can speed things up for you. Add a little fertilizer for your romance, so to speak."

She eyed him suspiciously. "Has Granny Weaver fixed a love potion at your request?"

"I hadn't thought of that. Does she make them?"

"Ernest claims that's the only way Betty Shetler got Henry to propose."

"Betty. Is she that tall, skinny woman with a big, hearty laugh?"

Sarah rolled her eyes at him. "She is tall, but I would never describe her laugh that way."

"And he's the short fellow with thick glasses? I don't see that they would need a love potion. I do see the need for a stepladder when he wants to kiss her. Then again, maybe he simply waits for her to sit down. Say on a swing on her front porch. Kind of like this one."

He placed a hand beneath Sarah's chin and lifted her face. Slowly, he bent near and kissed her.

CHAPTER FOURTEEN

SARAH FROZE IN SURPRISE. She should have turned aside or moved away but she didn't. The tenderness of Levi's lips against hers sent her pulse leaping. The sounds of the late afternoon faded away until she and Levi were the only living things in the world. It should have felt wrong, but it didn't. It was wondrous.

His kiss was gentle, coaxing her to respond. She lost herself in the sensations his touch brought to life. It was a marvelous, warm moment unlike any she had known. It crossed her mind that she had never really been kissed before. The awkward exchanges she and Isaac had shared in the past were nothing like this.

She wanted it to go on and on.

When he pulled back, she almost moaned with disappointment. Slowly she came back to her senses and took a deep, steadying breath. The earthy scent that was so uniquely his surrounded her. The sounds of the farm returned. The swing made little creaking noises. Why had he kissed her?

He rested his lips against her temple. "Isaac is watching. This should stir things up for you."

The kiss had been for show. It didn't mean anything to him. Sarah wanted to sink through the floor.

LEVI HAD SEEN Isaac watching them from the corner of his eye and decided a little prodding might benefit Isaac as well as Sarah. He lost sight of his purpose the moment her lips softened beneath his.

In that instant she became everything he'd never known he needed in his life. But she wasn't his. She wanted Isaac.

She tried to move away but he kept his arm around her. His purpose returned with the thud of a lead weight. "I want to make it look good."

He hated every word that came out of his mouth. It had started for Isaac's benefit, but it was more than that now. He was falling hard for his brother's girlfriend.

"Never do that again." Her whisper was ragged and harsh.

He forced himself to get up off the swing and walk past Isaac, who was standing at the end of the porch. "Hello, little brother."

He went down the steps with the taste of Sarah lingering on his lips. If he knew Isaac as well as he thought he did, Isaac would make a stronger play for Sarah just so Levi couldn't have her. He looked back at her sitting quietly on the swing with her hand pressed to her mouth.

What was she thinking? That he was a scoundrel? She wasn't far wrong. He walked away from her and found himself standing outside of Wing's stall. The horse put her head over the top board to beg some affection.

"You have a rival. I used to think you were the only one for me, but there is someone else now. Lucky for you, she isn't a horse. She'll never outrun you, but she makes my heart soar the way it does when I'm flying along behind you."

He rubbed the filly's cheek. "I'm a big heel. She is my brother's girl. I didn't know I could sink so low. Except it doesn't feel low when I'm with Sarah. It feels…amazing."

He could still feel the weight of her against his chest.

He went inside the stall and began brushing Wing's coat. The simple repetitive motion always soothed him, but it didn't tonight. Tonight he had stepped over a line he swore he wouldn't cross. If Isaac hadn't shown up, Levi knew he would've bared his soul to Sarah and asked her to choose him over his brother. Her answer would have been Isaac. He knew it, but that didn't change the need to pull her close and taste her sweet lips one more time.

He shook his head. One kiss was all he would have to remember. He kicked a pile of straw into the corner and sat down. He needed to stay far away from Sarah. As far as Lancaster, Pennsylvania. And he needed to go soon.

SARAH SAT WITH her hands covering her face. Why had she let Levi kiss her? She wanted to feel humiliation or shame. Instead she felt the loss of his wonderful touch. She finally looked up and saw Isaac standing at the corner of the porch. He hadn't moved. She reached out her hand. "I'm sorry."

He came forward, took her hand and sat beside her. "Levi is the one who should be sorry."

"I didn't know he was going to do that. I wasn't prepared."

"I'm not the only jerk in the family."

"Oh, Isaac. You aren't a jerk."

"I used to be."

"We all change and grow." She was changed. Levi had done that to her. The kiss didn't mean anything to him. He had done it to provoke Isaac. To make him jealous. For her, it had shone a bright light into the darkness.

Isaac slipped his arm around her shoulders. "I'll talk to him. I'll make him apologize."

"Can't we just forget it? It's not going to happen again. I won't let it."

He kissed the top of her head. "Okay, if that's the way you want it."

"It is."

She sat with him for a long time, trying to erase the feel of Levi's arms around her. Isaac's arm around her shoulders was comforting, but it didn't stir her heart the way Levi's nearness had. After a while she pulled away. "I want to go home now."

"Are you sure?"

"I am."

Sarah left the swing and hurried to her brother-in-law's tractor. She didn't relax until she was out on the road and headed toward home. A jumble of emotions churned in her mind. She should've felt cheapened by Levi's action, but she didn't. She pressed a hand to her lips. She felt treasured.

At home she went about her chores without thinking. She sat at the supper table with her family, but she wasn't hungry. She took a few bites and pushed the rest around on her plate.

She wanted to see Levi again. She wanted to know

if the kiss had really been for Isaac's sake or if there was something that Levi felt toward her.

"Sarah, are you feeling okay?" Laura Beth asked.

"I'm a little tired. I think I'll go to bed early."

She got up from the table and left the room, knowing her family would be concerned and worried, but she couldn't explain.

After talking endlessly about Isaac and her pursuit of him, how could she tell them a kiss by Levi had turned her world upside down? She had thought she was falling in love with Isaac the way she had loved him so many years ago. Only she wasn't. She liked him as a friend, but the closeness she had hoped for wasn't there.

She didn't know what she felt for Levi. It was so much more complex.

She got ready for bed and lay down, but it was a long time before she actually fell asleep. When she did, she dreamed Levi was kissing her.

"THERE'S TALK GOING around about you and Levi," Angela whispered on their way up the stairs to the room reserved for their class on Sunday morning.

The prayer meeting was being held at Seth Knepp's farm. The home was large enough to house the congregation downstairs. The main-level rooms had been designed with movable walls that opened to make a single meeting space.

"What kind of talk?" Sarah was pretty sure she already knew.

"Like maybe a courting couple got carried away and

wasn't looking where the horse was headed and the sheriff stopped them."

Sarah's mouth dropped open. "Are you serious? People are saying that?"

Angela giggled. "The real question is, are you and Levi serious about each other? I thought you had your sights set on Isaac."

It was hard for Sarah to keep her mind on what was being taught after that. The same church elders continued the baptismal instructions for her that morning, along with Isaac, Angela and Thaddeus. Isaac asked more questions and seemed more interested in the answers. She hoped that meant he was becoming serious about accepting the Amish way of life. After the class was over, she waited impatiently for the church service to end. Four hours of preaching had never felt so long.

Several times during the service, she glanced over at the men's side of the room. Twice she caught Isaac smiling at her, but Levi never looked her way that she saw. She was the object of more attention from the other women than the men. When the last hymn drew to a close, she shut the large black hymnal and tried to leave with as much dignity as possible. Outside a group of her friends were gathered beneath a large maple tree in the Knepps' front yard.

One of the girls grabbed Sarah's arm. "We heard you were pulled over by the sheriff for speeding with Levi Raber. Is that true?"

Sarah gave a long-suffering sigh. "I knew everyone would be talking about this today. I'm sure Granny

Weaver was delighted to repeat the tale. She likes to share a good story almost as much as Ernest does."

She kept her eyes on the door to the Knepps' house, waiting for Levi to come out. She knew the men were rearranging the benches into tables. She finally saw him leave and head toward the barn where a number of other men were already gathered.

She walked slowly toward the group. She didn't want to fuel more gossip by running after him in front of the whole church. She set her eyes on Owen Mast and strolled toward him. Owen was standing near Levi. She quickly thought of a reason to speak to Owen while ignoring Levi. Her sister had lost a goat to the coyotes recently and had wondered if they needed a guard dog or a llama. Pretending she didn't care if Levi was there or not might put a stop to any speculation that she and Levi were a couple.

She didn't even glance at Levi as she walked up to Owen. "*Guder mariye*, Owen."

"*Guder mariye*, Sarah. You don't look so very wind-blown to me." The men around him laughed.

She was going to be the punch line of a few jokes for a while. If she made light of the episode, it would be forgotten quickly. If she avoided the subject or Levi, then people would wonder why. Everyone knew she was working at the Raber farm.

She forced a smile. "When Levi Raber asks if you want to see how fast his horse will go, you'd better leave your hat at home. The ribbons of my *kapp* were standing straight out behind my head when the sheriff pulled us over. Took me an hour to iron them back into the right shape."

"Is that true, Levi?" Ernest asked.

"I didn't notice her ribbons, but her nose was pushed as flat as if it was up against the window glass. It still looks a little flat to me. What do you fellows think?" She was pleased that Levi was following her lead in making light of the episode.

Mr. Knepp scratched his beard. "I have a pretty fast trotter. I might like to see how my horse measures up to yours."

Ernest rubbed his hands together. "A match race. I like the sound of that."

Several men murmured their agreement.

"Did you need something?" Owen asked Sarah.

"I was wanting some information about the guard llama you recently purchased. My sister has a goat herd and we have been troubled by coyotes lately."

"Mr. Knepp, I'd like to see this horse of yours," Levi said.

"He's out in the pasture. I'll have one of my boys bring him in." The two men walked toward the pasture gate. Most of the other men followed behind them.

"Ruth is the one who made the decision to get the llama. You should talk to her." Owen joined the men at the fence.

"Do you think you turned the tide?" Ernest asked quietly in her ear.

Sarah arched one eyebrow toward him. "Maybe. Don't you start spreading any rumors about Levi and me."

"I wouldn't dream of it." He chuckled as he walked away.

Sarah drew a deep breath. She had done what she

could. Keeping things casual between her and Levi while they were in public would be her goal for the next few weeks until people found something else to gossip about.

She saw Isaac coming her way. He had a scowl on his face. "People are talking about you and my brother."

"It's okay."

"How can you say that?"

"I open my mouth, and what I'm thinking comes out."

His scowl deepened. "What should we do about the talk?"

"Nothing. Nothing happened. Nothing will come of denying that anything happened, so we do…nothing."

"Are you sure?"

"I am. Now let's go enjoy the meal and visit with Angela and Thaddeus. Maybe we can get up a game of volleyball after a while."

"Okay."

She saw Levi walking her way. He stopped beside them. "Have you eaten?"

"We were just on our way to the house." She saw the concern in his eyes and knew it wasn't because he thought she was hungry or angry. He wanted to make sure she wasn't upset by the gossip.

"We'd rather eat by ourselves," Isaac said.

"It will look better if I join you."

"He's right," Sarah said. Together they walked past Henrietta and a group of her friends watching them closely.

"My fish was the bigger of the two. Are you ready

to admit it?" Levi asked, his voice slightly louder than normal.

Sarah stopped. "You are *narrisch* if you think I'll admit anything of the kind. My fish was much larger than yours."

"Isaac, are you going to let your girl call me crazy?"

Isaac looked from one to the other. "I reckon I am."

She inclined her head. "*Danki*, Isaac."

Levi started walking again. Isaac and Sarah fell into step behind him. Isaac leaned close to her. "Did he just call you my girlfriend?"

She didn't want Isaac to feel trapped in a relationship with her after ending his previous one such a short time ago. "For this morning. You can dump me on the way home."

"I don't see the need to do that."

She stopped. "You don't?"

He turned to face her. "*Nee*. You and I are friends. We should try being boyfriend and girlfriend for a while and see how it works."

"What about your other friend?"

He scowled. "That's over. I'm going to ask you not to mention her again."

"Okay, I won't."

"*Goot*. It's time we started dating. We will enjoy each other's company, right?"

"Of course." And she wouldn't give Levi another thought.

She looked over Isaac's shoulder. Levi was waiting for them by the kitchen door. Had he overheard Isaac's comments? Was he satisfied that his ploy had worked?

His action had taken root in Isaac's mind and forced his hand. Levi wasn't ready to pat himself on the back just yet. It was a long way from being a dating couple to getting married. If his nudge had started Isaac along that path, Sarah should be grateful. Levi took his plate of food and cup of coffee outside to sit under the shade of a mulberry tree beside the pump house.

Isaac and Faron joined him. "How is that horse working out now?" Levi asked.

"He hasn't given me a lick of trouble. My thanks for your hard work. I sure will recommend you to anyone else with a problem horse."

Owen and Joshua stood leaning against the hay trailer. Owen pointed his fork at Levi. "Are you planning on starting a business training horses?"

"I haven't really thought about it."

"Why not consider it?" Isaac said. "*Daed* always used to say a trainer's job was to help the horse find his full potential and then get out of his way."

"He did say that." Finding a horse's full potential, any horse, was something his father had understood and loved doing. Levi had never thought about working outside of racing, but he could if he needed to.

"Are you going to set up a race with Seth Knepp?" Joshua put his coffee cup on the trailer.

Levi shook his head. "It wouldn't be a fair race."

"Why not?" Isaac asked.

"Wing would have to pull a buggy. She's never done that before. All she has ever had behind her is a jog cart or a lightweight sulky."

Isaac tapped his plate with his fork. "I don't see why

we couldn't find two carts of similar size and weight. It wouldn't have to be a buggy. She could get used to it in a few days. Faron, what do you think?"

"I think that's a great idea. And I know just the place we can get them."

As Isaac and Faron discussed possible locations along with the date and the time, Levi found the idea growing on him. It wouldn't hurt Wing to go head-to-head against another horse. It would be a good training exercise for her.

Angela, Thaddeus and Sarah came over to join the group. Faron leaned forward. "Thaddeus, do you still have those two-wheeled carts that your sisters used to use?"

He nodded. "I'm sure we do. Once the twins got married, *Daed* put the carts away, but he thought my two youngest sisters might want to use them when they're bigger. Why?"

Faron punched his fist into Isaac's shoulder. "I told you I knew where we could find carts. We're trying to set up a race between Seth Knepp's horse and Levi's."

Thaddeus shook his head slowly. "I'm not sure my grandfather would approve of that."

"Okay," Isaac said. "That's good to know. We wouldn't want to upset him."

Thaddeus looked relieved. "Are you all staying for the singing tonight?"

Faron and Isaac agreed they would stay. "What about you, Levi?"

"Not this time. I still don't feel I can leave Mother alone

for any length of time. She is certainly better. Thanks in large part to Sarah's help, and yours, too, Angela."

"Are either of you girls staying?" Thaddeus asked casually. Levi saw his attention was on Angela.

"I am," Angela said. "What about you, Sarah?"

"*Ja.* I enjoy singings. And Mrs. Knepp always makes those wonderful doughnuts for us."

It was common for couples to slip off together afterward. A boy would take the girl home and often spend a few hours visiting with her in her house. Levi smiled at Sarah. "I hope you find a ride home tonight."

SARAH KNEW LEVI was giving Isaac a broad hint. She hoped he would take it. It would be embarrassing to have to get a ride with someone else.

Over by the barn she saw a group of youngsters getting up a game of volleyball. The net was brought out and quickly set up on an open grassy area beside the barn. The teenagers were dividing up teams. Two of the young women raced over to Sarah. They each grabbed a hand and attempted to pull her to her feet.

"Come on, Sarah. We need you," one of them pleaded.

She looked at Isaac. "I will play if Isaac will. It's been a while since I've beaten him at this game."

Isaac's eyebrows almost disappeared under his hatband. "You think you beat me at volleyball?"

Sarah faced him with her hands on her hips. "That's how I remember it."

"Ha! Me and the boys never lost a game to you maids." He called out to Faron Mast, who was bounc-

ing the ball off his knees. "Do you have room for one
more on your team?"

Faron grinned. "We sure do."

Isaac took off his hat and laid it on his chair. "Prepare to be stomped."

Levi took off his hat and laid it beside Isaac's. "May
I join your team, Sarah? It looks like you only have
five players."

A sharp refusal hovered on Sarah's lips. Instead she
swept her hand toward the court. "Be my guest."

Levi sent a triumphant look to his brother. Isaac's
face grew rigid.

It wasn't going to be all men and boys against the
girls and women this time. She only hoped Levi was
a good player. Isaac had been particularly skilled at
spiking the ball.

She and Levi went to the far side of the net and arranged themselves with Sarah serving first while Levi
took the center position. She made sure to serve away from
Isaac. In spite of that effort, his team members fed the ball
to him at the perfect height for him to slam it over the net.
To her surprise, Levi dived under it and popped it up, giving Angela the opportunity to send it to the back corner.

"Out," Isaac yelled.

Sarah glared at him. "That was in. It was a perfect
corner shot."

Levi rose and dusted the grass off his shirt. "This
game might need referees."

"I volunteer." Joshua held up his hand. He stepped
off the length of the playing field and made a mark in
the grass with the heel of his boot. He raised his hand

and motioned to the group of men standing in the shade of the barn. "Owen, we need another referee."

Since the Sunday afternoon games were rarely competitive, Sarah was surprised to see the men all moving in their direction. Soon both sides of the field held spectators. Ernest had his arms crossed over his chest and a huge smile on his face. "Want me to borrow a dress for you, Levi?"

All the men started laughing. Levi wasn't fazed. For the next forty minutes it was a hardscrabble game that often came down to a competition between Levi and Isaac as they each tried to block the other's spike. When the score of twenty-one was reached by Sarah's team, there was cheering from the women who had gathered along one side. Sarah walked under the net to pat Isaac's shoulder. "Fine game."

Levi slipped under the net and offered his brother his hand. "Maybe you can stomp this team another time, but you're gonna need bigger shoes. These gals know how to play."

Isaac ignored his brother's hand. "You won't always be the winner." He marched away, anger evident in his every movement.

Sarah hurried after him. "Don't be a sore loser, Isaac. It's just a game."

He took a deep breath. "I'm sorry. He always tries to make me look bad."

"That's not true. You didn't look bad. You gave it your best." She glanced back and saw Levi watching them. She couldn't read the expression on his face.

She turned back to Isaac. "Don't let this spoil our first date."

"I ENJOYED THE EVENING. Didn't you?" Isaac held out his hand to help Sarah into his buggy after the singing let out.

"I did." She was happily surprised. Isaac's sour mood was gone and a pleasant young man like the one she remembered had taken his place.

He climbed in beside her. "*Gott* has given you a fine singing voice."

"*Danki.* You have a pleasant voice, too." She stared straight ahead with her arms clasped across her middle. Was she nervous? She was. This was their first real date.

"You don't have to hang out the side of the buggy." He winked at her.

Sarah scooted closer. She had dreamed of this day for years. Why did it feel so awkward? She knew the answer but hated to face it. It was because Levi had spoiled it for her. He had kissed her. She should be focusing on Isaac, but all she could think about was Levi.

"It's a nice night for a drive," Isaac said.

She rubbed her hands up and down her arms. "Driving at night makes me nervous. I'm always afraid a car will come up behind me too fast and run into me."

"It happens. I lost a good friend that way."

"We can't know when *Gott* will test our faith with such a trial." They had both suffered losses. They had that in common.

The drive up and down the hills of the Stumbling Blocks was pretty at night. As they topped each hill, Sarah could see the rising moon casting a silvery path across the lake in the distance. A pair of white-tailed deer jumped across the road and spooked the horse, but

Isaac quickly controlled him. It wasn't long before they reached the Y in the road that marked the start of her lane. Down and around the hill, across the low-water bridge and up the final hill could be tricky in the dark, but Isaac managed it without any trouble. He might like tractors, but he knew how to handle horses. He pulled to a stop in front of her house. It was dark except for a dim light glowing in the kitchen window.

"Would you like to come in?" It took a ton of nerve for her to ask the question. What if he said no?

It was customary for an Amish girl to invite her date in even though her parents would be in bed, but this was the first time for Sarah. The young man and woman were expected to be on their best behavior. It was a time couples often got to know each other the best. Laura Beth and Joshua would expect her to bring her date in to stay awhile.

Isaac shrugged. "Sure. I'll come in."

She led the way inside and closed the door quietly behind him. "I made some oatmeal cookies this morning. Would you like some?"

"Sure."

"Do you want to sit in the living room or in the kitchen?" She had her hands clenched tightly together.

"The kitchen, I guess. It's cozy." He took a seat at the table. "Smells odd. What is that?"

"We've been making lavender soap."

Moving to the cupboard, she took out a plate and placed several cookies on it. She sat down at the table and pushed the plate toward him. He picked up a cookie and bit into it. "Not bad."

"High praise."

"I meant it's *goot*."

She struggled to find something to talk about and finally settled on asking him about himself. "Tell me some of the things you used to do in Pennsylvania."

It was a good suggestion. He talked about his friends and shared a few funny stories about Levi. "We didn't always get along," Isaac admitted.

Sarah's heart filled with sympathy. "Things can change for the better between you."

"I hope so. I know he doesn't want to stay here. Frankly, I'll be glad if he does leave."

"What about you?"

"I like it here. I thought I wanted to go back because of her, you know, but now I'm enjoying farming and I like the countryside."

She reached across the table and took his hand. "I'm glad."

"Sarah, is there something between you and Levi?"

"Why would you ask that?"

"Just the way he acts."

She couldn't deny her feelings for Levi but neither could she put them into words. If only he hadn't kissed her. She had been so sure Isaac was the one for her until then. She had to forget it happened. Put it out of her mind. Somehow. "Levi and I are friends," she said lamely.

Isaac's smile grew stiff. "It's late. I think I'll go home."

Sarah let go of his hand. "Oh. Sure. That's fine. I'll be out to the house tomorrow."

"Do me a favor and don't mention Levi's race to *Mamm*. It might upset her."

"I didn't think you were going to hold it. Thaddeus said the bishop wouldn't approve."

"It turns out he doesn't object to the men having a bit of fun as long as we're safe about it."

LEVI HAD NOT intended to wait up for Isaac, but it was well after midnight and he was still sitting on the porch swing. He heard the clip-clop of Jasper's hooves before the buggy came into sight.

Isaac drove straight to the barn and put the horse away. He was walking toward the front door when Levi spoke. "How was your date?"

"Man, you startled me. I didn't see you there. Are you trying to give a fellow a heart attack?"

"I'm just hanging out to make sure my baby brother gets home okay."

"As you can see, I'm in one piece."

"And Sarah?"

"Safe and sound in her own home."

"Did you have a good time? I know Amish dating is not your speed."

Isaac shook his head. "Unlike you, my speeding days are behind me. I had a nice time. I think Sarah did, too. We talked a lot."

"That sounds like a good start."

"Why all the questions?"

"No reason. I'm just a little bored sitting here in the dark."

"Sarah is a pretty nice kid."

Levi shook his head. "Not really."

Isaac frowned at him. "What's that supposed to mean?"

"It means she is pretty nice, but she is no kid. She's a fine young woman."

"I think she's the kind of woman a man could settle down with."

"A man like you?"

"What's wrong with me?" Isaac went on the defensive.

"Nothing. I'm glad you're thinking about settling down. *Mamm* will be happy to hear it. Do you like her—I mean, really like her?"

Isaac shrugged. "I'd like to get to know her better. Maybe spend some time with her family."

"Now, that sounds serious."

"Don't turn it into a joke, *brudder*."

Levi got up out of the swing and laid his hand on Isaac's shoulder. "I don't think of this as a joke. We're talking about your happiness. I know you'll make the right decision about asking her out again. Is she coming back today?"

"She said she was. *Mamm* really likes having her here."

"Everyone likes Sarah."

"She's loyal. That's what I like about her the best," Isaac declared.

"I think you are smitten, little *brudder*."

"Love makes a fellow stupid," he said bitterly.

Levi was taken aback. "I've never heard you speak that way before."

"Maybe I'm just tired. I haven't been sleeping well."

"Is there anything I can do to help?"

"*Nee*, but thanks for the thought. Tell me something. What do you think of Sarah?"

He thought she was wonderful, witty, brave, a little foolish sometimes, but most of all Sarah was kind. It wasn't something she did; it was something she was deep inside. When she loved, she would love wholeheartedly. "I think she's a great catch."

"I think she would make a *goot* wife. *Guten nacht.*"

Isaac went in the house, leaving Levi alone with his thoughts. They were all thoughts of Sarah. Was he doing her a favor by pushing Isaac in her direction? The more he saw of her, the more he wanted to tell her how she made him feel.

It wasn't gonna be like that.

He prayed Isaac would mature into the kind of fellow that would make Sarah happy.

CHAPTER FIFTEEN

LEVI EXPECTED THINGS to be tense between Sarah and himself, but he soon discovered that wasn't the case. She seemed to have shrugged off the kiss as if it were of no importance. She never mentioned it, but she made sure to never be alone with him either.

He hadn't been able to forget it. Having her in the house was a constant reminder that she might one day live there with Isaac.

Levi spent more and more time in the barn.

He entered the house in the afternoon a few days after his brother's date and heard laughter coming from the open cellar door. He went down the steps to see what was going on. Sarah was standing on a three-legged stool, trying to reach the canning jars on the top shelf. She was about four inches too short.

"Let me get that for you."

She jumped at the sound of his voice and had to grab at the shelves to keep her balance. "I appreciate your offer, but don't sneak up on a body like that."

"I assumed my tromping down those creaky steps would alert you."

"We were too busy laughing," his mother said, holding a basket full of fruit jars.

He crossed to Sarah's side. "What are you trying to get?"

She cleared her throat. "Um…the quart jars of peaches. I'll get down out of your way."

He wrapped an arm around her waist, pulled her against his side and lowered her feet to the floor in one easy movement. She jumped backward and dusted at her apron with both hands. "That wasn't necessary."

He allowed a slow grin to spread across his face. "I always enjoy helping you with your awkward predicaments."

She raised her chin. There was a glint of defiance in her eyes. "At least this time you didn't get wet."

"The day is young."

His mother shifted her basket to her other hand. "What are you two talking about?"

"Levi thinks he needs to rescue me when I am perfectly capable of taking care of myself. Except when I fell in the lake, of course. I can't swim and I do owe him my life for that."

He bowed slightly. "I'm pleased to hear you say so."

She dusted off her hands as though she were dusting him out of her life. "Peaches?"

He gave his attention to the task. "How many?"

"Four should do it," his mother said. "Sarah and I are making peach cobbler today. Sarah and some friends are coming over for the next several days to help me can beans. The garden is overrun with them. I don't know what Helmuth was thinking when he planted so many."

"I'm sure you'll enjoy the company." He handed

Sarah the jars of peaches and allowed his mother to go up the stairs ahead of him.

At the top she pressed a hand to her chest. "Let me catch my breath."

He waited a minute. "Are you okay?"

She nodded. "I am now." She went to the stove and set out a large black kettle.

"What are you doing today?" Sarah asked without looking at him.

Was she really interested or was she making conversation? He found it hard to tell. They both enjoyed teasing each other, but he wasn't sure of her real feelings. He wanted to ask her about her reaction to his kiss, but he knew that wasn't going to happen. He didn't want to know if she hadn't been as affected by it.

"Isaac is getting the harvester combine tuned up. It won't be long before we'll be cutting wheat. My only plan is to take care of some bills and order fuel."

Sarah turned to his mother. "I will let you get started on the filling while I go check on Priscilla."

Levi couldn't put a face with the name. "Who is Priscilla?"

His mother handed him the peach jars to open. "She's the sow that had piglets two weeks ago."

He struggled with the stuck lids. "I didn't know she had a name." He opened the jars and set them on the counter for his mother.

"I named her. Actually, I named them all. I'll let you guess which one is Levi," Sarah quipped and went outside. He was tempted to follow her but decided some distance between them was best. He went to get the mail.

His mother was stirring the peaches in the pot on the stove when he came back in. The mouthwatering smell left him hoping to sample the cobbler before all her friends arrived.

He went through the mail piece by piece. There was a bill from the hospital, two auction flyers. Several pieces of junk mail—but the last piece was the one that caught his attention. It was from Arnold. He tucked it in his pocket to read later.

He left the house and went down to the barn. He stopped at Wing's stall. The filly came over to nuzzle his arm. He pulled out the letter and opened it. Arnold wrote that Stormy Seas Sailor been entered into an upcoming stakes race. He thought Levi might be interested to know they thought Stormy was ready to race.

"What I wouldn't give to be there and watch him," Levi muttered to himself. He crumpled the letter into a ball. His mother was getting better, but without constant help, she wouldn't be able to run the household. Walking up the basement stairs left her breathless. Isaac would be in the fields all day when harvest arrived. His mother could afford to hire help, but would she? She liked Sarah and didn't object to her help, but he was paying Sarah's salary. He couldn't see his mother parting with her own funds for a "needless expense." Isaac didn't have money of his own. He'd rarely held a job for more than two or three months.

A squeal made him look down. A little white piglet raced over his boots, heading for the open barn door.

"*Nee, nee, nee.* Come back here," Sarah called out

from the back of the barn. A second piglet raced behind his boots, heading in the same direction as his sibling.

Sarah appeared with a squealing little animal in her arms. "Did you see where they went?"

He pointed toward the barn door. "They are gone to freedom."

"And you didn't think to stop them. Here, hold this one." She shoved the pink-and-white squealing babe into his arms and ran out the barn door.

Levi heard a crash and then loud grunting coming from the back. An angry sow came around the corner, charging down the alleyway. He quickly climbed to the top of Wing's stall gate. The baby he held continued to squeal in fright. Mama sow reared on her hind legs to try to reach him. He jumped into the stall to escape her.

Wing started charging around in fright. She nearly knocked him down. He plastered himself against the wall and moved to open the Dutch door that led to the corral. She dashed out and he closed the bottom half to keep her from coming in again. The sow was trying to break down the gate by flinging herself against it. Suddenly she went running back the way she had come.

It grew quiet. He moved closer to the gate. Sarah entered the main barn door with two piglets in her arms.

Sarah noticed him inside the stall and stopped at the gate. "What are you doing in there?"

He heard the sow squeal and heard her come tearing back. He opened the gate and pulled Sarah inside. He managed to slam the gate shut and jam the bolt in place before the pig hit. The gate bowed but held.

The piglets, hearing their mother's grunts, all began squealing and struggling in earnest.

"What is all the commotion in here?" Isaac asked, coming in the main door.

"There's an angry sow loose. Watch out," Levi shouted, knowing the animal could do some serious damage with her massive weight, sharp teeth and hooves. The sow charged Isaac.

He scaled the gate of the adjacent stall. "How did she get out?"

Sarah was trying to calm the piglets she held. "Priscilla became upset when her babies got out through a broken board. She must've broken out of her pen. She just wants her babies back."

"Give them to her," Isaac said. The sow was throwing herself against the gate of his stall and starting to tear at the boards with her teeth.

"She's so upset she may accidentally hurt them," Sarah said. She handed Levi another piglet and held out one to Isaac.

"I don't want it. You keep it."

"I need to get Priscilla back in her pen. Hold him."

Isaac moved closer to the half-wall partition between the stall and took the squealing piglet. "If she gets in here, I'm coming over with you."

The sow returned to attacking the gate where Levi held her two babies.

"Cover them up so they get quiet," Sarah said.

"Cover them with what?" Isaac asked. It was hard to hear him over the sow's furious grunts and squealing.

Levi took off his hat and put it over the babies' faces.

They quickly quieted. Isaac did the same. The sow stopped attacking the gate.

"I need to shut the barn door so she can't get outside." Sarah giggled as she climbed to the top of the stall gate and walked with her arms spread out for balance along the two-inch-wide boards that made up the stalls until she reached the bench that ran along the wall at the front of the barn. She jumped to the bench. "Distract her for a minute."

Levi uncovered his piglets and they began squealing. Mama was immediately back attacking his gate.

He covered the piglets again and they quieted.

In the silence he heard the main barn door being rolled closed. The sow heard it, too, and ran in that direction. "Sarah, look out—she's coming your way."

There was only silence. Levi and Isaac looked at each other. After several long minutes, Levi leaned out to look over the gate. "Sarah, are you okay?"

"I'm fine," she said from behind him. He spun around. She came in the Dutch door.

"What did you do with the sow?"

"I tempted her back into another farrowing pen down the other alleyway with her remaining piglet and some grain. I'll take the babies now." She took the one from Isaac and the two from Levi. She bundled them in her apron and went out the Dutch door. "Did you have a scary time of it? You poor little *bobbli*. Let's go see your *mamm*." She closed the bottom of the door.

Levi turned to stare at his brother. "I guess it's safe to go out."

"I'm not opening that gate until I hear an all clear."

Levi caught the sound of the front door being rolled open. "It's safe to come out," Sarah called.

Both he and Isaac still held their hats in their hands. Levi looked at his brother. "You can never reveal what happened here today. Never."

"Do you mean because two grown men with piglets in their hats were trapped in the horse stalls by a mad sow and a quick-thinking little woman walked along the tops of the stalls to get out and coaxed the outraged mama into another pen?"

"Yes, that. It never happened," Levi said.

"Never happened," Isaac agreed.

The two men cautiously opened the stall gates and walked out to the alleyway.

"She's scary," Isaac said.

"The sow?"

Isaac shook his head. "Sarah. She just takes charge."

Levi nodded. "She's the one you want in a crisis." She had a heart for adventure and didn't hesitate to take risks.

Isaac slowly shook his head. "Doesn't she make you feel…I don't know…inferior?"

It was a troubling comment from Isaac. Levi shook his head. "Not at all. I admire her. I'm a little in awe." Was she the kind of woman who would understand the risks of his business and not shy away? He could see her behind a quick-stepping trotter circling the track. She would be laughing.

Isaac shook out his hat. "It's too bad she's in love with me and not with you. You'd make a great pair."

"I think we might at that." Levi found himself wondering if Sarah was in love with his brother. Maybe she wasn't.

They started walking toward the door. Isaac put his hat on his head. "I know one thing for sure. That's the last pig that's being raised on this farm."

ON WEDNESDAY MORNING Levi led Wing out of her stall into the center of the alley where he clipped her halter to short ropes on either wall. She tossed her head a little, testing how far she could move, but quickly grew still. She knew she was going out.

He ran a brush over her shiny coat, smoothing away a few bits of straw and any debris that would rub underneath her harness. When he bent down to wrap on her foot covers, he could feel her excitement rising. The covers would protect her legs if she accidentally struck herself while she was trotting. She knew when he put them on that she was going to do more than jog. She was going to go fast. There was nothing Wing liked better than to go fast. She did it so easily that she never seemed to understand exactly how fast she was.

He secured the light harness and bridle with the blinkers that would keep her vision focused straight ahead and away from another horse coming up beside her. There would be another horse today. He was taking her out on a dirt road where she would go head-to-head with Seth Knepp's gelding.

She whinnied loudly and pawed the ground impatiently. He laughed. "I'm working as fast as I can. Hold your horses."

When he had the harness secured, he unhooked her

and led her out to where the borrowed jog cart was waiting. It was bigger than his practice sulky with wider tires, but it wouldn't feel much different to her. He backed her between the shafts and attached them to her harness, making sure the connection was secure.

He sat down on one of the fenders and let her walk toward the road. When they reached the place where the race was to start, he swung his legs into the cart and centered himself on the seat. He didn't bother with the racing whip. Although a driver would use one to urge her on during an actual race, Levi had never needed anything but his voice to make Wing go faster.

He spent twenty minutes letting her jog up and down the dirt road to get used to it. Her hooves kicked up little puffs of dust each time they struck the earth. The ground was hard and fast. As soon as she was warmed up, he took her to the place that had been marked off as a starting point. Seth Knepp and several dozen men, including the bishop and the sheriff, were gathered there. The race was taking place on private land. The sheriff assured Levi he was only a spectator.

Trotters didn't normally start from a standstill, but there wasn't a pace truck to get up to speed behind. The sheriff raised a white flag and dropped it. A flick of the reins and Wing lunged forward, picking up her pace until the fence post marked as the beginning of a mile flew past. Seth Knepp was right beside him.

Levi urged Wing to stretch out. She did and was soon flying along at a beautiful ground-eating trot. Adrenaline pumped through Levi's veins and made him grin with joy. One of the best things about Wing was that she never broke stride. He didn't have to worry that she would break into a gallop and be disqualified in an official race. The quarter-mile pole went by and then the half-mile pole. Seth Knepp dropped behind them.

"Open up now. Let's see what you've got," he called out loudly, his pride in her almost choking him. Wing put it into high gear. He thought the first three-quarters of a mile was fast, but the last quarter of a mile was her best. She didn't fade. When the one-mile pole flew past, he clicked his stopwatch and saw she had done it in under two minutes. Wing was destined for greatness. Not for racing along a dirt road on a Kansas farm. He pulled her up. She slowed gradually, and he turned her around.

The group of men at the finish line surged forward to congratulate him. Faron, Ernest and Thaddeus were the first to shake his hand. "She's amazing," Faron said.

"I told you," Ernest said. "She's a beauty."

Levi let her catch her breath a few minutes. He leaned out to shake hands with Seth when he came alongside.

"I thought I knew what a fast horse looked like. Now I know for certain. All my horse saw was her tail. Thanks for a mighty fine race."

"My pleasure. You have a *goot* horse there."

"I'm sure gonna have to stop bragging on him."

Granny Weaver worked her way in. "You have a fine horse, Levi Raber. The two of you were a pleasure to watch. Where is Sarah?"

"Sarah stayed with *Mamm* today."

"The girl will be sorry to have missed this. It was the most fun I've had all year." She chuckled as she walked away.

Levi waved goodbye and left to cool Wing off on the walk home. She should have been racing in front of thousands of people, not a few dozen Amish farmers and their families. The September race where he had planned to start Wing's career was drawing closer. She'd need several months of intense work to be ready, and he couldn't do that on the farm.

As he neared the turnoff to the farm lane, he saw the white mail truck stop at their mailbox. The driver waved as he drove past to finish his route. Levi maneuvered Wing over to the side. He leaned over, opened the mailbox and withdrew several letters and the local newspaper. He took them under his arm and headed back to the barn. After giving Wing her rubdown, he turned her out in the small pasture where she trotted over to stand beside Jasper in the shade of an Osage orange tree.

Levi scanned the mail as he was walking toward the house and noticed one of the letters was from Arnold. He tore it open and pulled out a letter and a newspaper clipping. The letter said only, *I thought you would want to see this.* The clipping was of a horse in harness, with a driver holding up a trophy.

Levi looked closely at the name. It was Stormy Seas Sailor. Arnold hadn't meant to be unkind, but to Levi it was like holding a hot wire in his hand. The horse's winnings wouldn't go to improve the stable his father had poured his life into. The story wouldn't bring men with promising horses to Levi to train. It was the dream, but Levi Raber wasn't in it.

He crumpled the newspaper clipping into a ball. He walked into the house and tossed it toward the trash can.

He missed. The sound of his mother's hearty laughter reached him. It was a sound he hadn't heard in more than a year and it lightened his heavy heart. He walked to the doorway of the living room. Sarah was sitting beside his mother. Laura Beth sat on the other side of her. Caleb was up on his mother's bed while Isaac was on his hands and knees at the foot.

Isaac growled like a lion and rose up, pawing the air with his hands. Caleb shrieked with happy laughter and pulled the covers over his head. Isaac sank back onto all fours and waited. Giggling, Caleb peeked out from beneath the covers. The moment he did, Isaac roared and rose up, starting the whole game over again.

His mother caught sight of him. "Levi, come in and join us."

"I've got some work to do yet. I'm happy to see Sarah and Caleb are keeping you entertained." He hadn't told his mother about the race. She would hear about it sooner or later, but the deed was done. He realized as he glanced about the room that his mother, Sarah and Isaac were doing fine without him.

"Isaac is helping keep your mother entertained," Sarah said. She and Isaac shared a warm smile before he growled and made Caleb duck under the covers again.

Levi watched them for a little longer. His mother's face was pink and glowing from her laughter and from the time Sarah insisted she spend outside each day. Her cheeks had lost their gaunt appearance. She was getting better. He'd been afraid to believe that until now. His brother was happy farming with his loud, smelly tractor. Sarah and Isaac were getting along better all the time.

They were doing fine without him. Soon he wouldn't be needed here anymore.

He returned to the kitchen and picked up the newspaper clipping. He smoothed it out and looked at the schedule of upcoming races. There were half a dozen for the first week of September, when he knew Wing would be ready if he stepped up her training and if he could get her onto a real track. He would call Arnold and see if he had room to board and train her.

Sarah came into the kitchen with Caleb on her hip. "He wants a drink. How did the race go?"

Levi forced himself not to think about holding her and kissing her before sharing the story of his victory. Every day it became harder to ignore those impulses when he was near her. "We won."

"I knew you would. I wish I could have been there."

"I wish you had been, too, but thanks for staying with Mother."

"You're welcome. What do you have there?" She nodded toward the paper in his hand.

"One of my *daed*'s most promising colts has won his first race."

"Oh." Her smile faded. "He won, and you weren't there to see it."

"Or share in his winnings."

"Sort of a sad, happy thing, then."

"Sort of."

Isaac came in. "Did you win?"

"Of course he did," Sarah said.

"We were all cheering for you here." Isaac smiled at Sarah and she smiled back at him.

Levi stared at the clipping in his hand. Every day it became harder to see Sarah with Isaac. She had what she wanted. Levi faced the fact that he was losing the best thing that had ever come into his life.

SARAH NOTICED A change come over Levi. She couldn't put her finger on exactly what it was, but she sensed that he had withdrawn from her. She wanted to corner him and find out what was wrong, but he avoided her the rest of the day. He didn't come in for lunch. Some part of her was frightened by his behavior. She didn't know why.

She went out to the shed to see if Isaac had an explanation. "Do you know what's bothering Levi?"

"Is something bothering him? I didn't notice." He was on his back under the harvester.

She folded her arms across her middle. "I get the feeling he's upset about something."

"He won the race. What could be bothering him?"

"I don't know. He's avoiding me. Can you talk to him?"

"Sarah, I have to get this header reel straightened. You'll see him at supper." His exasperated tone told her to stop bothering him.

She left the machine shed and went back to the house. Levi didn't turn up for supper or return before she had to leave that evening. She spent a restless night trying to convince herself that she was worrying about nothing and that he was fine, but she wouldn't believe it until she spoke to him.

She was finishing up in Henrietta's kitchen the next

morning and getting ready to seek out the elusive Levi
when the screen door banged open. The man she wanted
to see rushed into the house, startling her. He went straight
to a lower cabinet by the refrigerator, opened it and pulled
out a black bag.

"Levi, we need to talk."

He unzipped the case, checked inside and stood up.
"Where is Isaac?"

She heard the fear in his voice. "He's in the garden
with your mother. What's wrong?"

"Wing has colic. I need Isaac's phone to call the vet."

"Isaac doesn't have a phone anymore. He lost it in
the lake."

"Do you have yours?"

"I loaned it to Laura Beth. I can go to the phone
hut for you." She quickly dried her hands. "How bad
is she?"

"I can't tell yet, but she's in pain. She's kicking at
her belly and lying down to roll."

"Do you want the vet to come here?"

"As soon as he can. I'm not taking any chances. Give
him this information." He handed her the corner of a
feed sack with writing on it. "And send Isaac to the barn.
I may need him." He rushed out of the house with his
bag in hand.

Sarah hurried to the back door. Isaac and his mother
were on their way in. "Isaac, Levi needs you down at
the barn. Wing has colic. I'm going to call the vet."

Isaac rushed past her and out the front door without
hesitation. He knew exactly how serious the condition

could be. Wing might recover within a few hours or she might die in terrible pain.

Henrietta came in with a bowl of cherry tomatoes in her hands. "I'll put on some coffee and make some sandwiches. Levi won't leave her. There's no telling how serious a bout of colic will be. For some horses it's a matter of walking until their gut clears. Others can be dead in a few hours."

"I know." Sarah headed out the door and ran as fast as she could to the phone located a quarter of a mile from the house. An Amish neighbor was inside talking to someone. She rapped on the window. The man immediately hung up and came out. She explained briefly and thanked him.

She slipped in and made the call, giving the veterinarian all the information that Levi had given her. She took down the doctor's instructions, hung up and then ran back to the farm. Levi and Isaac had Wing on her feet and were walking her slowly around the corral. The normally energetic filly walked with her head down, breathing heavily.

"Dr. Oslo can be here in about an hour. He said to give her pain medication and walk her until he can get here."

"I've done that."

"At least she is on her feet," Sarah said. A horse that was rolling in pain on the ground could sometimes hurt themselves and anyone trying to get them up. She saw the worry and fear in Levi's eyes. More than anything she wanted to comfort him. Wing meant so much to him.

Levi spoke softly to the horse, encouraging her. "You

have to be okay, Wing. Do you hear me? You're a good girl and you're going to be okay. You were spectacular yesterday." He led her across the small enclosure.

Isaac stepped out of the corral and stood beside Sarah. "We have a horse trailer, but we will need someone with a pickup to haul it if we have to take her for surgery. There isn't an equine surgery center close enough for us to use the tractor. It would be too slow anyway. Levi has the phone numbers of several people we can call."

Sarah looked up at him. "Has she had problems with colic before?"

"*Nee*, but Levi doesn't leave things to chance. As soon as he knew we were coming here, he located a vet that was close by and found out where our horses would have to go for surgery. The broodmare farm was our business and the horses were our livelihood. Some of them, like Wing, were worth thousands of dollars. Levi learned to be prepared."

"Is there anything I can do?"

"I don't think so. We will know more after the vet gets here." He slipped his arm around her shoulders. "It's going to be okay."

"It will break him to lose that horse." She tried to swallow past the tightness in her throat.

Isaac nodded. "I know."

CHAPTER SIXTEEN

LEVI WALKED WING as he waited for the vet to arrive. He stopped every twenty minutes to listen to her heartbeat and her breathing. Changes in either of those would be a sign that she was getting worse. The pain medicine he had given her seemed to be working. He prayed she would have a quick recovery and not need surgery. He prayed she would live. He'd faced too many losses already.

The young veterinarian was thorough and competent. After his exam he put his instruments in a tan case. "I'm optimistic about Wing's chances for recovery. However, I have to caution you that the horse's condition could deteriorate rapidly. I suggest someone stay with her constantly, even through the night."

"I will."

It was something Levi was already expecting to do. Over the years he and his father had had several mares that developed colic. The term covered a range of different illnesses from simple painful gas to an obstruction in the horse's digestive tract. One of their mares had died only four hours after showing symptoms. He would stay with Wing until he was sure she was out of danger.

His mother brought him food at noon and again at

supper. He barely touched it, but he was thankful for the coffee.

It was after midnight before Wing showed signs of improvement. She drank some water and quietly lay down in her stall. She hadn't been thrashing or kicking since her second dose of pain medication. He sat down beside her in the straw and lifted her head into his lap. She closed her eyes as he stroked her cheek.

"How is she?" Sarah asked quietly, looking into the stall.

He was surprised to see her. "What are you doing here? I thought you would've gone home hours ago."

SARAH SMILED AT HIM. He looked so tired. "I decided to stay so that Henrietta wouldn't be alone in case you and Isaac had to leave with Wing. I brought you some more coffee." There was little she could do to comfort him.

"That sounds great."

She opened the stall door and came in. She knelt beside him and handed him a mug of steaming black coffee. "Shouldn't you be walking her?"

"If a horse with colic is tired and is comfortable lying down, then it's okay to let them rest."

Sarah stroked the horse's face. "It's easy to become attached to them, isn't it? They do so much for us and ask so little in return."

His eyes grew sad. "I have been with her since she was born. I've seen her every day of her life. She's not just a horse. She's a friend. I think she feels the same way about me. I hope she does."

"Her affection for you is easy to see. Does the vet know what caused this?"

"No. That makes it scary because if she recovers it can happen again."

"When she recovers. Do you think it will affect her racing career?"

"I think you mean if she recovers."

"*Nee*, I mean when," she insisted.

"Sarah, the woman of faith. It shouldn't affect her ability to race."

It was peaceful in the barn. There was a feeling of closeness between the two of them that had been missing recently. She was glad she had sought him out tonight. She lifted a hand and brushed a bit of straw from his hair. It was a simple, intimate gesture. He met her gaze and held it for several long moments. She looked away first. "Are you still planning on going back to Pennsylvania?"

"If *Gott* is willing. So far His plan for Wing and me isn't clear."

"Your mother is doing better every day." Sarah scooted over to rest her back against the wall beside him. Close but not touching.

"Thanks to you and your family."

"We help each other. That is our way. Is it the same in Pennsylvania?"

"It is. The Amish communities are larger and more varied than they are here, but the focus on God, family and community is the same. If one man has trouble, his neighbors step in to help. We hold mud sales in the spring, you know, auctions to raise money for our schools and for those families that have medical bills they can't pay, as well as for children with special needs."

He sipped his coffee and she enjoyed the comfort of having him near.

"Is it pretty there?"

He smiled and closed his eyes to describe it. "Lancaster has big rolling hills and broad valleys. The farms are neat as pins with beautiful flower gardens in the spring and summer. The Amish houses are white and so are the barns. You do see some red barns but not many. In the fall the corn is cut and stacked into teepee-shaped bundles. You can see hundreds of them lined up in the fields as you drive along our highway."

"Are there lots of Amish farms?"

"Plenty. Horses and buggies can be seen everywhere traveling along the blacktop. Tour buses clog the narrow roads and our small towns. In the fall the colors are amazing in the hills. In the winter we get enough snow to turn the world into a sparkling wonderland. The best part is the horse farms. White board fences with grazing standardbred mares and foals frisking in the spring. *Gott* willing, they will someday be my mares and foals again."

"It sounds nice. I'd like to see it someday."

"You and Isaac will come to visit." He rubbed the back of his neck and grimaced.

"I pray your dream comes true." It was plain to Sarah that Levi was worried and tired. "Would you like me to leave you alone?"

He leaned his head back against the wall and closed

his eyes. "Please don't go. Talk to me. What about you? Tell me what your dream is, besides marrying my brother."

She wrapped her arms around her drawn-up knees. "My dreams are small. I want to marry and live near my sister and her husband. I want to help them harvest the lavender as we've done for years. I want babies of my own. I want my children to play with my sister's children. I want them to be taught by Miss Julie in school. It sounds ordinary when I talk about it."

"No, it doesn't. It sounds comfortable."

Sarah pulled her shawl tightly around her shoulder. Comfortable. That was a good description of the things she wanted out of life. A comfortable husband, a comfortable home, a comfortable way to earn a living. Would it be enough? She studied Levi as he stroked Wing's neck. He would not be a comfortable husband. He would be an exciting husband for the woman willing to bear the risks he took.

The sound of the barn door opening made them both look up. Isaac came in with some blankets in his arms. "I thought you might want to bed down out here. I'll take a turn watching Wing while you get some rest."

LEVI COULDN'T BELIEVE his little brother was offering to sit up with a sick horse. He opened his mouth to say he didn't need help, but he caught Sarah's eye and something there made him stay quiet.

She stroked Wing's face. "You're going to be fine. The Raber brothers are watching over you." She rose to her feet and took the empty mug. "Let me know if I can do anything."

"We've got this," Isaac said.

Levi nodded. "Isaac and I can take care of things."

Her bright smile told him that was the answer she was hoping for. She left, and Levi missed her comforting presence more than he cared to admit.

Isaac came into the stall and handed Levi a quilt and a pillow. Then he knelt by Wing's head and stroked her neck. "You're going to get well, pretty lady. Sarah said so, and there's no arguing with her. She's almost as stubborn as our *mamm*."

Levi scooted back and let Wing rest her head on the straw. "I appreciate the help."

"I was afraid you'd tell me to go back to bed like a good little boy and stop bothering you."

"I'm sorry if I've treated you that way in the past."

"I reckon I acted that way. How often are you checking her temperature and pulse?"

"Pulse every thirty minutes or so. Temp every hour. If she starts acting uncomfortable, don't stay in here with her. I'd hate to have her roll on you."

"Got it."

"Watch out for any piglets."

"Oh, ha ha."

Levi took the quilt into the empty stall next door. After gathering a big enough mound of hay, he spread the quilt over it and lay down. He didn't intend to sleep, but he welcomed the chance to close his eyes and rest. He made himself comfortable and closed his eyes. When he opened them again, it was growing light outside the windows.

He turned his head to see Wing was on her feet. Her eyes were brighter. She was nibbling on some hay. Isaac was brushing her.

Levi sat up. "Someone looks better."

Isaac chuckled. "I know it ain't me."

Levi rose and stretched his stiff muscles. "What's her temp?"

"Normal ever since I took over. She got restless once. I gave her another dose of pain medication and that seemed to help. She's been on her feet ever since."

Levi leaned on the stall divider and held out his hand. She came over to investigate and nibble at his fingers. "You are feeling better."

"Do you think she is over the worst?"

"We'll keep her on light feedings for a few days to make sure it doesn't come back, but she is starting to look like her old self. Thanks, Isaac."

"I didn't do anything but sit in the corner and sing her a lullaby."

"You always did have a sweet voice."

Isaac laughed. "That's not what you usually say about my singing."

Levi grinned. "Maybe my hearing is getting better."

THREE DAYS LATER Sarah was sitting with Laura Beth and Ruth on the front porch while Grace pushed Caleb and Henrietta in the swing. Caleb was standing up and peering over the back at Grace. He tried to grab her each time the swing came back to her. Henrietta kept one arm around him so he couldn't tumble off. Sarah, her sister and her friend were all busy snapping beans as they chatted.

When the children grew tired of their game, Caleb got down. Grace took his hand. "Do you want to go see Pumpernickel?"

Sarah glanced at the others. "Who is Pumpernickel?"

Grace grinned at her. "The new calf. Levi said it didn't have a name."

"I guess it doesn't," Henrietta said. "But why call her Pumpernickel?"

Grace shrugged. "I like that name."

The children went off, with Grace holding Caleb's hand and walking slow so he could keep up with her.

Henrietta chuckled. "I guess our new little heifer has a name."

"Grace gets quite creative with the names for our bottle-fed baby lambs. This year we have Cotton Ball, Muddy Feet, Sprinkles and Popcorn. Muddy Feet will be easy to pick out when she's older because she does have black feet. Sprinkles has tiny black dots in her wool, but Popcorn and Cotton Ball are plain white."

Sarah noticed Henrietta was biting on her thumbnail. "Is something wrong?"

"I was trying to think of a way to ask Laura Beth a personal question."

Laura Beth stopped snapping beans. "Just ask."

"I know you are recently remarried, as are you, Ruth, so I will ask you this, too. Do you sometimes feel that you're being unfaithful to your first husbands?"

Laura Beth shook her head. "I never felt that way. I know Micah only wanted what was best for me."

"I struggled with that question," Ruth said. "I had a hard time letting go of my belief that he was the only man I should love, not the only man I could love."

"What made you change your mind?"

Laura Beth and Ruth smiled at each other. "*Gott* changed our minds for us," Laura Beth said. "He brought me a man who needed to be loved and He gave me the courage to love him."

"That's exactly right," Ruth added. "Owen needed a home and someone to love him. I resisted for quite a while, but Grace helped win me over. She can be a very persuasive little girl."

"Are you thinking of marrying again?" Sarah asked.

Henrietta looked down. "There's not much point to it at my age, or at his age, for that matter."

Ruth chuckled. "I don't believe age has anything to do with our hearts. We are just as capable of loving someone at eighteen as we are at eighty."

"There's no time limit on loving someone," Sarah said. "At least that's what Ernest told me."

Henrietta leaned back in the swing. "He said that, did he?"

Sarah nodded. "He told me that when you were in the hospital and he was worried about you."

"Worried about me! He had a funny way of showing it."

"He was deeply ashamed that he upset you that night. I know you have forgiven him."

Henrietta considered the statement and then nodded. "*Ja*, I have forgiven him for that. He needs to return the favor. I've waited a long time to hear him say he has forgiven me."

"For what?" Sarah asked softly.

"For betraying his trust. I'd rather not talk about it."

Ruth shook her bowl. "I think we have enough for our first batch." She and Laura Beth took their bowls of snapped beans inside.

Henrietta stared off into space for the longest time.

"What are you looking at?" Sarah followed her line of sight.

"Levi."

Her son had come out into the corral with Wing. The horse was making a remarkable recovery. She began prancing around him. He took a step to the left and Wing altered her course to brush by him, tossing her head and shaking her mane. He took two quick steps back and she circled him again, just brushing past his shoulder.

As Sarah watched, the filly trotted up behind him and snatched his hat off his head then galloped away with it in her teeth. Levi sank cross-legged to the ground with his elbows propped on his knees. Wing came charging back to him, skidding to a stop a few feet away. She shook her head, still holding on to his hat. He put one hand in the air as if to take it from her. She wheeled away and made a big circle before coming back to him.

Sarah had never seen anyone play with a horse like it was a big dog. Levi put his hand in the air again. She dropped the hat in his lap and lowered her head to his chest. He stroked her neck then looped his arms around her, and she lifted him to his feet. He stood with his arms around her and she laid her head on his shoulder. They remained motionless for several long moments. Then he rubbed her forehead and she darted away.

"I was wrong to make him leave Pennsylvania," Henrietta said. "He has those horses in his blood the same way his father did. Walter would never have been happy here. I made a mistake insisting Levi come with me and now I don't know how to undo it."

"You could tell him he is free to leave."

Henrietta turned to gaze at Sarah. "I don't want him to go. I'm afraid I'll never see him again. I want him to be happy here with me and his brother."

Sarah turned her gaze back to Levi. He was watching Wing trot around the small corral. Her heart expanded with emotion when he looked her way and smiled. There was no doubt about it. She was falling for him.

She had tried to resist the temptation, argued her way around it, but she had to face it. She cared deeply for Isaac, but it was Levi who came to her in her dreams. Levi who made her heart beat faster. She didn't want him to leave, but Henrietta was wrong. Levi would never be truly happy away from the world of his racing horses.

Sarah heard the familiar *putt-putt* of Ernest's tractor coming up the lane. Henrietta heard it, too. She sat up and straightened her dress. "Sarah, is my *kapp* on straight?"

"It looks fine."

Ernest pulled up and stopped in front of the house. He waved, climbed down and strolled up to the porch. "It's good to see you enjoying your swing, Henrietta."

"I haven't gotten around to repainting it yet, but I will."

He chuckled. "I don't doubt it for a minute. How have you been?"

"Fair."

"Well, you look better than fair. You look down-right healthy."

"That's kind of you to say so. Proves you're no doctor."

Sarah choked back a laugh. Ernest hooked his thumbs in his suspenders. "I was wondering if you'd like to join me for a picnic at the lake. You and your family, of course." He saw Ruth come out of the kitchen. "I'm hosting a picnic at the lake, and I'd like your family to come, too. What do you say, Henny? Will you join me there?"

Henrietta turned pink and then pale. She straightened her shoulders. "It will be good for the boys to have some relaxation before the harvest starts. We'll come."

"*Goot*. You know the place."

She frowned at him. "I know it as well as you do. Go on, you mean old man. We'll meet you there."

He nodded and drove away. Sarah took Henrietta by the elbow. "Are you okay?"

"Dying might have been easier," she muttered. She looked at Sarah. "I'm okay. Tell my sons we're going on a picnic."

An hour later Isaac drove the tractor into the clearing by the lake below the Miller farm. Ernest was waiting for them, but he wasn't alone. Owen, Ruth, Faron and Grace were there, too. The men were already fishing while Ruth sat on a quilt spread in the shade of a walnut tree. Grace came running up to meet them with her growing puppy at her heels.

Sarah and Levi carried their basket and quilt over beside Ruth. Isaac took his pole down to the lake.

"Nice day for a picnic, isn't it," Ruth said.

"Very nice," Sarah agreed.

"Do you do this often?" Levi asked.

Ruth shook her head. "We don't. Ernest announced he was hosting a picnic at the lake and asked us to be here."

"I wonder what he's up to." Sarah was watching the older man fidget with his rod and reel.

"I'm sure we'll find out," Ruth said.

"*Mamm*, may I have a cookie?" Grace asked hopefully.

Ruth opened her blue-and-white cooler and rummaged in it. "I think I left them in the trailer." She rose and went back to their tractor with Grace and the puppy skipping along beside her.

Henrietta had walked to the edge of the water where Ernest was fishing. After a moment, she returned to Levi's side. "I believe I'll take a short walk."

He got to his feet. "I'll come with you."

"I'd rather be alone, dear. *Danki*. Go ahead and eat without me." She strolled into the woods, following a narrow path.

A few minutes later Ernest came up to Levi. "The fish aren't biting here. I'm going to try a better spot."

Sarah looked up from the plates she was setting out and saw him walking down the path that Levi's mother had taken a short time ago. He wasn't carrying his fish-

ing pole. She tugged on Levi's hand. "I think he is following your mother?"

"Grace? Where are you?" Owen's voice interrupted
their conversation as he stopped beside the quilts. "Have
you seen her?" he asked.

"She was with Ruth a few minutes ago by your tractor," Sarah said.

Ruth was already on her way to Owen's side. "One
minute she was with me and the next time I looked
down she was gone."

Sarah looked at Levi. "Let's see if she followed the
path down to Ernest's fishing spot."

"I agree."

"We'll check and see if she went up to visit the
Millers." Ruth and Owen headed in that direction.

Sarah and Levi walked through the woods with
Sarah in the lead and Levi a few steps behind her. Several times they called for Grace but got no answer.

They reached the clearing where Levi had first
pulled Sarah out of the water. Did he remember the
episode as fondly as she had come to regard it? She
glanced at his face and saw a look of tenderness in his
eyes. He quickly looked away and walked to the water's
edge. "Check for her footprints in the mud."

They searched along the water's edge but found no
trace that a child had been there before them.

"We found her!" The shout came from the direction
of the Millers' farm. Sarah thought it was Owen's voice,
but she couldn't be sure.

She grinned at Levi. "That's *goot*."

Suddenly he held up one finger. "Do you hear that?"

Sarah listened intently. "It sounds like voices."

"It sounds like my mother."

Sarah saw a second path leading away from the Miller farm and deeper into the woods. She and Levi ventured along it until he stopped. She looked around him and saw another smaller clearing where a knee-high shelf of rock provided a perfect seating place under the spreading branches of an enormous walnut tree. Two people sat together on the bench-like rock. Ernest and Henrietta. They had their arms around each other as they kissed. Sarah tugged on Levi's arm, trying to get him to come away. Instead, he cleared his throat and stepped into the open.

"It's clear the two of you have settled your differences. Would you mind telling me what's going on, Mother?"

CHAPTER SEVENTEEN

ERNEST SMILED AT Levi over Henrietta's head then gazed at her face. "Beautiful woman, are you ready to face everyone?"

Henrietta pulled away from him and turned to Levi. "I'm sure you would like an explanation."

"I would," he said, staring at them.

Sarah moved in front of him and gently pushed him backward. "No explanations are necessary. We will leave you in peace."

Henrietta laughed. "It's all right, Sarah. I know our actions have confused you." She looked at Ernest. "Do you mind if I tell them?"

He patted her cheek with his hand. "It is your story to tell."

She caught his hand beneath hers and turned her face to place a kiss on his palm. Then she looked at Sarah and Levi and drew a deep breath. "Come and sit down. Where shall I start?"

"With the first time I kissed you?" Ernest suggested with a glint of mischief in his eyes.

"We were in the first grade, and you did it on a dare. I think that's a little far back."

He chuckled. "It was the day I knew you were the one I would marry."

"It was the day I learned you were an incorrigible mischief maker. I think I will start with the year we were both eighteen."

"It's your story, dear. This was our meeting place."

"We had been friends since grade school, you see," Henrietta said.

"We would both sneak away to spend time here together. As we got older it seemed only natural to plan on spending the rest of our lives together." Ernest patted her hand. "I thought we had an understanding between us. We were going to be married."

Henrietta nodded and grew somber. "Then Walter came to spend the summer with Ernest's family, and I fell head over heels in love with someone new and exciting who loved me as deeply as I loved him."

"With my father," Levi said, making sure he had the facts straight.

"With my best friend," Ernest added, sadness filling his eyes.

"We never intended to betray you," Henrietta said softly.

"I believed that, but it didn't lessen the hurt. I saw the two of you together, here at this spot. Our place, Henny. I couldn't believe my eyes. You were in his arms. I knew I'd lost you. I was such a fool. I never saw it coming."

Henrietta cupped Ernest's cheek. "We were trying to decide how to tell you when you came upon us that day. I'll never forget the look on your face. I knew then what a terrible thing I had done to you. I betrayed our friendship. I never imagined it was possible to love two men at the same time. I didn't know how to choose between you."

"But you chose Father." Levi waited for her to confirm what he already knew.

She looked at Ernest. "Ernest made the choice for me. He told me to marry Walter."

"I believed he was the man you wanted. The better man."

She tipped her head to gaze at him. "If you had only told me that you loved me, I would've stayed with you. You never once said those words."

He gave her a wry smile. "Henrietta, I had been in love with you since the first grade. We were as close as friends could be. To my shame, I didn't know you needed to hear those words. I thought they were etched in your heart the way they were etched in mine."

"When you told me to go with him, I thought you didn't love me the way Walter did. If you had only spoken up. When I got your shawl in the mail, your wedding gift to me, and read your note that said..." Her voice trailed away.

"That since I would never hold you in my arms again, I wanted you to think of me every time you wrapped it around your shoulders and know I was sending you comfort and warmth," he said softly.

Henrietta nodded. "I knew then that I had hurt you more than words could express. But I was married, and I couldn't undo my vows."

Levi tipped his head to the side. "I still don't understand—why were you so angry with Ernest when we first arrived here?"

"Because I was ill. I thought it wouldn't be long before I joined your father. I came all this way to apologize to Ernest, beg his forgiveness and spend my last days near him." She glared at him. "But he didn't come to see me."

She slapped him playfully on the chest. "The first thing he does is ask my boys to go fishing with him! I spent a lifetime believing I had broken this man's heart. When he told me he was taking you boys to this spot, I thought he was going to tell you the story of how I went behind his back to be with Walter here in the place where Ernest and I had made plans to marry. I thought he was implying that he refused to forgive me."

She laid a hand on Ernest's cheek. "It was guilt that clouded my thinking. I should've known you wouldn't do something so unkind."

"To tell the truth, Henny, when I saw you standing on those porch steps looking as beautiful as you did thirty years ago, every word I had ever dreamed about saying to you flew right out of my head."

"I hope you have remembered them all," Sarah said with a kindly smile for him.

"I might need another kiss or two to jog my memory." He leaned over and gave Henrietta a smooch. He looked at Levi and Sarah. "You two *kinder* should run along and leave your elders to mend their mistakes."

Sarah rose and kissed Henrietta on both cheeks. "He's not much of a catch. If you grow tired of his foolishness, I suggest you throw him back."

Ernest laughed. "Sarah, how can you say such unkind things about me?"

She grinned, leaned over and kissed his cheek. "Because I know you so well."

Sarah straightened, held out her hand and pulled Levi to his feet. "I don't understand." He continued staring at his mother.

Sarah cupped his chin and turned his face to look at her. "Ernest is in love with your mother. Your mother is in love with him. She loved your father dearly—never think otherwise. Now she's about to receive a proposal of marriage from someone who has quietly loved her for thirty years. What's not to understand? We should get back to the picnic."

She led him back up the path. A few yards on, Levi pulled her to a stop.

"Should I tell Isaac about this new romance?"

"Let your mother do it. It's her moment."

He squeezed her hand. "Wise words from a wise woman. I'll take them to heart."

They arrived back at the picnic to see Isaac beaming over a catfish that must have weighed twenty pounds. Owen, Ruth, Faron and Grace were exclaiming over it. Isaac grinned at Levi. "Top this, big brother."

Levi shook his head. "I'm not even going to try."

Isaac lowered his prize. "Where have the two of you been?"

Levi gazed at Sarah's beautiful face. "We were searching for Grace."

"She was found quite a while ago. Didn't you hear

Owen shouting that?" Isaac's voice held an edge of annoyance.

"We did, but then our stroll took an interesting turn." Levi hadn't taken his eyes off Sarah's face. She gave a tiny shake of her head. He smiled. Let Isaac stew about what may or may not have happened between them.

"They ran into us," Ernest said as he walked out holding Henrietta's hand. His eyes widened at the sight of the fish lying at Isaac's feet. "Oh, that's a fine blue cat. What bait were you using?"

Henrietta jerked on his hand. "Do not even think about putting a pole back in the water."

He straightened. "Right." He looked over the people gathered in front of him. "We have an announcement to make, and I wanted my family and Henny's family to hear the news from us first. She has agreed to marry me."

There was stunned silence from everyone. He gave Henrietta a beseeching look. "Can I go back to fishing now?"

She rolled her eyes. "Oh, if you must."

He gave her a quick peck on the cheek. "That's what I love about you." He went down to his chair and picked up his fishing pole.

Henrietta held out her arms to her sons. "I hope you won't mind having him for a stepfather."

Levi embraced her. "Not at all. I know he will take great care of you."

"He will," she whispered.

Everyone gathered around to voice their surprise

and offer delighted congratulations except Isaac. He was still standing over his fish with a bemused expression on his face.

SARAH TOOK PITY on Isaac and moved to lay a hand on his arm. "It will be okay. You should be happy for your mother."

"I am, I guess."

Levi joined them, standing close to Sarah. "It seems that love blooms everywhere when spring is in the air."

Isaac looked him up and down. "Has it?" There was a challenge in his tone.

Levi smiled at Sarah. "I think so."

"What does that mean?" Isaac demanded.

Levi laughed. "While you were angling for a catfish, I was angling for something much sweeter. Isn't that right, Sarah?"

"Did you sneak off to try for another kiss?" Isaac demanded. "I told you to watch out for him."

She opted to remove herself from what was clearly becoming a tense situation between the brothers. "I think I'll make everyone sandwiches. And please behave, both of you. I don't want you to ruin your mother's big day."

Levi touched the fish with the toe of his boot. "You should put him back in the lake before he dies."

"You don't need to tell me what to do anymore. I'm old enough to make my own decisions." Isaac picked up the fish and stomped off.

Sarah went back to the quilt. Ernest's family was still gathered around Henrietta down by the lake, talking about wedding plans. Sarah sat on the blue-and-white quilt and opened the red cooler she had hurriedly packed.

Levi sank down beside her. "That went well. I'm surprised he didn't punch me."

"I'm surprised I didn't punch you." Sarah wasn't happy with his behavior. "You should be thankful we Amish are against any type of violence."

She layered ham slices on bread and spread mayo over it with a plastic knife. "He thinks we were necking out in the woods. What possessed you to goad him with your well-chosen innuendos? I'm not a bone for the two of you to squabble over."

"Hey, I thought you agreed to pretend to like me?"

"I'm not that good of an actress." She shoved the sandwich at him. "Now that your mother has someone to take care of her, your brother is all that stands in the way of you getting back to Lancaster, is that it? Is that what you were doing? Trying to make him jealous?"

He laid the sandwich aside. "Going back was always my plan. Do I need to remind you of your plan to settle with a hardworking man here in your little slice of paradise and have tons of babies?"

She looked down. "Don't make it sound like that."

"Like what?"

"Like it's something to be made fun of. It isn't."

"I'm sorry. I was unkind while you have been nothing but wonderful taking care of my mother, Isaac and… me."

"I forgive you."

"Maybe you shouldn't just yet." He placed a finger under her chin and raised her face to his. He kissed her gently. Sarah leaned into his touch, wanting more as her heart began hammering in her chest.

He pulled away and rose to his feet. "You're a fine actress. I could almost believe you like me."

He walked away, and Sarah closed her eyes. *Oh, Levi. I wasn't acting.*

She didn't look to see if Isaac was watching them. She wanted to believe Levi had kissed her because he wanted to. One brief kiss that she would cherish for the rest of her life.

HE SHOULDN'T HAVE kissed her.

Levi jammed his hat down on his head and went to pretend he was fishing until his mother and Ernest decided it was time to go home. He didn't bother baiting his hook. He simply tossed the line in the water and watched the bobber float on the placid lake. If only his insides were as calm. Sarah had him twisted up as bad as any tangled fishing line.

Did she know how sweet her kiss was? Did she know how hard it was for him to walk away when all he wanted was to take her in his arms?

His pretend courting of Sarah Yoder was officially over.

He wasn't going to put himself through pain like this again. He glanced her way, but she had joined the group with his mother.

Why did he have to fall for someone so wrong for him and so right for his brother? He understood how his father must have felt falling for his best friend's girl.

Gloriously happy and sick inside all at the same time. It wasn't a comfortable way to live.

"Levi, are you upset with me?"

He looked up to see his mother standing beside him. He managed a smile for her. "Of course not. I'm happy for you. Surprised but happy."

"You were looking lost in thought a moment ago. Care to tell me what's on your mind?"

"Were you happy with *Daed*? I mean, really happy? Did you love him more than Ernest? Or did your love for him grow over time?"

"I wondered if that was what was bothering you. You are so like your father. I see him in you every day, and I feel his love looking out of your eyes. I can't say I loved one man more than the other. I do know I had shared so much with Ernest that we never seemed to need words between us. It wasn't like that with your father. I had to learn to know him. In that way I grew to love him more."

"But you hated his work."

"I saw a terrible accident on the training track when I was pregnant with you. Two of the trainers were racing each other. One man was killed in front of my eyes. Your father wasn't involved, but it could have easily been him. I had a child on the way. I was hundreds of miles from everyone I knew. I couldn't bear the thought of losing him. I made him promise never to race again. He agreed. That was when I knew how much he loved me. He gave up training, the thing he loved most."

"Did he grow to resent that promise? Can a man be satisfied doing something he doesn't love?"

"Did we quarrel about it? Sure. It was less money and more work for him, but he never raced against another driver. Was he satisfied with his life? When you were born, he was over the moon. I don't think he ever looked back."

She gripped Levi's shoulder. "You can give it up, settle here with us and be happy. I know you can."

He looked toward Sarah playing a game with Grace. Was it possible to leave one love for another and find happiness? As he watched her, Isaac came to sit beside her. She smiled and laughed at something he said. Grace demanded a piggyback ride. Isaac swung her to his shoulders and charged off at a gallop while Sarah called encouragement.

She met his gaze and stopped smiling. He looked down. Sarah, Isaac and himself. Which one of them was going to own a broken heart when it was all said and done? He couldn't do it to Isaac or Sarah. That meant he was the one who had to leave.

CHAPTER EIGHTEEN

THAT EVENING SARAH sat on the stone wall overlooking the lavender fields as the sun set. Lightning bugs began blinking in the dusk. Their flashing seemed in time with her thoughts. *Isaac, Levi, Isaac, Levi.*

She had been so sure of what she wanted, of what she thought was God's plan for her. *Foolish, foolish, foolish*, the tiny lights said.

She had grown to care for Isaac dearly, but she was in love with Levi. She pressed her hands to her chest. The warmth of happiness that filled her heart as she admitted her love proved it was real. Aggravating, annoying, marvelous man that he was, she had fallen hard for Levi while trying to fall in love with Isaac.

But Levi wanted her to marry his brother.

The sobering thought drained the warmth from her chest. Levi had convinced her that was his goal until he kissed her.

She pressed her fingers to her lips, remembering the feel of Levi's mouth against hers. Would a man who wanted her to marry another kiss her so tenderly? Was he the one who was good at acting?

She had to know.

The only way to find out was to ask him.

What if he did admit he cared for her? He wasn't staying in Cedar Grove. So what was the point of telling him how she felt, only to watch him leave and take her heart with him?

"What if he says it was all an act? How silly would that make me feel?"

About as foolish as a woman talking to fireflies in the darkness.

Only Levi could answer her question. She got up, went into the house and up to her bedroom, but she never really slept.

Bright and early the following morning, Sarah arrived at the Raber farm ready to confront Levi and find out where she stood. What happened after that was up to him, but she couldn't go on like this.

Ernest turned into their lane ahead of her. He tipped his hat to her. She saw Henrietta was sitting on the porch swing looking as bright and happy.

He took the steps two at a time and came to a halt in front of her. "Have you had a change of heart?"

"You old goose, why would I do that?"

"*Goot.* I was hoping you might want to take a little walk with me this morning. Only if you're feeling up to it."

"I believe I would like that." She gestured to Sarah. "Would you fetch me my cane, please?"

"It's on the back of your chair." Sarah walked over and handed it to her.

"How silly—I forgot I brought it out with me." Henrietta seemed flustered.

Ernest came closer and helped her out of her chair. "If my head wasn't tied on, I would forget it most days."

Henrietta smiled at him. "I imagine it's our age."

"I reckon you're right."

They walked off together along the lane, smiling at each other and holding hands. Sarah was happy for them both.

She looked for Levi, but he and his horse were nowhere in sight. She wanted to speak to him before she lost her nerve because it was only hanging on by a frayed thread.

She walked down toward the barn. She didn't see Levi or his horse inside. She heard something toward the back and followed the sound. Isaac was stacking bales of hay along the wall of the alleyway. He lifted his hat and wiped the sweat off his forehead with the back of his shirtsleeve. "Hi, Sarah. You're just the person I was hoping to see."

"I was looking for Levi."

He frowned but quickly smiled at her. "I haven't seen him. Faron told me there is a singing tonight at the school. It's a program for some of the senior citizens. I thought it would be fun if we went together."

"Not tonight, Isaac."

His cheerful expression vanished. His disappointment almost made her change her mind. She truly cared for him. Hurting him was the last thing she wanted to do. "I'm sorry. I have a lot on my mind right now."

He nodded. "Sure. Another time, maybe. Well, the hay bales won't march out of the meadow and stack themselves in here. I'll see you later."

"Of course." She watched him walk outside, wishing she cared for him as much as she cared for Levi.

"What is wrong with you?"

Sarah almost jumped out of her skin, startled by Levi's harsh whisper behind her. She spun around. He pulled open the top half of the Dutch door and leaned in, frowning at her. Wing stood behind him, stretching her neck to scratch it on the door frame.

Sarah looked at Levi in disbelief. "Are you spying on me?"

"Of course not. I merely happened to be passing by and overheard some of your conversation."

She glared at him. "You were spying. You should be ashamed of yourself, Levi Raber."

"I should be ashamed of myself?" He pointed a finger at her. "You are the one who messed up a perfectly good chance to go on a date with my brother."

She planted her hands on her hips. "I'm not in the mood to go to a singing tonight. I need to tell you something."

"Maybe you can't carry a tune in a bucket, and you don't want my brother to know that."

She took a deep breath. "I've been trying to convince myself that you are not an awful person, but you are making that really hard. There is nothing wrong with my singing voice."

Wing nudged him with her head. He pushed her aside. "Okay, I'm sorry. That was harsh of me. I apologize."

"For spying on me or just for insulting me?"

"Now who is trying to be an awful person? I said I was sorry. We Amish must forgive those who insult us."

"I can forgive but that doesn't mean I have to like it."

His mouth dropped open. "I'm not sure that counts as forgiveness."

"It's the best I can do. Take it or leave it."

She turned away, not even sure why she was so mad at him except that he was pushing her toward Isaac and not pulling her close for another kiss. Tears stung her eyes and she fought them back, but it was a losing battle. She sniffled and wiped her eyes. Crying didn't help anything. All it did was give her a headache.

"Hey, are you crying?" He almost sounded concerned.

"What if I am?"

She heard him open the lower half of the door. A moment later Wing was nuzzling at her face. Levi appeared at her other side. "Wing doesn't like it when people cry. It makes her feel sad."

Sarah couldn't look at him. She put her arm around Wing's neck and laid her face against the filly's silky soft warm hide. "I don't know why she would feel sad. She's not the one acting like a jerk."

"I told her that. I guess it makes her feel sad that her owner is being a jerk. I didn't mean to make you cry." He offered his handkerchief. "It's clean. Mostly."

She choked on a laugh. "What does 'mostly' mean?"

"I used it to wrap my biscuit in so I wouldn't get dirt on it while I was grooming Wing this morning."

She took it from him and blew her nose. "It does kinda smell like dough." She dabbed at her eyes then put the handkerchief in her pocket.

"Do you want to tell me why you're upset, or do you want me to disappear and leave you alone?"

She shook her head. One instant he was making her cry and the next instant he was making her laugh. Life around Levi was not dull. She struggled to find a way to say what she was feeling without making a fool of herself.

"Well?" he asked. "Should I go get Isaac for you?"

She closed her eyes. This had been a mistake. She couldn't bare her soul and have him say he didn't love her in return.

THE DESIRE TO take Sarah in his arms was so strong Levi had to use every ounce of willpower he possessed to keep his arms at his sides. Of all the women in the world to choose from, why was he attracted to the one who wanted his brother? The Lord had surely designed a painful test for him. He would not covet his brother's wife.

"Tell me why you are unhappy," he said gently.

"It's nothing. Women cry sometimes. It doesn't always mean we're unhappy."

He was pretty sure that wasn't what she wanted to tell him. "That's confusing. How is a fellow supposed to know if you are crying because you're unhappy or for some other reason?"

"Your mother is getting better by leaps and bounds. She's out taking a walk with Ernest now."

"How is that a bad thing?"

"It's not. It's a wonderful thing. Only it means you don't need me to take care of the house anymore. She'll be able to do it soon. If it gets a bit much, you can have Angela and Mary Jane come over and help once a week or so."

"So that's why you're sad."

"*Nee*, that's why I'm happy, because your mother's getting so much better. These are happy tears."

He pushed his hands into his pockets. "Okay. Happy tears. You know you can always come over just to say hello. I know Mother would like to visit with you. And so would Isaac."

"What about you?"

He took a step back. "What about me?"

"Are you going to miss me?" she asked softly.

He turned his face away and began petting Wing. "Sure. I'll miss you. I'd like to say I'll write, but I'm no better at that than Isaac is."

"Oh. You're going to Pennsylvania, aren't you?"

Why did she have to sound so sad? He blew out a deep breath and looked her way. "Yeah, I'm going to Pennsylvania."

"When?"

"The end of next week."

She spun around to face him. "So soon? When did you decide this?"

"Yesterday at the lake."

"I see. Does your mother know?"

"I've been waiting to break the news to her. I was hoping that Isaac would have some good news to tell her before I unloaded my bad news on her. Isaac swallowed my performance at the lake hook, line and sinker. He thinks I'm trying to steal you away from him."

"Your performance?" A dull blush crept up her cheeks.

He didn't know pushing her away would be so hard.

"I see. Is there anything or anyone that could convince you to stay here?" The quiet pleading in her voice cut his heart like a jagged piece of glass.

She had her dream and he couldn't be a part of that. He had a promise to fulfill. "Not a thing that comes to mind."

He saw her flinch then lift her head. "You know, I think I'll go to the singing with Isaac after all." She walked away with lagging steps.

His hands ached from wanting to touch her face. His chest ached from the pain of losing her. How was he going to live the rest of his life without her?

SARAH RODE BESIDE Isaac in his buggy as they traveled home from the singing at the school. As the light faded, Sarah wondered if her affection for Levi would fade in the same way if she gave it enough time.

She glanced at Isaac. She should've been happy to be alone with him, but she struggled to find something to say that wasn't boring.

She never had that trouble when she was with Levi. There always seemed to be something to talk about. Until he told her he was leaving.

"You're quiet this evening," Isaac said, looking her way.

"I'm sorry. I was just enjoying the sunset." The air was cool with a slight breeze that kept the bugs away after the heat of the day. On either side of the road the green wheat fields waved in the breeze, rippling like the water on the lake. It was mid-May and the wheat would soon turn golden, the color of the sunset.

"Things could use a rain." Isaac surveyed the corn on his side of the road. It was two feet high already. It was hard to believe it would grow to eight feet by the end of the summer.

"We've been blessed with fine weather so far this year," she said. "Last year was dry. The year before that we had more water than we knew what to do with." Was the weather really all they had to talk about?

"Your mother seems to be getting along well." She tried to change the subject to something more substantial.

"She sure enjoys having you around."

Sarah smiled softly. "I enjoy her company. We've become good friends."

The silence stretched on for another few minutes. Isaac cleared his throat. "There is something I want to talk to you about."

She turned to look at him. "Okay."

"I wonder if I might court you."

Once, being courted by Isaac had been exactly what she wanted. Levi had ruined that for her. She didn't want to hurt Isaac. Maybe he could make her forget Levi if she gave him the chance.

"I reckon it would be okay."

"I thought maybe you might prefer Levi. He has paid a lot of attention to you."

Only to make you jealous.

"We want such different things, and besides, he's

leaving." Levi had a dream to follow but it didn't include her.

"I know he has his heart set on going back to Pennsylvania." There was a wistful tone in Isaac's voice that made her look at him sharply.

"Is that what you want? Do you want to go back to Pennsylvania?"

He shook his head. "There's nothing there for me now. I like it here. I can learn to be a good farmer with Ernest's help."

"She is still there. The girl that made you throw away your phone."

"That's over and done. I'm never going to see her again."

"Then we are both free, and courting is the next step. Let's see where it leads." Maybe she could even grow to love Isaac in time if Levi wasn't around.

"Great. I know *Mamm* will be thrilled to hear it. You've made a big change in my life, Sarah. I found where I belong. I think we might be meant for each other."

Why did it sound like he was trying harder to convince himself than her?

He smiled brightly, but his smile didn't reach his eyes. "What are you doing tomorrow evening?"

She stared at her clasped hands. "Nothing. I'm free all week."

"Levi, can I talk to you about something?"

Levi lowered Jasper's hoof to the ground and patted the gelding's hip. He was trying to get as much work done around the place as he could before he left at the end of the week. He worked hard at everything he could think to do to keep his mind off Sarah. It hadn't helped. At least he didn't have to worry about avoiding her. She hadn't been around since the afternoon he told her their kiss had been an act on his part. He must be a far better actor than he'd ever imagined because she believed him.

"If you can talk while I work." He turned to face his brother. Isaac was standing outside the stall, leaning on the top board.

"Maybe later, then." Isaac started to turn away.

It dawned on Levi that his brother had something serious on his mind. "Hold on. I have time now."

"You sure? *Goot.* I need your advice."

"About what?"

"I asked Sarah if I could court her, and she said yes."

"Is that where you've been every evening this past week?" Levi had suspected as much.

"*Ja*, I've been seeing her. I think she's the woman I should marry someday."

Levi hoped he didn't look like he had just been kicked in the stomach. He bent over to retrieve the horseshoe he had pried off Jasper's hind hoof as he tried to catch his breath. This had been his plan all along, but he wasn't thrilled. His victory was like ashes in his mouth. The faint hope he cherished in his heart that he and Sarah could somehow be together flickered out. "Is that so?"

"*Mamm* loves her. She'll be happy about it for sure."

Levi loved Sarah, too. He hadn't realized how much until this very moment. "What's not to love? She's a wonderful woman." A woman who could never be his. He kept his face averted so Isaac couldn't read the pain in his eyes.

"I think she is, too. You and I have had our differences and I know you wanted to court her, so I need to make sure you're okay with this."

Tell him no. Tell him he's wasting his time. He'll listen to me. Then I can court her.

He couldn't do that to his brother. Or to Sarah.

Isaac was the right man for her. If only Levi hadn't kissed her, leaving would be so much easier. "Sarah's a great gal, but if you are that serious about her, I'll step aside. I think she always liked you better anyway."

"It means you won't get the farm."

Levi almost laughed out loud. "I'll get over it. You're the real farmer anyway."

Isaac concentrated on straightening the harnesses on their hooks. "I know I talked a lot about not wanting to marry, but I'm ready for a new start. I want to stay here and farm this land. I want to make something of myself. I know Sarah could help with that. She's good for me. It may seem like I'm rushing into this, but I'm ready to give it a chance and see if we are meant for each other."

"It doesn't sound like you need my advice."

"Maybe I just needed to say it out loud. *Mamm* is almost well. I think she'll be back to her old self in a few weeks. She's happy with Ernest. They'll be married soon. Sarah and I can take care of her if anything happens. The way I see it, you can return to Pennsylvania without worrying about us."

"That's good because I'm leaving on Friday." Going back wouldn't be the same now that he had met Sarah. Now that he had fallen in love with her.

Isaac stopped fooling with the tack and faced Levi. "You are?"

"I've hired a trailer to transport Wing to Arnold's stable. I'll train her there."

Isaac smiled. "I'm happy for you. I know it's what you wanted. Have you told *Mamm*?"

"I will today."

"You'll be glad to be free of me. I've been a millstone around your neck long enough."

Levi shook his head. "You have never been that to me."

"Maybe not, but I've always been the little brother you needed to look after. Anyway, if I can work up the courage to ask Sarah to marry me, you'll have to come back for the wedding."

"What will you do if she turns you down?" What if she did? Levi held his breath as he waited for his brother's answer.

"I'll probably pester her until she says yes. *Gott* brought her into my life for a reason at a time when I needed her the most. I do need her. Without her I'm going to fall apart or go back to my old ways. I have to believe it means we are meant for each other."

"You'll have to join the church. I know you weren't keen on that at one time."

"It won't be that bad. It's not like I have much choice if I want to wed Sarah, and think how happy *Mamm* will be."

"Then I wish you the best of luck."

The ceremony couldn't take place until after they finished their baptismal classes and joined the church. It would be several months at the earliest. Unless distance dulled his feelings for Sarah, he couldn't stand by and watch her wed his brother. He would be back in Pennsylvania by then and he'd find a good excuse not to attend. "You'd better treat her right from now on."

"I will."

As his brother left the barn, Levi sat on a bale of hay in the alleyway. He had heard it called a broken heart often enough, but he never knew it was a true physical pain that would slice through his chest and make it hard to breathe. He might love Sarah with all his being, but his brother needed her. How could he be selfish enough to contemplate wooing her away from Isaac?

Would it be right to tell Sarah how he felt? She cared about him. He'd known that the moment he had kissed her because she had kissed him back. But how could he ask her to choose him over his brother?

He sat for a long time trying to imagine a scenario where no one ended up being hurt. He couldn't see a way out of his dilemma. Levi knew he had to leave.

It was the best thing he could do for Sarah and for Isaac. That way the two people he cared most about would be happy. They deserved their happiness more than he did. He hadn't fulfilled his promise to his father yet.

He got up and headed to the house to break the news of his leaving to his mother.

"I'D LIKE TO talk to you for a little bit, Sarah."

She looked up from the mending she was doing for Henrietta. "What is it, Isaac?"

He shot a glance at his mother and Ernest playing a game of checkers on a small table in between their chairs.

He gestured toward the door with a nod of his head. "Come outside with me."

He sounded unusually serious for Isaac.

She followed him outside, where he sat down on the swing. She took a seat, too, remembering the way Levi's lips had felt against hers when he first kissed her in this very spot to make Isaac jealous. The wonderful kiss she shared with him at the lake was the one she would remember him by.

Isaac seemed preoccupied. Sarah looked across the farmyard to see if Levi was exercising Wing. The horse had made a complete recovery, but Levi keep a close eye on her so that the colic didn't recur. Sarah couldn't see him. Maybe he was in the barn. She hadn't seen him in more than a week. If she was being honest, she would have to admit that was why she had suggested they spend the day at Isaac's home instead of hers for a change. Levi was leaving and she needed to see him.

"I have something I want to ask you."

She turned her attention back to Isaac. He sounded so serious. "All right."

"We've become pretty good friends, haven't we? We've gone out every day for almost two weeks. You aren't tired of me, are you?" He looked so nervous that she almost laughed. What was going on?

"We have become wonderful friends, and I'm not tired of you." She answered slowly, wondering where the conversation was going.

"My mother likes you a lot. I hope you know that."

"That's *goot* because I like her, too."

He rubbed his hands on his thighs. "I mean...she almost thinks of you as a daughter."

"That's wonderful, but didn't you say you had something you wanted to ask me?"

"I did. Sarah, would you consider marrying me?"

She was shocked speechless.

He noticed. "I'm sorry. I know this is sudden. I don't mean right away. You don't have to answer now. I meant if things continue to go well between us. I think you're a wonderful woman. I know you will make a wonderful wife."

She heard one of the horses whinny. She looked toward the corral. Levi was bringing out Wing.

Isaac leaned forward to see her face. "Sarah?"

"I heard you, Isaac. I'm humbled that you wish me to be your wife."

He leaned back. "Do I hear a 'but' in that statement?"

"I'm afraid you do."

He shrank back. "What is it? Do you need more time? Is there someone else?"

Was there someone else? She could admit it and end her relationship with Isaac, but that didn't mean she would have one with Levi.

Levi had overshadowed Isaac in her heart. She cared for them both, but she knew without a doubt that if Levi asked her the same question she wouldn't hesitate to accept him. She needed to know how Levi felt about her. She had to know if the kiss had simply been to make Isaac jealous, as Levi claimed, or was there something else behind it? She wanted to believe it meant something to him because she was in love with him. She had to know for sure, even if it meant hearing he didn't care.

She took Isaac's hand between hers. "This is very sudden, and I thought you were in love with someone else."

He got to his feet and moved a few paces away. "I wondered if that might be the reason for your hesitation. I did care for someone else." He turned back to face her. "That relationship is over and done with. In time we'll grow to care for each other like in the old days. It will make Mother happy to see me join the church and marry you. Even Levi is thrilled for us."

She blinked several times. "You spoke to Levi about this?"

"I did. He doesn't have any objections."

"He doesn't?"

Isaac sat beside her again. "I'm handling this badly, aren't I? If Levi had an objection, it would not sway me. I don't need his permission."

She stared into his worried eyes. "Do you love me?"

He looked down. "I know I will in time. Maybe not the way you want just now, but I can see spending the rest of my life with you. You make me a better person. I'll never give you a reason to regret saying yes."

She cupped his cheek with her hand, knowing what she was about to say would hurt him. "If the woman you thought you loved in Lancaster was standing here beside me, would you still be asking me to marry you? Or would you be asking her?"

He flinched and turned away. "That's not a fair question. She isn't here."

"You're right and I'm sorry. I'm honored by your proposal and I will consider it."

He looked up and smiled. "*Danki.* I know you'll make the right decision. I'll spend my life proving that to you if you say you'll have me." He got up and walked away.

The right decision. What would the right decision be? Sarah stared at him as he crossed the farmyard to the tractor shed. She searched for Levi and found he was leaning on the corral fence looking her way. What was he thinking? Did he want to hear her answer, or didn't it matter to him? If he didn't love her, then he wouldn't care what she said.

As she stared at him, he turned away and went back inside the barn. Was that her answer?

SARAH ARRIVED HOME later than usual. She was surprised to see Laura Beth and Joshua were still up. They were sitting in the kitchen. She went in to join them.

"Is Mrs. Raber worse?" Laura Beth asked.

"She's upset about Levi leaving but otherwise she is fine. Getting better all the time."

"Then why the long face?" Joshua pushed a plate of banana bread toward her.

She broke off a piece and nibbled at it. "Isaac asked me to marry him."

She saw the astonishment on Laura Beth's face and knew exactly how she felt. "Already?"

"I was stunned, too."

Joshua leaned back in his chair. "Don't leave us in suspense. What did you say?"

"I told him I had to think about it."

Joshua wagged his eyebrows. "You are getting more sensible by the day."

His wife gave him a stern look. "This is no time for teasing. Sarah, do you know what you want?"

"I thought I did. I've spent years waiting for this very day to come, not knowing who my future husband would be but convinced I would know him the moment I saw him. It was a childish fantasy. Now that the day is here, it's not quite what I expected."

"I'm sorry. Being in love with the idea of being in love is a common problem for young people."

"Is that what I was doing?" She felt tears sting the backs of her eyes.

"It is real while you are going through it. It takes time for the newness to wear off a relationship. Do you know what you want to do?"

Sarah shook her head because her throat was too tight to speak.

Laura Beth recognized what was wrong and put her arms around Sarah. "Everything will be okay."

"No, it won't." Sarah burst into tears and sobbed on her sister's shoulder.

Joshua got to his feet. "I think I forgot to shut up the henhouse." He hurried outside.

Sarah drew a shaky breath. "He never forgets to take care of the chickens."

"I know. He's a wonderful man, but he doesn't handle crying women very well."

"Tell me what to do," Sarah said as she sat down at the table.

"It's late but you could start mending. The pile of Caleb's clothes with rips and tears is growing larger."

Sarah shook her head as she rolled her eyes. "You know that's not what I meant."

"You want me to tell you whether or not to accept Isaac's offer of marriage."

"Yes, that's what I need to know."

"And do you really expect me to have the right answer?"

"You're my big sister. You know everything."

Laura Beth chuckled. "I know a lot, but not everything. I'm afraid in matters of the heart only the owner of the heart can answer that question. Do you love him?"

"I care about him deeply. I don't want to hurt him. He isn't a strong man. He needs me."

"When he kisses you, does the whole world fade away until you are the only two people standing on it?"

"Isaac hasn't kissed me." Her voice cracked.

Laura Beth's eyes widened. "Does someone else make you feel that way?"

"Levi. He only kissed me twice and he said it was to make his brother jealous, but, Laura Beth, they were the most amazing kisses." Sarah's eyes filled with tears.

Laura Beth leaned back in her chair. "That complicates matters. Are you in love with Levi?"

"I think so. I don't know how he feels about me, but he is leaving tomorrow. His mother is upset about that but she is so happy I'm going out with Isaac."

"I think it best not to base your future on what Mrs. Raber thinks."

"I know that, and I know I have to make up my own

mind. Honestly, I think Isaac would be a good husband. I think he would be a comfortable husband."

"Oh, I see. Sarah wants comfortable?"

"Is that so wrong?"

"Of course not. As long as both of you can live with that decision. I take it you don't believe Levi loves you?"

"I'm not sure. But I do know he doesn't want to live here. He wants to go back to Pennsylvania and raise racehorses."

"Is that unacceptable to you?"

"To leave you and Joshua and Caleb, not to mention all my friends, Ernest and Henrietta? I can't imagine doing that. Would you want me to go that far away?"

"I would miss you terribly, but you have to do what your heart says is right. A woman leaves her family and clings to her husband. That's the way it has been done for thousands of years."

"By braver women than I am." She took another bite of banana bread.

Laura Beth chuckled. "This is my advice. Pray the Lord will show you the path to take. Sleep on it, and in the morning I think your decision will be clear."

"Why do I think I'm not going to get much sleep?" Sarah rose and kissed her sister on the cheek before making her way upstairs to her bedroom.

Early the next afternoon, Sarah drove to the Raber farm still in a state of indecision. A sleepless night of prayer and soul-searching hadn't given her the answer she was looking for.

Levi held the answer. She had to speak to him.

She found him in the barn packing harnesses into a large box. "Hello, Levi."

"Hey, Sarah. Haven't seen you in a while. What's new?" He didn't look at her.

"A lot, actually."

"Like what?"

"Your brother asked me to marry him."

Levi paused but he didn't turn around. "What was your answer?"

"I told him I had to think it over."

"That's reasonable, but isn't this what you wanted?"

"I thought so."

He turned around then. "Isaac is a great guy. He loves it out here. You are getting exactly what you want. Why get cold feet now?"

"Don't you know?" *Please say you do. Am I making a fool of myself?*

He shook his head. "I don't."

"I have feelings for someone else. You. I can't forget the way you made me feel when you kissed me."

He bowed his head and slowly shook it side to side. "Sarah, Sarah, we were playing a part. I was, anyway." He looked up at her. "The point of the whole thing was to get Isaac jealous and it worked. Now I can go back to Pennsylvania because I know you'll take good care of him."

Her heart plummeted to her feet. "Is that all it meant to you?" she whispered.

He turned away. "That's what it meant."

She had her answer. She pressed a hand to the ache in her chest. She could feel her heart breaking.

"What if I don't marry Isaac?"

Levi didn't look at her. "Then I'll have to delay leaving until he finds a woman who will. I promised my father I'd take care of him."

"I see. Then you'll be happy to know you won't have to stay here. I'm going to say yes."

Sarah quietly left the barn and went toward the house. It was amazing that she could keep walking as if nothing had happened when her heart was broken into a million pieces. He didn't love her. But she loved him enough to keep her end of their bargain. She would see that he got his freedom.

In the house, she found Henrietta mopping the kitchen floor. "What are you doing?" Sarah tried to take the mop away from her.

"I can do it. Leave me be. If I get tired, I'll take a rest."

"I want you to stop right now. I have something to tell you."

"Oh?"

"Isaac has asked me to marry him," Sarah said quietly. Henrietta smiled. "What did you tell him?"

"That I needed more time. That I wanted to be sure." She was sure now. If she married Isaac, Levi would go back to what he loved.

"And are you sure?"

Sarah managed a little smile. "Henrietta, I was in love with Isaac when I was sixteen years old." It wasn't quite all the truth. She had been in love with the idea of being in love with him. The reality was much different. She cared deeply for Isaac. Maybe it was love, but it wasn't the heart-pounding, soul-stirring kind of love that she had for Levi.

"I would be delighted to have you as a daughter-in-law." Henrietta reached out and pulled Sarah into her embrace.

"I will make Isaac a good wife," Sarah whispered.

"I know you will. You are exactly the kind of woman he needs."

Sarah prayed that she had spoken the truth. That the affection she had for Isaac would grow into love.

The outside door opened, and Isaac walked in. "That combine is a piece of junk. I need to replace half the cutting blades."

Henrietta threw her arms around her son. "I've been sad because Levi is leaving us, but you have made me very happy."

"What did I do?"

"You asked the right woman to marry you."

He smiled at Sarah. "What did the right woman say?"

Sarah tried to smile but couldn't. "She said yes."

Isaac pulled her into his embrace. *"Danki."*

Henrietta looked out the window. "Ernest is here again. I can't wait to tell him."

Henrietta smiled. "You two should go see the bishop right now and pick a date for the wedding. We have a lot to get done before the banns are read."

Isaac looked at her. "What do you say?"

"Sounds like a good idea. I would like to say goodbye to Levi first." She couldn't let him leave without seeing his face one last time.

Isaac looked at her closely. "Okay. I'll ask Ernest

what he thinks he can do for the combine. Don't be long."

"I won't." She squared her shoulders and headed out the door.

CHAPTER NINETEEN

LEVI DREW THE brush over Wing's soft hide in slow, steady strokes. The task was repetitive and calming. Normally. Today wasn't a normal day. He wondered what one would look like in the future. How could a day without Sarah ever feel normal?

Brush, brush, wipe with a cloth, brush, brush, wipe with a cloth again.

"Aren't you worried that you will rub away all her hair?"

He stopped the motion. Why did she have to show up now when his emotions were so raw? It cost him every ounce of strength he possessed not to turn around and beg her to come away with him.

"I like to keep her shiny. I think she likes it, too."

He didn't turn around. He couldn't look into her eyes and not tell her that he was in love with her.

"When are you leaving?" she asked.

"My ride will be here at four o'clock."

"You'll come back for the wedding, won't you?"

"Sure."

"Isaac and I will understand if you can't make it. We know it's a long way."

He was going to need an excuse because there was no

way he could watch her vow to love, honor and obey another man. "A lot will depend on Wing's racing schedule."

"You must be happy to know it has all worked out."

He stopped brushing and looked at her. Did his brother know how fortunate he was to have this wonderful woman care for him? "What makes you think I'm happy?"

"I know it can't be easy to leave your mother and your brother behind, but you're going to have a chance to do the thing you love above all else. I'm truly happy for you, Levi."

He gazed into her beautiful eyes and realized his loss wasn't important. Her happiness was all that he wanted in life. "We both got what we set out to do. I'm going back to Pennsylvania to race horses and you are going to begin a wonderful life in your slice of paradise. We are both blessed."

He thought he saw a flash of pain in her eyes, but she looked away so quickly he knew he had to be mistaken.

"Isaac needs me."

Levi stepped up to the stall gate and laid his hand on hers. "I hope he tells you that he loves you every day. You deserve to be loved like that. I hope he tells you that he can't breathe when you're not near him. I hope he tells you that your happiness is like the moon, the sun and the stars in his universe."

"Isaac isn't one for romantic talk like that."

"Then I need to have a discussion with him before I leave because God has chosen a very special woman for him and he needs to let her know just how special she is."

Isaac walked into the barn. "There you are. Didn't you hear me calling?"

She gave him a bright smile. "I was just about to answer you. I wanted to say goodbye to Levi before he left us."

Isaac blinked hard. "I wish you weren't leaving today, brother. Sarah has agreed to marry me."

"She told me. Congratulations to both of you. I'd stay longer but I want to get Wing back in time to rest up before her first race." Levi opened the stall door and stepped out into the alleyway. He held out his hand. "I wasn't going to leave without saying goodbye."

Isaac took his hand and pulled him into his embrace. Isaac stepped back and wiped his cheek. "I'm going to miss you."

Levi cleared his throat. "I'm going to miss you, too, pesky little brother. I've got one piece of advice before you go. Don't ever let the sun set without telling this amazing woman how much you love her."

Isaac nodded as he slipped his arm around Sarah's shoulders. "That's pretty good advice. I wish I had heard it sooner."

"We should go," Sarah said, looking out the door.

"Where are the two of you off to today?" Levi asked.

"We're going to see the bishop and pick a wedding date."

Levi made himself smile at her, but Sarah didn't smile back.

"The first step in making it official." Ernest came

from the tack room at the back of the barn. He had several leather straps in his hand. "I promised your mother I would fix the handhold straps on the passenger side of her buggy. She claims my driving makes her want to hold on to something tight."

"She never enjoyed going fast." Levi stepped back inside the stall and resumed brushing Wing.

Isaac tugged on her hand. "We should get going."

Isaac led her away. She looked back over her shoulder. Levi lifted his hand in a wave. She waved once and then she turned away.

"It isn't very often a fellow gets to watch a man make the biggest mistake of his life," Ernest drawled.

Levi resumed brushing Wing's already gleaming coat. "What's that supposed to mean?"

"I'm going to tell you about another man, one just about your age, who also made the biggest mistake of his life."

"I'm really not in the mood for one of your stories."

"That's too bad. I'm going to tell it to you anyway. There were two men who were as close as brothers and they were both in love with the same woman."

"I've heard this one."

"Then listen again. These two men, close as brothers, loved the same woman. They knew she would have to choose between them. Now, this woman cared for each of these men. But one fella loved her so much that he knew he couldn't ask her to make that choice. So he bowed out and he let his best friend marry the woman that meant more to him than life itself. Know why? Because her happiness was everything to him."

"It sounds like he made the right choice."

Ernest shook his head. "No, he didn't make the right choice. He didn't trust her enough. She wasn't some weakling that needed a man to decide for her. She deserved the chance to make that decision. To tell both men where her heart lay. So one man stepped aside and has regretted it every day since."

"It isn't the same with Isaac and me. Isaac will give Sarah all the things she wants. They'll have a life here in the community she loves. She'll raise her children with her family close by. Isaac will be content farming with tractors instead of horses."

"You only forgot one thing."

"And what is that?"

"You didn't tell her that her happiness was the sun and the moon and the stars in *your* universe. Are you brave enough to give her a choice? Are you going to bow out as cowardly as I did? Is believing you gave her something she wanted better than hearing her choose another man over you?"

Ernest walked away, leaving Levi's emotions in a whirlwind. He wasn't a coward. He was as brave as the next man. And yet Ernest was right. The one thing Levi couldn't face was hearing Sarah's rejection. He loved her, but the life he wanted wasn't the life she wanted.

Wing whinnied softly and nudged him with her nose. He laced his fingers together around her neck. "I want to see you be the best you can possibly be. I want to raise your foals and see them win. But what will that be worth if Sarah isn't there with me? If she can't share those moments with me?"

Without Sarah, he wouldn't feel like a winner. There wasn't a trotting trophy in the world he wanted to hold without Sarah by his side. It would be meaningless.

He left Wing's stall and walked out into the farmyard. A pickup pulling a horse trailer turned in from the county road and came to a stop in front of the barn. The driver rolled down his window. "Are you the fellow going to Lancaster, Pennsylvania, with a horse?"

Levi looked toward the house, where his bags were packed in the living room waiting for him to throw them in the back of the pickup. Ernest and his mother came out of the house and stood on the front porch and waved. Ernest was right. Sarah deserved to make her own choice.

And maybe he deserved to have the woman who put the moon and the stars to shame cast her light on him.

He turned to the driver. "I'm the fellow that's sending a racehorse to Pennsylvania, but I'm not going with her. I want you to call the owner of Arnold Diehl Stables and tell him I'll be in contact with him about my plans soon."

"I didn't know the Amish owned racehorses."

"In Lancaster, Pennsylvania, they can. Here in Kansas we stick to tractors."

"A fellow learns something new every day."

"I'll help you load her."

Ernest approached Levi after Wing was safely loaded in the trailer. Levi stepped in with her and laid his head against her cheek. "I hate to let you go. You know that, don't you? *Gott* has given you the heart of a champion. You were born to race and to win. You can't do that here. You go be the winner I know you are. I'm gonna try and convince a Kansas gal that I can't live without her. If she says no, I'll follow you."

He gave Wing one last pat on the cheek and left the trailer. He closed the end gate and signaled the driver to pull away. Ernest clapped his hand on Levi's shoulder. "You'd better go find Sarah and let her make the decision."

"Ernest, if this goes the way I hope it does, you're going to have to teach me how to drive that combine."

"It's easy. And you won't only be farming. We need a good horse trainer in Cedar Grove."

Levi smiled. "I'd like that. I may just hang out my shingle. Can I borrow your tractor?"

"Of course."

Levi climbed aboard and the engine turned over on the first try. As the motor roared to life, he took a moment to pray for Sarah and for his brother. If Sarah chose Isaac, Levi could wish them well and leave for Pennsylvania tomorrow. If she chose him, Levi wasn't sure what his relationship with his brother would be like.

CHAPTER TWENTY

ON THE DRIVE to the bishop's home, Sarah wrestled with her conscience. She was doing this for the right reason, but it didn't feel that way. Was she wrong? Isaac needed her. She saw that Levi didn't need her. He didn't love her. Why was she planning a wedding date when neither brother loved her?

She deserved to be loved the way Joshua loved Laura Beth. That was all she really wanted. Isaac deserved to marry a woman who loved him. One who thought he made her life complete, not someone who hoped that love would grow in time.

This marriage was a lie tied up in a bow to look like a gift to Henrietta and Isaac, but it was still a lie. As much as she cared for Isaac and his mother…she simply couldn't go through with it. She grasped Isaac's arm and leaned close to his ear. "Pull over and stop." She had to shout to be heard over the tractor engine.

"Why? Did you forget something?" he shouted back.

She nodded. "I forgot to tell you the truth."

He pulled the tractor over to the side of the road and turned off the engine. The sudden silence was unnerving. Gradually the sound of the wind sighing through the waving golden wheat in the fields beside the road and the noises of insects filled in around them. Isaac stared at her intently. "What do you mean by that?"

She laid her hand on his arm as he gripped the steering wheel. "I care about you, Isaac, but we would both regret it if I married you. I'm sorry. I never should've let it go this far. I thought I could do it, but I can't. Please say you understand?"

He didn't look angry or hurt; he simply looked like a lost child. "Why are you saying this?"

"Because I don't love you, Isaac. And you don't love me." She looked away. "I love someone else, and even though you deny it, I think you still do, too. The man I love doesn't want me, but that doesn't matter. It's not right for us to get married just because it's comfortable. We both deserve to be loved."

Was Levi already on his way? Would she ever see him again? The pain of losing him pressed down on her until she couldn't breathe. Tears burned the backs of her eyes. Why did she have to love someone who didn't love her?

She took a steadying breath and turned back to Isaac. "What matters is that I don't hurt you more than I already have."

"It's Levi, isn't it? And he's leaving today."

She smiled through her sadness. "He's doing what he has dreamed of doing since your mother sold your property in Lancaster. He's going to reclaim what your father built. His heart is there, and I'm happy for him."

Isaac took off his hat and raked a hand through his hair. "Are you sure about this? I would be a good husband to you."

She laid her hand on his cheek. "Oh, Isaac, I know that. But you deserve someone who loves you unconditionally. And so do I."

"I thought I had found love once, but I was wrong. Maybe I don't love you enough, but I want you to be happy. I could make you happy if you gave me a chance."

"Isaac, you love me exactly enough. I know you would do anything for me. I won't let you sacrifice yourself because someone broke your heart and I'm the bandage you chose to fix it. I have too much respect for you to do that."

"I can't stand it when you sound so wise. I reckon there's no point in going to see the bishop now, is there?"

"Not unless we want to raid Granny Weaver's cookie jar like we did when we were kids?"

He chuckled a little and covered her hand with his own. "She makes the best gingersnaps. It might be worth the risk. What do we do now? Should I try and stop Levi? He needs to know that you are in love with him."

"He knows I have feelings for him, but he doesn't return them."

"Poor Sarah. I didn't treat your affection as the gift that it was when we were young. Now you're in love with another man who is going away and leaving you behind again. We might have made a good life together, Sarah. I think I'll always wonder if we made the right choice today."

"I'm not sure what God's plan for us is, but I have faith that everything will work out as it should."

The sight of another tractor approaching from behind them made them draw apart. Sarah was amused to see it was Bishop Weaver. He stopped beside them. "Are you having trouble?" He yelled to be heard over the sound of his engine.

Sarah shook her head. "We're fine." She looked at Isaac. "Aren't we?"

He nodded. "*Ja*, we're fine."

The bishop waved and turned down his own lane.

"I reckon I should take you home. Is your family going to be upset?"

"I'm more worried about how your mother will take it."

"I'm a little worried about that myself, but she's a grown woman. She'll have to get used to the idea. Besides, she'll be Ernest's problem soon."

He started the tractor and continued through Cedar Grove. Julie Temple was standing in her front yard watering the flowers. She waved, and Sarah waved back.

About a mile outside of town, Sarah saw a red car parked at the side of the road up ahead. A woman was standing in front of it holding something high in the air. She leaned over to Isaac. "What is she doing?"

"Trying to get a signal on her phone. Reception is terrible out here."

"Should we stop and see if we can help?" The woman looked toward them and waved.

Isaac didn't answer. He stepped on the brakes so hard the tractor skidded on the gravel. Sarah had to grab hold of his arm to keep from being dumped off the fender. He shut down the tractor.

"Brittany?"

The word was barely more than a whisper. Sarah

glanced from Isaac's stunned expression to the woman's equally shocked one.

Isaac seemed to recover first. "Brittany, what are you doing here?"

She lowered her phone. "I was trying to find you. My GPS isn't working. I haven't been able to reach you."

"I sort of lost my phone."

She leaned back against her car. "Who is your friend?"

Isaac didn't appear to have it all together yet. Sarah climbed down from the tractor and held out her hand. "I am Sarah Yoder. I'm a friend of Isaac's family. I've been helping take care of his mother, but she is much better."

The relief in Brittany's eyes touched Sarah's heart. "I'm very glad to meet you. I'm Brittany Delaney."

"You must be the girl Isaac has told me so much about." Sarah raised one eyebrow as she looked up at him.

He blushed and climbed down from the tractor seat. "I can't believe you came all this way."

"I couldn't think of another way to let you know I've changed my mind. If it's not too late."

"But what about your parents?"

She shrugged one shoulder. "They're going to have to learn to live with it. I should've told them I was old enough to make my own decisions months ago. It's my life." Her lower lip trembled. "And I want you in it because I'm so empty without you."

He reached for her and she threw herself into his arms. He held her close and stroked her hair. "I love you, Brittany. Don't cry. I've been miserable without you. I thought I would never see you again."

Sarah took a couple of steps back and then walked around to the other side of the tractor to give them a few moments of privacy. She wiped the tears from her eyes. She wished Levi would look at her the way Isaac was looking at Brittany. Like she was the moon and the stars to him.

Poor Isaac was going to have a lot of explaining to do to his mother. At least he hadn't been baptized into the Amish faith. He was free to marry where his heart led him. If he chose to follow Brittany to her world, he would become Henrietta's *Englisch* son, and if he and Brittany were blessed with children, they would be Henrietta's *Englisch* grandbabies. It was nothing new in the Cedar Grove Amish community. Even the bishop had *Englisch* grandchildren. Or perhaps Brittany would want to become Amish. Stranger things had happened.

After a few minutes, Brittany and Isaac came around the tractor. They were both smiling, their eyes so full of love for each other it was almost painful to see. "What about your schooling?" he asked.

"All my credits will transfer to the University of Kansas. I checked. I can finish medical school there."

"You're going to be a doctor?" Sarah winked at Isaac. "Good choice, farm boy."

"She wanted to become a pediatrician."

Brittany smiled shyly at him. "I love babies."

He tore his gaze away from her. "I'll take you home, Sarah, and Brittany will follow us. Then I'm going to introduce her to my mother. Here's hoping that goes well."

Brittany tipped her head to look up at him with a puzzled expression. "What do you mean by that?"

He opened his mouth and closed it again. Sarah took pity on him. "His mother was hoping he would settle down with a nice Amish girl. She had me picked out, but Isaac and I are just friends."

"I have to admit I'm a little frightened of his mother," Brittany said.

Sarah smiled at her. "Henrietta has been ill, but she is getting better. In fact, she will be getting married soon. Having someone to help her plan a wedding is exactly what she needs."

"Will it be an Amish wedding? I don't know what that entails. I'm not sure how much help I'll be. What if she doesn't like me?"

"She will," Isaac assured her.

Sarah patted the girl's arm. "I agree with Isaac. His mother knows we are all, Amish and *Englisch*, simply God's children with very little difference between us. Well, that is except for Ernest. He is a little different. Maybe a lot different."

Isaac laughed, happier than Sarah had seen him since his arrival. "Ernest will love her. She likes to go fishing."

Brittany blushed a pretty pink. "Fly-fishing. Does that count? Do people go fly-fishing in Kansas?"

"I've heard it is catching on," Isaac said. "You'll have to show him how it's done."

"Isaac, why don't you ride with Brittany. I'm sure you have a lot to catch up on. I'll take the tractor. My family will be delighted to meet you. You must stay for supper."

Brittany looked suddenly worried. "I hate to just drop in on them. Shouldn't we call first?"

Isaac and Sarah exchanged amused glances. He gave Brittany a playful hug. "The Amish don't have telephones, sweetheart."

"Oh, that's right. Does that mean I will have to give up my phone while I'm visiting your mother?"

"Is that a deal breaker?" Sarah asked.

"No, but it's going to be awkward. Everyone I know has a phone."

Sarah chuckled. "Don't worry, dear. Isaac is not technically Amish. You may keep your phone even at his mother's house."

She pressed her hand to her chest. "Oh, good."

He kissed her forehead. "Not that it will do you much good out here. Our cell service stinks."

Levi got to the bishop's house as quickly as he could. He didn't see his brother's tractor. Had they already come and gone? Was the date set? Would Sarah consider backing out of her engagement to Isaac now that the bishop and his mother knew about it? Would Isaac agree? Did he even have the right to interfere in his brother's happiness?

The bishop came out of the barn carrying two buckets of milk in his hands. "Good evening, Levi. We had heard you were leaving."

"Not yet. Has my brother been here?"

"I saw them out on the road, but they didn't come to the house. Were you expecting to meet them here?" The bishop set his pails on the ground. A black-and-white kitten came running up. He was just big enough to get one paw over the lip of the milk bucket and into the milk. He sat down and licked his foot as fast as he could.

Relief filled Levi. They hadn't met with the bishop to schedule a wedding date. What did that mean? Was Isaac getting cold feet? He wouldn't do that to Sarah. "I must've gotten the message wrong. If you see them, tell my brother I need to speak to him right away."

"Is your mother ill again?"

Levi shook his head. "Nothing like that, but please tell him to come straight home."

"I'll do that." He picked up his milk pails and carried them to the side of the house where he poured a generous amount into an old hubcap. Kittens came running from everywhere to enjoy their supper.

Levi turned the tractor around and left the bishop's farmyard. Where would Isaac and Sarah have gone? To see her family, maybe? There was only one way to find out. He turned toward Cedar Grove and the Stumbling Blocks beyond.

Some twenty minutes later, the scent of lavender filled the late-afternoon air as Levi drove the tractor across the bridge and up the lane toward the King farm. The sun was low in the sky, a bright ball of orange behind the clouds gathering on the horizon.

It was a beautiful sight, and Levi had never been more frightened in his life. What if she said no? What if Isaac was the one she truly wanted? Did he have a right to ask her to choose between them? Sarah deserved to know that he loved her, but what if it didn't change her decision?

What if he laid his heart bare and she didn't believe

him after the way he had brushed aside her feelings for him? Would telling her he was staying be enough to make her choose him? Was he willing to risk hurting Isaac in the process? His fingers grew ice-cold as he faced the biggest decision of his life.

He pulled the tractor to a stop in front of her house and got down. His brother's tractor was parked beside the barn. There was a red Ford Escort sitting beside it. He didn't recognize the car.

Joshua came out onto the porch. "Good evening, Levi. We heard you left to go back to Pennsylvania today. Have you changed your plans?"

"That depends on Sarah."

"Does it, now? Perhaps you would like to come in?"

Levi rubbed his sweaty palms together. "I'd rather speak to Sarah alone."

"I'll get her. Your brother is here. Are you sure you don't want to come in?"

"I must speak with Sarah first."

The screen door opened behind Joshua, and Sarah walked out. "Levi, what are you doing here? Why aren't you on your way to Pennsylvania?" she asked in a shocked tone.

Joshua winked at her and gave her a little push toward Levi. "He wants to speak to you. There's a pretty view of the lake from the rock wall beyond the lavender field. I think you should show it to him. It's a good spot to hash things out."

Sarah's expression grew more puzzled. "All right. Levi, would you like to see the view of the lake?"

"Sure. Thanks, Joshua."

Sarah walked down the steps and headed toward the low rock wall that bordered the lavender fields. When they reached it, she gestured toward a gap in the trees and the shimmering lake beyond it. "As you can see, there is the lake. Now, why are you here?"

"Because I realized that everything I thought I wanted doesn't amount to anything if I don't have you."

She blinked owlishly. "What are you saying?"

"When I suggested we pretend interest in each other to make Isaac jealous, I never intended to fall in love with you, but, Sarah, I have." He stepped up to her and cupped her face with his hands. "You are so easy to love."

She laid her hands on his chest. "I can't believe it."

"Please believe me. I love you, Sarah Yoder. With all my heart and soul. And you said that you had feelings for me. I want to be with you, but more than that, I want you to be happy. If my brother is the man you want, I will step aside and never bother you again, but I want us to raise a family here in Cedar Grove. I want my mother to spoil our children. I want Miss Julie to teach them in school. I want you and your sister to harvest lavender together for years to come."

Sarah turned away from him and his heart stopped beating for one long, painful moment. She sat down on the wall and stared at her hands clasped together in her lap. "What about your dreams of racing Wing and a Prayer? Of seeing her in the winner's circle at the Hambletonian? What about your father's farm? I've heard you talk about that place and I know that's where your heart is."

He sat down beside her and took her hands in his. "It's

a very easy choice for me. I can stand in the winner's circle with a horse I've trained or I can hold you in the circle of my arms and know I have won a prize far greater than anything racing has to offer."

She looked into his eyes. "Levi, are you sure?"

"I know that I am putting you in a terrible position, but I couldn't let you marry Isaac without telling you how I honestly feel. I can't leave without hearing from your lips that you don't want to be with me. If you don't, I'll go back to Pennsylvania and I will wish you and Isaac every happiness. Because as much as I want you, I want your happiness more."

"You would give up everything you have dreamed of for me?"

"Sarah, you *are* everything I have dreamed of and never knew it. Will you marry me?"

SARAH WANTED TO shout "Yes!" at the top of her lungs and throw herself into Levi's arms, but she knew what he was giving up for her and she couldn't let him do it. She loved him too much.

"Please say something, Sarah."

"I'm trying to find the right words."

He rose to his feet and walked a few steps away to gaze out at the lake. "You don't have to say anything if your choice is Isaac. I'm sorry if I've upset you."

"I'm not going to marry Isaac."

He tensed but didn't turn around. "You're not? When did you decide this? Does he know?"

"I told Isaac this afternoon that I couldn't go through with it. I care for him but not enough to marry him. As it turned out, it was a good decision on my part because Isaac loves someone else."

Levi spun around. "I don't understand."

"Isaac has been in love with an *Englisch* girl whose parents did not approve of her marrying a simple Amish boy."

"I know. He told me."

"She broke up with him a few weeks after your family moved here. Actually, the same day that Isaac asked me to go to the first singing with him. I was something of a rebound in spite of our efforts to make him jealous. He threw his phone in the lake that day. Brittany has been unable to reach him to tell him that she changed her mind and has told her parents that it will be Isaac or no one. She drove here all the way from Pennsylvania to speak to him. We met her on the way here."

Levi took her hand. "I'm so sorry."

She laid a hand on his cheek. "Don't be. I think they will both be very happy, although I'm afraid your mother will be upset if Isaac doesn't end up joining the Amish church."

"I don't believe he will. Our faith isn't for everyone and *Mamm* knows that. Dear Sarah, always thinking of others. Your heart must be broken."

"I think my pride is dented more than my heart. My heart belongs to a wonderful man who was willing to give up everything he loves for me."

Sarah had rarely seen such joy on someone's face. "Do you mean that? Do you love me? Because I have been in love with you since our first argument in the barn."

"I think I've been in love with you since you whispered 'guess who' in my ear. I might not have known your name then, but you were the one who made my heart race. Will you marry this poor Kansas farmer and horse trainer?"

"Nee."

He drew back in shock. "What? But you love me."

"I do love you more than you will ever know. I won't marry a farmer from Cedar Grove, Kansas, but I will marry an amazingly talented horse trainer and breeder who resides in Lancaster, Pennsylvania."

"I can't ask you to give up your family."

"And I can't ask you to give up doing what you love. Are we going to argue about this or are you going to accept that I am right?"

"I don't know what to say."

"The appropriate answer is *ja*, my dear, whatever you want, dear."

He stood up and gathered her close, knowing that he could never express how much he loved her or how thankful he was that God had seen fit to bring them together. He pulled her closer. She fit perfectly against him as if God had fashioned her exactly for him. His heart surged with joy before realization returned. He wanted to keep her in his arms forever. If he could spend the rest of his life holding her, he would be the happiest fellow alive.

He moved his lips to her cheek and then to her temple, and finally he turned his face away.

He breathed in the sweet smell of the flowers around

them and laid his cheek against her hair. "I am the most blessed man in the world."

She chuckled. "Remember that statement the next time I do something that drives you to tear out your hair."

He drew back to look into her eyes. "I might look good bald."

"That's what you say now because you want to kiss me."

"I do want to kiss you."

She raised her face to his. "Is there anyone watching us?"

He looked over the top of her head. "I don't think so."

"I just wanted to be sure that this kiss isn't for anyone else's benefit," she murmured before pressing her lips to his.

Soft yet firm, the touch of his warm mouth against hers sent her mind reeling. The same wonderful feelings she remembered exploded in her chest, an exquisite ache that made her press closer to him. All she wanted was to keep on kissing him. Her arms crept around his neck and he pulled her closer still.

He was the first to break away, drawing a deep, unsteady breath that made her smile. He tucked her head beneath his chin. She pressed her face to his chest and forgot everything else except the wonder of being loved by the man God meant for her alone.

CHAPTER TWENTY-ONE

ONE WEEK LATER, Levi lay back with his hands crossed under his head on the quilt Sarah and her sister had made. He stared up through the leaves of the tree. The sun was high in the sky, but the dappled shade made the summer day bearable. He turned his head to look at the woman who sat beside him. Sarah was gathering up their dishes and utensils and stowing them in a wicker picnic basket. She looked at him and cocked her head to the side. "Are you listening to me?"

He yawned. "Of course I am."

"Then what is your answer?"

He hadn't really been listening. He had been too caught up in the bliss of his life. "The answer is, yes, I love you."

She arched one pretty eyebrow. Of course, the other one was equally as pretty, especially since they were the same color as the lashes that framed her amazing blue eyes. "That was not the question."

He was in for it now. He rolled to his side and smiled at her. "Then the answer is, yes, I will marry you."

She crossed her arms over her chest. "You're getting warmer."

"I am. Let me see. The answer is six children. I believe we should have an equal number of boys and girls."

She tipped her head to the side. "Now you're getting way ahead of yourself. Can you just admit that you were not listening to me?"

"Your smile is like the sun coming out on a cloudy day. It brightens everything around me."

"Next you will tell me that holding my hand is as exciting as racing Wing and a Prayer."

He reached out and closed his fingers over hers. "Much more exciting than that."

She looked mollified. "Now that I have your attention, I will repeat my question. Would you like some more watermelon?"

"*Nee*, for having you near me is sweetness enough to last a lifetime."

"I'm not sure I like this flowery new you."

He knew he shouldn't do it, but he just had to see that flash in her eyes again. "If that's the way you feel, finish cleaning up and go put the hamper away like a good little *frau*."

Her mouth dropped open. Her eyes, first wide with shock, suddenly narrowed, and he saw that spark of independence he adored. "You can clean up after yourself, Levi Raber."

"You are so much fun to tease." He laughed and she slowly relaxed.

"You are shameless."

"If I was, I would kiss you in front of all these people." He swept a hand toward the families spread out across the lakeshore below the Miller farm.

Dozens of friends and family members had gathered for a picnic to celebrate Granny Weaver's ninetieth birthday. Six men and Granny were seated on chairs at the water's edge with their fishing poles in hand. One chair was empty. Ernest had gone off somewhere.

"If I was shameless, I would *let* you kiss me in front of these people. Are you paying attention to me? I'm about to ask you another important question."

"More important than do I want some more watermelon?"

She leaned toward him with a come-hither gleam in her eyes. "Much more important. Would you like to go for a walk?"

"I'm mighty comfortable right where I am."

"Then I am going to go for a walk and see if there is someone in the woods who would like to kiss me where no one is watching." She got to her feet and sauntered toward the path that led to the place where she had fallen out of the canoe.

He jumped up and hurried to catch her. When he reached her side, he leaned toward her. "A rendezvous in the woods at the place where I first held you in my arms. What an excellent suggestion."

She turned her face away. "I was not suggesting anything." She stopped walking. "Doesn't your mother look wonderful?"

He followed her line of sight and saw his mother walking toward them. In the two months since her hospitalization, she had put on weight and regained energy. Best of all, she had acquired a brighter outlook on life. Isaac's courtship of Brittany aside, Henrietta was basking in the glow of the love in Ernest's eyes. While Henrietta might have wanted her son to join the church, she was content to know that he was going to continue farming and would raise his family around her.

"It has turned out to be a lovely day," his mother said as she walked by them.

Levi realized she was headed in the same direction that he and Sarah intended to take. She seemed to be in a hurry. Puzzled, he looked at Sarah. "Where do you think she is going?"

"For a walk. The real question is, where are we going now?"

He leaned close to whisper in her ear. "It's a big lake. I'm sure we can find another secluded spot."

Sarah put her hand on his chest. "I like the way you think."

SARAH HAD A hard time thinking straight when he was so close. The sturdy muscles of his upper body tensed at her touch. He pulled her against him.

He overwhelmed her senses. She could feel the beating of his heart beneath her palm. His shirt smelled of sun-dried linen and leather and the scent that was uniquely his own. She couldn't describe it but she would never forget it.

She looked up at his dear face. "How is it that I am so blessed?"

The warmth in his eyes brought a flush to her skin. "The ways of God are hidden from us, but we see His grace all around us. In the words of my *Englisch* friends, you just got lucky, honey."

She chuckled and he let her move away. "That should be the name of our next foal. Lucky Honey."

"I kind of like that. Maybe We're So Lucky Honey, so we are reminded that the Lord showers us with gifts we have not earned. Tell me, how may I earn a kiss from you today?"

She took his hand and pulled him toward a nearby cedar tree. Once they were behind it and screened from the other picnic goers, she rose on her tiptoes.

"My kisses will always be given freely. You never have to earn them." She pressed her lips against his and sighed when he wrapped his arms around her and held her tight. Nothing had ever felt as right as this did.

When he finally broke the kiss, he lifted his head and tucked hers beneath his chin. "How many days until the wedding?"

"A lot," she said in her most mournful voice.

"Four weeks after your baptism, that's all the longer I'm going to wait."

"I can't see a way to do it any quicker. Besides, there's a lot of work involved in preparing for a wedding and you are going to miss most of that process. I wish you didn't have to return to Pennsylvania so soon."

"A man has a lot of work to do when he intends to bring a new bride home. I will be back before you know it. I will write you every day."

"Will I like Pennsylvania?"

"You will love the Lancaster area. There are many Amish. And best of all, none of them will be driving loud, smelly tractors. Our Amish farms may be small, but our

Amish hearts are large, and you will be welcomed with open arms."

She pulled back to look at his face. "Your Amish arms and heart are all I need."

"If you miss your family, we will come back to see them or they may come and visit us."

"I will miss them, but I know my place is with you."

"You youngsters should find a more private place for your wooing," Ernest said from the other side of the cedar.

"You could just mind your own business," Levi suggested.

Sarah heard a woman giggle. "Is that you, Henrietta?"

The older couple stepped around the tree. "We seem to have had the same idea," Ernest said, wagging his eyebrows. "A little smooching in private."

"It's not so private now," Isaac said behind them. He had his arm around Brittany, who was smiling as well.

Henrietta laughed heartily. "This is *wunderbar*. We have all been blessed with the gift of love by a loving God."

Sarah gazed up at Levi. She had been blessed in many ways on her roundabout path to finding the man she was meant to love. She could hardly wait to see where the Lord would lead them next.

* * * * *